A DARKENED

FORGED by FLAMES

H.E. BAUMAN

First paperback edition June 2023

Cover design by MiblArt

Map by Cartographybird Maps

ISBN 978-1-7354553-7-2 (paperback)

ISBN 978-1-7354553-8-9 (hardcover)

ISBN 978-1-7354553-3-4 (ebook)

www.hebauman.com

Content Warning

Thank you for picking up *Forged by Flames*, the prequel to *Under Darkened Skies*. It is highly recommended that you read *Under Darkened Skies* before reading *Forged by Flames*.

This is a fantasy novel that follows Prince Varojin Auris from ages 18 to 26 as he navigates familial issues and fighting multiple wars. The story includes themes and events that may not be suitable for some readers:

- Fantasy and magical violence, including inuries, mentions of blood, and character deaths

- References to parental death

- Alcohol consumption

- References to sex, including questioning by main character if he is asexual or allosexual

- Nightmares

- Grief and loss

- Mildly disordered eating and exercising (not descriptive, tied to depression)

- Verbal and physical abuse by authority and parental figures

Readers who may be sensitive to these elements, please take note. If you need to put the book down at any time (including now), please do so and take care of yourself.

THE NORTH SEA
TALMARIS
GRAND DUCHY OF NOVARIA
ZINDIR
THE ZAIKUD EMPIRE
MACADIAN MOUNTAINS
THE WESTERN SEA
POSAN
FORT AVALON
NARIZON
CORSYCA
FORT BLACKROCK
FORT IRONWING
KINGDOM OF DELIA
SAPOI
CAPITAL CITIES
CITIES
NOTABLE TOWNS
FORTS
MEMATOS
ILESOURIA

IRVINA

THE LOST
ISLES

THE
HELOSIAN
EMPIRE

REPUBLIC OF
TORNAMA

THE
ADLANDS

RING OF
FIRE

KALAMA

SEZIA

THASIA

KATAVENA

TAIPOLI
ISLANDS

THE SOUTHERN OCEAN

THE EASTERN SEA

To those just trying to survive

PART 1: CHANGE

Chapter 1
Spring, Year 1012

Prince Varojin Auris didn't need special treatment. He was perfectly content being treated just like every other person in all of Helosia.

But did his father have to treat him *worse*?

Jin's jaw tightened as he finished packing his suitcase. He'd just turned eighteen a month ago. Twenty was, by law, the minimum age for enlistment. He was supposed to have two more years before he got sent off to his father's skies forsaken military. But, Jin supposed, his father made the laws. That meant he could also break them whenever he wanted.

He'd been dreading this morning for a week, and it was finally here.

"Ready to go, Your Imperial Highness?" The voice was cool, removed. Oskar.

Jin slammed his suitcase shut and turned to his guard. "Can't wait."

Oskar didn't react. He *never* reacted. "Would you like me to take your luggage, Your Imperial Highness?"

"No."

Jin grabbed the suitcase and followed Oskar out of his apartment. He'd never needed the three rooms when he was a child, but he was going to miss this place. He'd lived at the palace since his birth, had been welcomed in despite the fact that he was the product of his father's affair. He'd grown up here. Even if he didn't love the bright colors—especially that Auris-family red woven into the details of the sitting room—Jin was going to miss it. After one last look over his shoulder, Jin closed the door behind him.

His half-siblings were all on this floor of the palace, safe and asleep in their own apartments. They'd all said their goodbyes the night before. His eldest brother, Apelo, had seemed appropriately sad. Kaius, older than Jin by a mere six months, hadn't seemed sad at all. But Eliana, Jin's younger sister, had actually been upset. He'd saved their goodbye for last, and he'd made her promise not to wake up in the morning to see him off. One tear-filled goodbye in private was enough. Another one out in the open would simply make their father angry. Emperor Aelius Auris hated tears.

The palace halls were empty, eerily quiet compared to the usual bustle of visitors and politicians. It was just Jin and Oskar this close to sunrise. Courtiers wouldn't have yet made their way to the palace, and the palace staff had their own back corridors and stairways to use.

Even outside the palace walls, the world seemed to be waiting. The cool morning air was still. The usual faint sounds of city traffic were nonexistent. Even the seagulls, usually soaring overhead before making their way down to Tinale Bay, were absent.

It was like the stars knew what was about to happen.

A black car idled on the palace's long drive, just a few dozen feet from the bottom of the front steps. The driver, a red-haired man whose name Jin didn't know, stood at attention near the rear passenger door.

And at the bottom of the stairs stood Emperor Aelius Auris, watching as Jin descended. He hadn't expected his father to look sad, but the man didn't even look so much as worried. In fact, Jin swore Aelius's eyes were a little brighter than normal.

Fuck you, Jin thought as he passed his father.

"I trust you have everything you need, Varojin?" Aelius asked as he fell into step with Jin.

4

"Yup."

The driver opened the door for Jin, then lifted the brown suitcase from his hand. He brought it to the back of the car, opened the trunk, and set it inside.

Jin tried not to look in that direction. Truly, he did. But his traitorous eyes shifted anyway, focusing not on the driver but on the gray observatory tower peeking out from the garden's tree line in the distance. His heart squeezed.

"I know you're upset, Varojin," Aelius said, drawing Jin's attention back. "But this is for the best."

Jin hadn't planned on saying more than a simple goodbye to his father. He'd planned to keep this simple, swift. Cold, just like Oskar. Just like his father usually was.

Fuck plans.

"For the best?" Jin asked. "Please, Father, explain to me why this is for the best. Explain to me why you're not sending me to university like Kaius. Explain to me why you're breaking your own fucking laws to send me away."

"This is your problem," Aelius hissed. "I told you not to make a scene. You cannot follow simple orders."

"Orders? I'm not some soldier for you to command!"

Aelius sniffed, his eyebrows raising almost imperceptibly. "You will be soon. Sergeant Koyalis might be the one to finally break you."

"Break me?" Jin laughed, a dark sound. Behind him, the driver and Oskar both shifted on the gravel driveway. "Do you hear yourself? You want someone to break your child?"

Aelius's jaw tightened; it was a habit Jin had picked up, too. He hated that about himself.

"Children do not speak to their parents with such disrespect."

"Respect goes both ways."

Jin was sure that would earn him some sort of punishment. While his father had never been an involved parent—neither with Jin nor his half-siblings—Aelius did love doling out punishments. Jin was the only one of the four Auris children who had ever been on the receiving end of their father's magic, though. The lightning bolts of scars on the left side of his back were proof enough.

But now, his father simply stared at him. No flames. No lightning. No . . . anything.

"You are an Auris," Aelius sneered as he inched closer to Jin. "You are a prince. You are a powerful mage. You *will* learn to start acting appropriately for your station."

Jin lifted his chin. "And if I don't?"

Aelius straightened and took a step back away from the car. "You have one year, Varojin. When you next step foot in this city, I expect you to be more like Kaius. Do not disappoint me more than you already have."

A string of curses formed on the tip of Jin's tongue as his father turned and walked away. Before he could shout any of them, Oskar stepped back in front of Jin, blocking the sight of Aelius's retreat.

"You should be on your way, Your Imperial Highness," Oskar said. "Your airship is scheduled to leave in half an hour."

Jin looked east again, back toward the observatory tower. Should he try to convince Oskar to let him have just a few more minutes? Should he go try to wake Astrea up to somehow explain what was happening?

He'd known for weeks. He'd known this day was coming, but he hadn't told anyone. His father hadn't even told Jin's siblings until just two days prior. But Jin hadn't been able to bring himself to tell Astrea.

Astrea Sovna was his best friend. If something happened to him—*when* something happened to him—in one of his father's wars, she would be devastated. He didn't want her to feel that loss, the loss that thousands of families around the empire already felt. Cutting her off now was for the best. It would hurt, but when he eventually became another casualty, just one more lost to his father's war machine, she wouldn't be so sad. It would be easier this way.

He'd promised himself he wouldn't try to tell her at the last minute. He'd also promised himself he wouldn't fight with his father, and look how that had gone.

He had to keep this promise. It was for the best. It was for her.

"I'm ready," Jin said as he finally looked back at Oskar.

His guard, the man who had been assigned to protect him when Jin was still just a small child, simply nodded. "Have a safe trip, Your Imperial Highness."

And then Oskar, too, walked away without so much as a glance over his shoulder.

Jin slid into the backseat, flinching as the driver slammed the door shut behind him. And as the car started down the long palace driveway, Jin looked out the window facing east one more time.

Would he really make it those twelve months his father promised?

Jin wasn't sure he would ever see this place again.

CHAPTER 2
SUMMER, YEAR 1012

Flames spun out from Jin's hands in a torrent of heat and anger, consuming the bullet-sized pieces of earth headed straight for him. A water whip lashed at him from the right. Jin jumped back, skidding on the dusty floor of Fort Ironwing's training center.

It had been almost three months since Jin left Kalama. Three months that he'd been away from his home, his family, and his friends. Being away from his family—except for Eliana—was a blessing, actually. Not seeing Kaius's smug face every day was the best thing in the world.

But everything else was awful.

Another Fireweaver's flames arced toward him from his left. Energy burned under Jin's skin as he tore them from the other Fireweaver's control and into his own. He pushed them back at the woman, the flames surging bright and hot.

"Focus!" a rough, unwelcome voice shouted.

Jin hated that voice. Sergeant Koyalis's voice.

Koyalis advanced on Jin's front. The Tidebacker and Fireweaver moved in from his right and left.

Jin tensed.

The water came from his right first, fire from his left half a heartbeat later. This he could handle. Jin shot his arms out to each side, fire bursting free in identical shields that protected him. The other mages didn't relent. If he dropped his hands, his fire, he'd get hit.

And his front was fully open. Vulnerable. *Focus.*

Jin sucked in a deep breath as he pulled on that energy thrumming through his body. His fire roared to his right, consuming the water and heading straight for the Tidebacker. He didn't look to see what happened. As soon as the water stopped, he angled his body toward the Fireweaver and pulled the flames from her control again. He'd practiced that thousands of times back home with his old fireweaving teachers.

Easy.

As he began redirecting the fire, something rough slammed into his shoulder. The fabric of his maroon training shirt tore. Earth ripped into his skin. Jin staggered back, flames faltering. A heavy rock struck him in the gut. Doubling over, Jin nearly vomited.

"What did I tell you about focusing?" Sergeant Koyalis sneered.

Jin glanced up at the older man. He knew that pose. The wide stance. The tight shoulders.

"Do I really need to teach you this lesson again, Private Auris?" Koyalis shouted, more earth hovering in the air in front of him. His sand-hued skin turned red with his rage. "You are an embarrassment to this camp! To your family! How many times do we have to go through this drill?"

Jin knew he shouldn't say anything, but it didn't matter anyway. Koyalis wasn't done with him yet. "Fuck you."

Koyalis punched forward. That floating rock barreled toward Jin. Despite his aching shoulder and abdomen, Jin moved, his flames roaring to life with little effort at all. They ate the rock just as something hard hit his good shoulder, then his knee.

Jin stumbled forward, pain flaring through his wrists as he caught himself before he faceplanted.

He hated this place.

You are a powerful mage. His father's words from the morning Jin left Kalama still echoed in his mind every time he set foot in the training center. He was a powerful mage. He knew that. But as his trainers said, he lacked finesse. He lacked control and discipline and awareness. And they'd been beating that lesson into him day in and day out since he'd arrived at Fort Ironwing three months before.

Black boots stopped just in Jin's line of sight. He looked up at Koyalis, the man's brown eyes almost alight. That happened whenever Jin pissed him off.

"Your father will hear about this."

Jin forced a smile. "Good."

Koyalis's eyes narrowed, then he barked over his shoulder, "Auris is heading to the healers. Whelan, you're next! Come show everyone how it's really done."

Pushing to his feet, Jin staggered past Koyalis and out of the training ring. A group of privates stood there, their maroon uniforms identical to Jin's. Some of them raised their eyebrows at him, while others whispered to each other.

He'd been training with these same people for months. All older than him by at least two years. All of them mages. None of them his friends. He'd hoped to at least make one friend while away from home. Just one. He hadn't thought that was too much to hope for. But everyone else in his unit just avoided him when they could.

Almost everyone.

"Can't handle the heat, Your Imperial Highness?" asked Whelan, a young Tempest, as he stepped toward the front of the group. "Daddy pampered you too much at the palace?"

Jin clenched his teeth as Whelan shoved past him, knocking him right in the shoulder that had just been injured.

This skies damned place. These skies damned people.

Ignoring the whispers of the others, Jin headed for the stairs that would take him to the infirmary.

This was the third time this week Jin had been sent to the healers. He winced as the Lightbringer leaning over his cot began to heal his right shoulder, the last injury that needed to be taken care of. *Fucking Koyalis.*

"Private Auris." That soft, sing-song voice didn't match the woman it belonged to. Lady Zephyrine Kanakos, also known as Colonel Kanakos to those at the camp.

"You're good to go, Your Imperial Highness," the Lightbringer, a middle-aged man with russet skin, said. He helped Jin sit up, fine lines forming around his purple eyes as he smiled. "Just take it easy for the rest of the day. Magic can only do so much."

Jin nodded at the man; he didn't know his name, though he'd seen him a couple of times this week. The healers were always rotating in and out of the camp, taking turns on the front lines. His father was still fighting the Zaikudi to the northeast, and the fighting was moving into the Macadian Mountains. Based on the few reports Jin had overheard, it was a stalemate. He didn't know what they were fighting over. He wasn't sure the two sides even knew what they were fighting over. Helosia and its neighbors were constantly fighting over something.

"Colonel Kanakos." Jin rotated his shoulder, surprised when it moved without even the smallest twinge. That healer did great work. "Does Sergeant Koyalis want me back in the ring?"

"I have no idea what Koyalis wants, nor do I care."

Zephyrine was a strange sight in this place, and it wasn't because of her stark white hair at her young age. No, it was because she was a noble-woman and eldest child. Usually, only a family's younger children—the less important ones—ended up here, if nobles even ended up here at all. She'd transferred in a month ago, and after the handful of run-ins he'd had with Zephyrine, Jin had decided he liked her best of all the officers. She wasn't warm, but her reputation said she was fair.

"Then what can I help you with?" he asked.

Zephyrine pulled two envelopes out of her black uniform's deep front pocket. She was the only person in all of Fort Ironwing who wore black; everyone else wore some shade of red. When she extended the letters to him, Jin noticed a small, puckered scar marring the smooth, brown skin of her hand.

"Special delivery from Kalama," she said.

Jin's heart skipped a beat, then sank. He knew what this was without even reading the fronts of the envelopes. He did anyway, confirming his suspicions.

One was from Eliana.

The other was from Astrea.

"Thanks," he muttered as he tucked them away into his pocket. When he glanced up, Zephyrine was still there, watching him with those gray eyes. They reminded him of Kalama's summer storm clouds. "Isn't delivering mail a private's job?"

"Perhaps." Zephyrine settled onto the cot across from him. The infirmary was quiet, empty except for the two of them. The Lightbringer had disappeared into a small office on the opposite side of the room. "Perhaps I wanted to check up on you. That was a hard hit you took earlier."

"You saw that?"

"I did."

Jin's entire face heated. "Great."

"You're not the problem, Prince Varojin."

"Please, don't call me that." Hearing that title, that name, hurt. He'd never liked the formal title of his birthright, but now that his father had practically kicked him out of the family, Jin hated it even more.

"What would you prefer I call you?"

"Private," Jin said. "That's what the other officers call me. Or Jin."

It was a strange position to be in. In Kalama, in any other situation, Jin technically held rank over Lady Kanakos. He held rank over everyone at this camp. *Technically.* His commanding officers and trainers didn't go easy on him. He didn't expect them to, but he also wished that Koyalis and a handful of others didn't privately flaunt the fact that they had his father's permission to do whatever they needed to make him comply. And everyone else was uneasy around Jin. He may have worn a private's maroon uniform, but they still saw the invisible crown on his head.

Zephyrine nodded. "As I was saying, Jin, you're not the problem. You're a real talent."

"Tell that to Sergeant Koyalis."

"I planned to do so after I spoke with you about an opportunity."

"I've not been approved for anything beyond training here at Fort Ironwing."

"I can change that."

The hairs on the back of Jin's neck prickled. "What, exactly, is this opportunity?"

"While I cannot provide you with the specifics now—"

"Of course you can't."

She rolled her eyes. "While I cannot provide the specifics *now*, just know it will not be an easier assignment. In fact, it will likely be harder."

Why would he take on something *more* difficult? Jin's days already ran together, a never-ending blur of getting beat on by his trainers. What could be harder than this?

"It will be harder," she continued when he said nothing, "but it will be fair. It will suit your talents."

"What could you possibly know about my talents?"

"More than you realize." Zephyrine smiled. "So, do you want me to put in the request with Sergeant Koyalis?"

"Do you need my decision now?"

"No, but I do need it by tomorrow morning. I leave in two days, and you'll be coming with me if you accept. You can find me in the officer's lounge."

With that, Zephyrine stood and adjusted the cuffs of her jacket. Then she nodded at Jin and exited through the infirmary's narrow door, leaving him alone again.

The one good thing about Fort Ironwing was that even privates were given their own quarters. Jin's room was smaller than his closet back at the palace. He could take two short steps from his bed and be at his desk. If he took two steps in another direction, he'd be at the narrow wardrobe tucked in one corner. That was fine by him. He was just grateful to have a few moments of privacy every day.

He'd come straight back to his room after leaving the infirmary. Training was over for the day anyway, and he still had half an hour before dinner was served in the mess hall. The letters Zephyrine had delivered were burning a hole in his jacket, and he'd barely locked his door behind him when he tore them out of his pocket.

Eliana's first. Privates didn't get phone privileges, so this was the only way he could communicate with his sister.

Dear Jin,

I hope you're alright. I haven't heard from you in several weeks. Is training really that hard? You were always better than me when we had lessons with our mage tutor. I can't imagine you're not doing well.

I miss you. The only thing I can be grateful for is that Kaius is on a tour of the empire right now. Father agreed he could have a break from university for that reason. He's lucky. I'm still stuck in Kalama.

Did you read my last letter? Apelo is marrying Lady Thana the week before the autumn equinox. Do you think Father will let you come home for the ceremony? I know Apelo would like to see you. Father doesn't love that Apelo wants to get married so young. Hopefully he changes his mind. Thana is so lovely. I can't wait to call her our sister.

Please write back to me soon. I know you're probably too busy, but it's awful not having you around to talk to.

I love you. Please be safe.

Your sister,
Ellie

P.S. Are you going to write back to Az? She told me you haven't answered any of her letters.

Sighing, Jin set the letter on his bed and ran his hands through his hair. He tugged at a few of his curls, pulling them apart. He'd gotten the last letter, the one that said their eldest brother was getting married. Jin had been surprised by the news; Apelo was only twenty-three. He was more surprised that Apelo was being permitted to marry Thana; she was from one of the lesser noble families. The territory they ran in eastern Helosia was one of the smallest in the empire. She had to be bringing *something* to the dynasty for their father to agree to the marriage.

How was he supposed to tell Eliana he wouldn't be welcomed back to Kalama for three more seasons? That he wasn't allowed to come to the wedding? The knowledge that he wouldn't get to attend his eldest brother's wedding was like a stab to the gut. The fact that it wasn't even an option hurt. But how did he tell his fifteen-year-old sister that without breaking her heart?

And what to do about that postscript? Jin hadn't expected Astrea not to say anything. She was Jin's best friend—used to be his best friend—but she was close with Eliana too. How did he explain that to his little sister?

He needed to get it over with. This was Astrea's third letter in as many months.

Jin picked up the second envelope and tore it open.

Dear Jin,

Are you allowed to receive letters at training? Are you allowed to write them? I'm worried that I haven't heard from you.

You don't have to worry about things here. I'm making sure Ellie doesn't get into too much trouble without you around. She was so happy when she found out Kaius was leaving for a tour of the empire. I think she's looking forward to a summer without him. It's practically a vacation. Also, I hope it's alright that I got your address from her.

Why didn't you tell me your father was making you leave? Ellie says she only found out a couple of days before you left. Why did you feel you couldn't tell me? Honestly, I'm a bit furious with you about it. Maybe that's not fair, but I wish you would have told me. I wish I could've said goodbye.

My studies are going well. I'm going to apply to university this summer. I know it's a bit early, but Saros says my chances are good. I have to believe a Stargazer, right?

Please be safe, and please write back to me when you have the opportunity. I hope you're making new friends and learning new things.

Your friend,
Az

P.S. Cress wanted me to tell you hello.

If Jin was grateful for his private room before, he was even more so now. Tears stung the back of his eyes as he folded Astrea's letter in half. Here he was, missing the first major milestone he should've been celebrating with her. He was so proud she was going to apply for advanced studies early, nearly two years earlier than normal. She always had been so much smarter than him. Saros was right to encourage her.

But the third paragraph stung. Of course she was mad at him . . . and even still, after he'd ignored her for three months, she kept trying to reach out. She still wanted to be his friend.

Jin wiped his eyes with the back of his hand and stood. He wanted to sit down at his desk, skip dinner, and write back to Astrea. He could fill pages and pages with his apologies and stories.

He could, but he wouldn't.

What good was he, anyway? He was a bastard prince, exiled from his own family in the name of what? Discipline? Just for speaking out of turn one too many times? Now he spent his days getting his ass kicked by men twice his size.

The best thing Astrea could do was forget about him.

Jin opened the single drawer on his desk and slipped Astrea's letter inside with the first two she'd sent. Then he grabbed Eliana's letter and set it on top of his desk in hopes he'd actually reply to her. He needed to tell her to drop the wedding issue and simply enjoy her summer without Kaius. She only had a few more years before she would be going to university as well. If she was smart, she'd avoid following in Jin's footsteps. He wouldn't wish this on anyone, but especially not his little sister. If he could convince her to stay the course, maybe he wasn't entirely worthless.

"Sergeant Koyalis may be the one to finally break you." His father's stupid words bounced around Jin's head every day, but as he wiped at his tears again, Jin realized that his father was right. Sergeant Koyalis *was* breaking him, slowly but surely. Fort Ironwing was breaking him.

Jin couldn't let that happen. He couldn't. He couldn't give his father the satisfaction of being right.

He needed to train under someone who believed in him. And based on their conversation just minutes before, Zephyrine Kanakos seemed to believe in him. More than Sergeant Koyalis did, anyway.

"Auris!" Someone pounded on his door. "Dinner's in ten minutes!"

Jin didn't respond, but when the warning calls to the other privates stopped, he went to his door. While the other privates all moved as a group to the right, toward the mess hall, Jin went left.

He needed to find Zephyrine Kanakos.

CHAPTER 3
AUTUMN, YEAR 1012

Wind howled around Jin, slapping his face and pushing back his hair. "Harder!" he yelled. "Come on, I can take it!"

"You sure about that, Auris?" called Dorin Tysias, a Tidebacker and one of Jin's new teammates.

Across the makeshift sparring ring, Dorin bounced back and forth on the balls of his feet. Zephyrine's team had built it for their private use, away from the rest of the soldiers at Fort Avalon. It was high in the mountains, an hour's hike from the base, and the conditions were good for training. Challenging. Unforgiving. Just like real missions, according to Zephyrine.

"Hit me like you mean it!" Jin kept his fists near his face, ready to block whatever move the Tidebacker made. Dorin was the oldest and largest on their team, and when he landed an attack, it hurt. But the pain of training was better than the pain burning a hole in Jin's chest. "Come on!"

Dorin moved, sapphire eyes flashing. The punch was swift. Unforgiving. Jin blocked with his forearm, the hit reverberating through his bones. Another punch from the left. Jin skidded back as he put distance between them. Dorin circled the ring as sweat dripped down his warm brown skin. Jin followed his every move.

These fights were nothing like what Jin had taken part in with his siblings and their shared mage trainer. There was little, if any, magic;

Zephyrine's team learned how to fight without it. They weren't like the beatings he'd taken from Sergeant Koyalis for three months, either.

Jin still couldn't believe Zephyrine had managed to get the transfer approved. Had his father found out?

After getting the transfer approved, Zephyrine had finally disclosed more details to Jin. She was in charge of an elite group, just two teams of four. A spot had opened up after a Fireweaver named Neri died on a prior mission.

Maybe his father would be proud that Jin had been selected for this. Status, after all, was crucial for the Auris family. Or maybe he was glad Jin had been put in just as precarious a position as Neri had once been.

A boot connected with Jin's knee. He crumpled before he even had a chance to react. When Dorin reached a hand out toward him, Jin flinched.

"Easy, easy," Dorin said. "Just helping you up."

That was the other thing about Zephyrine and her team. If you went down during training, it wasn't an excuse to rain down additional abuse. Every time Jin fucked up during their exercises—losing spars, misunderstanding a drill, missing a target—one of the others was there to help him back up and offer some advice.

Jin took Dorin's hand and pulled himself off the cold ground. "Thanks."

"You were off your mark today." Dorin's tone was kind, but Jin glared at him. "You alright?"

"I'm fine."

He wasn't fine.

The wind gusted, blowing right through the thin fabric of Jin's gray shirt. Goose bumps prickled his skin. Autumn had set in, and all around them, deep auburn, orange, and red leaves rustled on the trees. It was nothing like autumn back home, where almost everything stayed green and the temperatures remained mild.

"We should get back to base." That soft voice belonged to Rasa Foscari, the Earthmover on the team. She was short—almost as short as Eliana—and narrow. Her light skin and lighter hair made her look almost like a ghost. Jin had learned very quickly not to underestimate her because of her size. "Boss'll be waiting for us."

"And it's going to get dark soon," added Lando Acordole, a Tephran with sand-colored skin and hair to match. His brown eyes narrowed as he squinted up at the setting sun. "Time to call it a day."

"Fine," Jin said. "Let's go."

Crisp air filled Jin's lungs as he ambled after his teammates. The path back down the mountain was clear thanks to their frequent trips back and forth. They went to their private training area at least twice a week.

Being on Zephyrine's team was better than his last station, but it didn't change the fact that he was missing everything at home. Apelo was married. Astrea would have started her university classes part-time by now. Eliana was growing up; her sixteenth birthday was in just two weeks. Cressida had filed for her first patent with her father's company. Even Kaius had sent one letter in the last six months.

Jin hadn't heard from his father at all.

As Dorin, Rasa, and Lando talked among themselves on the walk back to base, they left Jin alone. Maybe they knew he wasn't in the mood to talk, or maybe they didn't fully trust him yet. They'd been wary of his status and age at first, though they claimed to be over it. Jin had been working with them for a few months, but he still wasn't approved to go on missions. Not yet.

Not that there had been any missions to go on yet, even for the rest of the team; the skirmishes with the Zaikudi had ended. But, Jin guessed based on a few overheard conversations, they really needed time to recover after losing their last Fireweaver.

By the time they'd descended the mountain, the sun had fully sunk below the horizon and the night's chill had set in. Fort Avalon's outer walls rose up in the growing darkness, and the group slipped inside the large front gates. Compared to Fort Ironwing, Avalon was small, just a few low-profile buildings nestled at the base of the Macadian Mountains.

Jin shivered as the wind gusted again. As a Fireweaver, Jin could warm himself up, but he resisted the temptation. Zephyrine encouraged them to push their limits; that was part of why they only got access to healers for the most severe injuries. Growing up in Kalama, Jin hadn't experienced cold like this. It was too far south. Now was as good a time as any to build that tolerance for the chilly air.

His skin ached as he passed into the warm interior of the main building. Just as Fort Avalon was smaller than Ironwing, it was also far less state-of-the-art, but it had everything they needed. Besides, becoming a member of Zephyrine's team came with its perks. He was a second lieutenant now, an officer. And being an officer here meant he was spared the group barracks and had a private room set far away from anyone close to his age.

He'd just unlocked his door when Zephyrine rounded the narrow hallway's corner.

"Ah, you're back." She handed him a small box and two envelopes. "Mail arrived. If you want to send any replies, get them in by the tenth bell tonight. Airship's leaving first thing in the morning and won't be back for a fortnight."

"Thanks."

"I know it's not my business," Zephyrine said, "but are you ever going to write her back?"

"What?" Jin didn't actually need clarification. He knew exactly what Zephyrine was asking.

"That Astrea girl. That's the third letter I've given you from her, and you've never dropped one off addressed to her."

"All due respect, Colonel," Jin muttered, "but you're right, it's not your business."

"It might help if you actually write back to your friends and family. It makes missing them a little more bearable."

"I write back to Eliana."

"Yes, well." She shrugged a slender shoulder. "Supper's in twenty minutes. Clean up before you come to the mess hall."

Jin ignored her and pushed his door open. The room was sparsely decorated, with plain wood-paneled walls, a narrow bed, and a small desk and wardrobe. It wasn't much bigger than what he'd had at Fort Ironwing, but there was enough space for him to move around comfortably. Unfortunately, he still had to use the communal bathrooms.

Jin dropped his package on his bed. Twenty minutes. Could he open his mail and shower in twenty minutes?

He could if he was quick.

Jin pried open the box first. Kalama's palm frond symbol had been stamped in faded red ink on the top, and when Jin saw its contents, he knew who it had to be from. His sister. There was a large jar of the salve he'd requested, the one that helped numb pain. It was hard to sleep with so many bruises and sore muscles, and he couldn't wait until after dinner when he could use it and relax for a couple hours.

That was all he'd asked her to send, but tucked next to the jar were two chocolate bars wrapped in gold foil. He reached for her letter first.

Dear Jin,

Sorry it took me so long to get the package sent to you. I had to sneak it past Father and Oskar. He's on my guard detail now. He's so boring.

How do you like Fort Avalon? I found it on the map in Father's office. It's so remote. How are you tolerating the cold? I may freeze to death if I ever visit someplace so far north.

I'm sorry you couldn't come to Apelo's wedding. It was lovely, though Kaius managed to make part of the cocktail party about himself. We got it sorted before the reception. Apelo and Thana are going south for their honeymoon. Do you think we'll get a new niece or nephew next year?

Train hard. I know you'll be the best one on your team.

Love,
Ellie

P.S. Enjoy the chocolate. That's from my personal stash, the kind with the nougat pieces. I'm very nice for sending that to you since it's my favorite.

Despite himself, Jin laughed. He pulled one of the bars out of the box and unwrapped the foil. He broke off a piece and popped it in his mouth, and sure enough, milk chocolate and nougat melted on his tongue. He hadn't had sweets in months, not since he left Kalama. Soldiers didn't get such luxuries.

Jin swallowed the chocolate, then sighed. There was no point putting off what came next. He reached for the second letter.

Jin,

I know I'm a fool, but I'm hoping you write me back this time. I also know you've been writing Ellie back, so you can't be too busy.

I don't know why you won't respond to me. Did I do something wrong? Did I hurt your feelings? If so, I'm sorry. And if I didn't, would you please just write back to me? Even one sentence. I miss talking to you. I have so much to tell you.

It's been six months since you left. This is my sixth letter. If I don't hear back this time, I'll stop writing to you.

You're my best friend. I hope you know I miss you and that I'm sorry if I did something wrong.

Even if you don't write back to me, please stay safe.

Az

Jin blew out a harsh breath. Before he could stop himself, he imagined Astrea in her bedroom in the observatory. He'd only been in a handful of times over the years; her uncle didn't like him being there. Even still, Jin could picture her at her desk, hunched over as she wrote in that hurried scrawl of hers. What was that like for her, finally realizing they couldn't be friends anymore? That he wasn't going to write back no matter how many times she wrote to him?

Jin went to the narrow wardrobe and opened it. He pulled out a fresh uniform, then reached for his luggage, where he kept all of the letters from Eliana and Astrea. He tucked Astrea's inside, next to not only the letters he'd received from her, but all of the ones he wrote her that he never sent.

It had become a regular ritual for him. He wrote down everything that happened that he would've told her if he was still in Kalama. Astrea would never see those letters, but somehow, that hurt less than not writing to her at all.

He slid the luggage back into its spot at the bottom of the closet.

Knowing that Astrea finally understood he wasn't going to write back hurt more than he'd expected. He wished more than anything that he could go back home, that he could go knock on the observatory door and hug her. That he could tell her he was sorry and explain why he'd made the choice he had.

That deep ache settled in his bones, the one that had been there since the day his father told him he was leaving Kalama.

He'd made the right decision to end that friendship. Joining Zephyrine's team inevitably meant greater risks than with the regular army. For skies' sake, he was replacing the team's *dead* Fireweaver. How long would it be before they were bringing in *his* replacement and sending his body home?

CHAPTER 4
WINTER, YEAR 1012

Jin had never been so cold in his life.

Kalama's mild winters rarely required more than a sweater or light coat. In his eighteen years, he'd only seen snow a couple of times. And now, here in the Macadian Mountains, hundreds and hundreds of miles north of the capital, Jin was sure he was going to freeze to death.

Just two more days, he reminded himself. They were supposed to be here for a full three days, backpacking through the mountains, trudging through half-frozen rivers, camping outside, and pushing their magic and stamina to the limit. Exposure training, Zephyrine called it. It was good for them, she said.

Jin wasn't even allowed to use his fireweaving to warm himself. He'd contemplated disobeying orders and doing it anyway, but Zephyrine would notice if he stopped shivering.

"When you're out at night, trying to find your way back to your camp, base, or transportation," Zephyrine called over her shoulder, "what star do you want to try to find first?" She was at the front of the group, Dorin and Rasa right behind her.

"The North Star," Jin called back. Talking kept his teeth from chattering. "You can use the moon to orient yourself south, too, depending on what phase it's in."

"Well, kid, you know a few things after all," Lando said from behind him. "Haven't even covered that one in your training yet. Maybe you aren't as soft as I thought."

Lando had been giving Jin grief like this for weeks. Suggestions that he was too pampered, too soft from growing up at the palace. That he needed to get used to military life.

While it was true that Jin had grown up with every creature comfort imaginable, he had never found his home life comfortable at all. Every day as a child, he'd dreaded finishing his lessons and mage training; that meant he was more likely to run into his father. Growing up at the palace meant walking on eggshells, interpreting double-speak, and wearing a mask to avoid upsetting the wrong person.

Jin said nothing, instead focusing on Zephyrine's quiz about celestial navigation. She asked them about the constellations, which ones to use to orient their direction and which ones were their favorites. She talked about how to estimate time of night with the stars and how to remember the phases of the moon.

None of it was new to Jin. These were conversations he'd had with Astrea as recently as the spring of that year. Just weeks before he learned he was being sent away, she'd snuck him into the observatory one night to show him the Warrior constellation. *Ironic.* He tore his gaze off the snow-covered path and glanced skyward.

The stars had been out for almost two hours and still, Zephyrine hadn't stopped for the night. Jin couldn't feel his body anymore. He was ready to simply drop to the ground when Zephyrine paused.

"Another ten minutes, then we'll be at the clearing."

A clearing? Had she lost her mind? That would only leave them more exposed to the cold and the wind. They needed a cave or sheltered location. But nobody else questioned their leader. Lando, Rasa, and

Dorin all followed her without another word. Sighing, Jin adjusted his knapsack and hurried after them.

Zephyrine was, at least, true to her word. They reached a clearing not too long after. One side of it was buffered by a large rock formation, though the rest was just more endless forest.

"I'll clear space for a fire," Zephyrine said. "Lando, get wood. Rasa, go keep an eye on him. Dorin, start dividing the rations."

As everyone else scattered to do their jobs, Jin looked at Zephyrine. "What about me?"

"You're going to start said fire for us," she said, "and then sit by it before I get court-martialed for letting a prince die under my care. I know you're freezing."

His jaw tightened. "I'm fine."

"Some advice for you, Jin." Zephyrine walked toward the rock formation, then extended her hands in one smooth motion. Wind swept in from behind Jin, chilling his already frozen body as it blew snow toward the far side of the clearing. She turned back toward him. "Don't be proud. We're all cold. That's the point. Now, when Rasa comes back, get the fire started. Nothing too big."

And then she was gone, stomping through the remaining snow toward Dorin.

When Rasa returned a couple minutes later, she dropped a bundle of sticks onto the area Zephyrine had cleared. That was barely enough firewood to burn for ten minutes, but Lando had gone in search of some, too. Hopefully enough to keep something burning through the night.

"Don't feel bad," Rasa said as Jin shivered. "We all struggled the first time we did this hike."

"I don't feel bad." Jin sucked in a breath, relishing in the heat of the flame now dancing over his gloved hand. He pushed it toward the kindling and watched, grateful, as the campfire burst to life.

Rasa clapped Jin's shoulder. "Neri used to struggle with that, too. Said it was hard to pull on his fire when he was so cold."

This team didn't talk about Neri, the Fireweaver they'd lost, often. Not in front of Jin, anyway, though he was sure they did when he wasn't around. It had to be hard seeing a prince—a child—take your dead teammate's spot.

Jin shrugged. "It wasn't that hard." And it wasn't. Jin had heard that Fireweavers typically had trouble conjuring their flames in freezing temperatures, but it felt no different to him now.

"Then I'm very glad you're here. I wasn't going to last if Zephyrine made us go much longer." Rasa said nothing else as she joined Dorin.

Jin finally shrugged off his pack and let it fall to the hard dirt underneath him. He dropped down next to it and pulled off his gloves. His skin was a little red and dry, but it didn't look too bad.

How were they supposed to continue in these conditions for days? Eliana would never believe this.

Eventually, everyone else joined him around the fire. Jin silently took his rations from Dorin, just dried meat and crackers. He wasn't hungry, but he forced himself to eat.

"The thing I miss most about home," Rasa said as she swallowed a bite of jerky, "is my wife's stroganoff. I swear, it's the best on the entire continent."

"And where'd she find the best recipe on the whole continent?" Dorin asked.

"Family recipe from where her mother grew up in northern Tornama." Rasa sighed and snapped a cracker in half. "Who do you all miss?"

"My brother," Lando said. He ran a hand over the top of his hat. Jin didn't know he had a brother; Lando had never mentioned him before.

"My children," Dorin replied. "Skies, I miss my children. And my wife, of course."

"What about you, Zephyrine?" Rasa asked. "Who do you miss?"

Zephyrine swallowed a mouthful of water from her canteen, slowly recapping it before she set it on the ground. "You three always get sentimental when we go on these excursions."

"Something about the stars and the night make you realize how far away from home you are," Rasa said. When Lando chuckled, Rasa glared daggers at him. "So, who do you miss the most, Zephyrine?"

Zephyrine studied the group for a moment, then gave a tight smile. "My pet bird."

Jin raised an eyebrow and tore off another piece of jerky. It wasn't much, but the knot in his stomach had started to loosen.

"Your bird?" Lando asked. "I don't think I realized you liked animals."

"Yes, well, it was a gift from my sister. That bird now lives with said sister. But the thing has grown on me."

"You don't miss your sister?" Dorin asked.

"Skies, no." Zephyrine laughed and shook her head once. "No, we never got on that well. I think she got the bird to try to annoy me. Now she's stuck with the damn thing."

It sounded like something Kaius would do, especially to Eliana. Actually, Jin could see Eliana doing it to Kaius, too. Those two were always arguing, though Jin supposed that came with the territory. They *were* competing to be their father's heir.

"What about you, Jin?" Rasa asked.

"No one," Jin lied as he pushed the pain back, back as far away as he could. He snapped a cracker in half, watching as a few crumbs fell to the ground. "I miss no one."

"There has to be something you miss about Kalama," Lando said after a moment. "I know I give you a hard time, kid, but it can't be that bad."

Jin watched the small fire. He could make them larger, give them more warmth, but that would burn through the wood faster. Instead, he cracked his knuckles.

"My sister," he finally said. "I mean, I actually miss her, unlike Zephyrine."

That earned him a chuckle from the group.

"And nothing else?" Lando asked. "Not even the food at the palace?"

Jin shrugged. The food was always good back home, but the company usually soured the meal.

"It helps, you know," Zephyrine said. "Talking about those we miss."

"Makes it hurt a little less," Dorin agreed. "Helps to know that we're all just fighting to get home to our people."

Jin tore into another piece of jerky, chewing slowly. Could it actually hurt less to talk about everything he missed? Instead of forcing it down, would it be better to share? They'd probably think him a fool. Maybe he was. Still, he nodded.

"My best friend," he finally said. "I miss my best friend."

"And what is this best friend's name?" Zephyrine asked.

She already knew. Jin knew that Zephyrine knew. Wasn't she the one keeping tabs on his mail?

"Her name is Astrea." How long had it been since he'd said her name out loud?

"And what do you miss most about her?"

Everything.

But Jin didn't say that. Instead, he fixated on the sky again. Thousands of stars twinkled above them, a thick band of purple, white, and blue slicing through the middle of the sky. He'd been able to see it much more faintly in Kalama. Here, it was a hundred times more brilliant. Astrea would love it. Maybe someday she could see it for herself.

"You gave me crap for knowing the night sky, Lando," Jin said. "Well, Astrea was the one to teach me. That's what I miss most. That she always taught me something new."

There was so much more he missed about her, of course. The novels she picked for him at the shops in Kalama when he couldn't join her. Her laughter as they hid deep in the gardens for a break from Saros and the other tutors. Her recent obsession with coffee. Her appreciation for all things sweet. How she always seemed to know what he was feeling even when he hadn't told her something was wrong. The way they'd both just seemed to understand each other. Those were just a few of the many things he missed about Astrea.

"Very generous of her to take the time to do so," Lando quipped. Jin didn't have it in him to even glare; he was too cold, too tired.

"She was," he agreed, swallowing past the lump in his throat. "She is, I mean. She is very generous."

Astrea had always been willing—eager, even—to help Jin when he needed it. Sometimes he pretended to need help with his studies just to spend more time with her. He never gave her extra work to do, just said he needed the structure she set. Astrea took her studies very seriously. He'd always bring her coffee or cookies from the palace kitchens to make up for it. Maybe, in hindsight, he should've just studied on his own and left her to do what she needed to do, but what he wouldn't give to spend time with her again.

"A real gift," Rasa mused. "I mean, if you think about it, she taught you how to find your way home."

As the conversation shifted to Dorin's children and everyone's families, Jin tried to listen. He tried. But he couldn't stop staring up at the stars and wondering if he'd actually get to go home to her soon.

CHAPTER 5
SPRING, YEAR 1013

Jin supposed this birthday, his nineteenth, was better than the year before. After all, his father had already given him the worst possible gift. Sure, there was no cake, no celebration, no friends, no anything, but at least he didn't have to see his father. That was a gift in itself.

As he walked into Fort Avalon's mess hall, the last of the soldiers about to go on their morning shift shuffled out past him. The hall was bare bones, its gray brick walls depressing first thing in the morning. The only splashes of color were the red and maroon accents on the soldiers' uniforms. Then Jin spotted the familiar all-black garb of his group seated at a table near the middle of the room. Rasa waved Jin down. He got his breakfast quickly—eggs, sausage, toast, and coffee—and joined them.

"Do you eat the same thing every morning, kid?" Lando asked.

"Oh, leave him alone," Rasa said. "At least he doesn't take ten minutes to pick what he wants."

"I do not take *ten* minutes," Lando protested as Jin shoved a forkful of eggs into his mouth. "Just five."

"Which is about four too many. The menu never even changes."

"So?" Lando asked. "I like a little variety. Maybe the kid needs a little encouragement to try something new."

"Jin certainly doesn't need your bad influence in his life," Dorin quipped.

This was part of their morning routine before going to run drills. Rasa and Lando traded jabs for a while, Dorin would throw in his two cents, and they'd try to get Jin to join them. It wasn't that he didn't like his teammates; he just preferred to listen. With them all being at least a decade older than him, it was hard to find much in common. Lando continuing to call him 'kid' proved that point.

This was how he learned about them, though: listening to their chatter. Rasa and her wife, Coral, had been married for nearly ten years. Coral still lived near Kalama and ran a café. Dorin's wife, Meri, stayed at their home further north of the capital with their two young children. Lando was a bachelor, though his brother still worked their family farm toward the central part of Helosia.

Just as Rasa directed a series of curses at Lando, Zephyrine appeared in the doorway on the far side of the room. She strode toward them, her long braid swinging with each step.

"Boss incoming," Jin murmured, and the other three stopped their bickering.

Zephyrine sometimes joined them for meals, but today, it looked like she was on a mission. She was doing *the* walk, the one she always used when she had news or assignments for the others. Dorin, Lando, and Rasa had been on a couple of missions without Jin in the last few months.

Jin took another sip of his coffee as Zephyrine closed the rest of the distance to their table.

"Dorin, Rasa, Lando, Jin." Zephyrine scanned their table, her gray eyes finally settling on Jin. "We're headed to the Badlands for the summer. After breakfast, pack your things."

"Headed out today?" Dorin asked.

"First light tomorrow," Zephyrine said. "Jin, come with me."

Jin glanced at his teammates. Rasa, seated next to him, shrugged.

"Go," she said. "I'll clean up your tray."

"Thanks." Jin swallowed one more giant mouthful of coffee before he jumped up and hurried after Zephyrine. Wherever they were going, she was going fast.

Was he in trouble? He didn't think so; he was doing well in training, kept up with whatever chores he was assigned for their unit, and kept his head down. Still, Zephyrine didn't even look over her shoulder at him. As they moved deeper into the fort and the hallways narrowed, Jin realized they were going to her office.

Maybe he *was* in trouble.

Zephyrine motioned for him to go into the room first. Her office was small by most standards, and he'd only been in it a couple of times for team check-ins. It barely fit the five of them.

"Sit." She nodded at the chair behind her desk.

Jin hesitated. Had he seen right? "What?"

"Sit in my chair," Zephyrine said. "You have fifteen minutes. I suggest you pick up that phone now."

Jin hadn't noticed before, but the desk phone was off its receiver. Someone had to be on the other end of the line.

He turned toward Zephyrine, but she was already closing the door.

Swallowing hard, Jin crossed the few paces to the desk. As he sat, he picked up the phone. "Hello?"

"Jin!" Eliana sounded almost like herself, slightly tinny and crackled thanks to the long distance. And he thought he heard a sniffle or two. "I can't believe it's you. Happy birthday!"

"I can't believe it's *you*," he croaked. He stared at the oak door across the room from him. He wasn't allowed phone privileges—his father's order—so how, exactly, had Zephyrine pulled this off? Was this some kind of birthday gift? He hadn't told his team it was his birthday, but he supposed Zephyrine would have access to that information. Maybe she even remembered from some past birthday party of his at the palace; he couldn't be sure.

Jin didn't even know what to say. It had been so long since he'd gotten to speak with his baby sister. The last time he'd seen her, talked to her, was the night before he had to leave Kalama.

He'd been closest to her when they were growing up. Kaius had never been thrilled to have a half brother just six months younger than himself, and Apelo had always been aloof, even with Kaius and Eliana. But Eliana and Jin got on well, and she never held it against him that he was the product of their father's affair. They had their differences, of course, especially since she was being prepared to possibly take over Helosia, but Jin didn't hold that against her, either. It wasn't like either of them had chosen to be born to their parents.

He simply missed his sister.

"Lady Kanakos said you don't have much time," Eliana said quickly. "Something about needing to pack?"

"We're going to the Badlands."

"Why?"

"Training, I guess? I just found out a few minutes ago. I don't have any details."

"Well," Eliana said, "I want you to tell me everything you can in the next ten minutes."

And so Jin did. He told Eliana about Sergeant Koyalis, Zephyrine asking him to join her team, that skies forsaken winter training in the mountains, and his new teammates. He couldn't go into much detail about any of it, but Eliana didn't interrupt him even once. That had to be some kind of record; she almost always interrupted.

"I miss you," Eliana said when he was done. "I wish we had more time."

"Me too, Ellie."

"Are you coming home soon?"

Jin wiped at the tears springing up in his eyes. Aelius had said Jin had one year in the military before he could go home, and they were nearly at that milestone. But as far as Jin knew, his father hadn't reached out. And with their new training location for the summer, Jin doubted he'd be headed back to the capital anytime soon. Zephyrine would've told him if his father had requested Jin's return. That wasn't the kind of summons either of them could ignore. Jin didn't even want to see his father, but he would've liked to see Eliana again.

"I don't think so," Jin muttered.

She scoffed. "Father's such a prick."

"El—" Jin didn't disagree, but she didn't need to be thinking or talking like that. He ran a hand over the top of his curls, then sighed. "Eliana, listen to me."

"Wow." She laughed, the sound distant and hollow. "You never use my full name."

"I'm being serious."

"Serious, sure."

"Eliana, *please*." Jin leaned forward against the desk and pressed the phone closer to his ear, as if that would somehow make her absorb what he had to say. "I am where I am because I mouthed off to him too many times. I disobeyed him too often. You may be higher in line as an heir, but do not test him."

He'd worried about this so much since leaving the city. Eliana may have been just sixteen, but she was already starting to understand how corrupt their father was. She could see what Kaius couldn't and what Apelo wouldn't. And though Jin knew the chances of their father sending Eliana—one of the *real* heirs—away from the city was low, he needed her to listen.

"Please, Ellie. Promise me."

"Jin—"

"Promise me."

She huffed. "I promise."

"Thank you."

The office door cracked open. "Wrap it up, Auris," Zephyrine said. The door closed again.

"Ellie, I have to go," Jin said, using the back of his hand to wipe away the last few tears in his eyes. There was still so much he had to tell her and so much he wanted to ask—about Apelo and Thana, about Cressida, about Astrea. "I don't know when I'll get to call you again, but I'll ask Zephyrine to tell you where to send me letters this summer."

"Oh, you don't have to ask. She already told me."

Jin half-smiled. "Of course she did."

The line went quiet for one heartbeat, two. Then, Eliana whispered, "I love you, Jin."

"I love you too, Ellie."

"Stay safe."

"I will."

He hesitated, but then the line went dead. Eliana had hung up. Jin was glad, too, because he wasn't sure he would've had the strength to end the call first.

Zephyrine strode into the office without so much as a single word. How she could act so aloof at a time like this, Jin didn't know. And whether or not he was allowed to hug his commanding officer, Jin also didn't know.

That didn't stop him from jumping up and throwing his arms around the woman. "Thank you," he said as he quickly pulled away. "Really, thank you."

Jin was tall by most standards, and Zephyrine stood just a few inches shorter than him. Though she barely smiled, fine lines formed around her eyes, and she nodded.

"Family's important," she said. "I thought you'd like to speak with her . . . especially today."

"I really appreciate it."

"Good." Zephyrine tilted her head back toward the door. "Now go pack. First light tomorrow."

"Yes, ma'am." Jin stepped around his boss and headed for the door.

"And remember this moment, Auris!" she called after him. "You're not going to be thanking me after you see what's in store for the summer."

CHAPTER 6
SUMMER, YEAR 1013

Jab. Duck. Cross. Block. Jin skipped backward as Dorin hurled a water whip across the sparring circle. The liquid shot over Jin's left shoulder as he punched out with his right fist. His fire blasted toward Rasa. She cursed. A chunk of earth shot up in front of her, barely blocking the flames as they licked the air.

They'd been going like this for fifteen minutes, and Lando had already tapped out after a nasty fall. Three against one, now two against one.

Dorin came in close, aiming a hook punch for Jin's cheek. He blocked. As Dorin sidestepped, Jin kicked at his knees, sending the Tidebacker to the ground. Jin didn't even need to look as he punched out toward Rasa again. Fire shot toward her. She had just one choice: drop to her knees or get a nasty burn.

She dropped to the ground with a grunt. Jin's chest heaved.

Outside the ring, Lando clapped dramatically. "Well, well, Your Imperial Highness!" he called. "Well done."

"Shut up, Lando," Jin shot back, and the Tephran laughed, a warm, deep sound. Jin offered his hand to Dorin first, helping the Tidebacker off the ground. Then he went to Rasa and did the same.

"Don't go getting a big head," she joked as she brushed sand and dirt off her black pants. "That's only the fourth match you've won this week."

"Four out of five," Jin said, smiling. Rasa laughed. "But don't worry, I won't."

"At least all the work you're putting in is paying off," Lando said.

"Yeah," Jin mumbled as he followed his teammates out of the sparring ring and into the arid desert beyond.

They saw him training his body and magic at all hours of the day; he was first to practice every morning and went back out on his own every night after dinner. Any time he wasn't doing chores or being briefed on tactics they'd need in the field, Jin trained.

What his team didn't know was *why*.

He'd been gone from Kalama for over a year, and he hadn't been invited home. Hadn't been invited home even for his birthday. Hadn't even gotten a phone call or letter from his father to mark the occasion.

Jin knew what this was. He wouldn't be welcomed home anytime soon. It didn't matter how much he trained. It didn't matter how powerful of a mage he was. It didn't matter if he was recruited for an elite team. His father didn't want him in Kalama.

It hurt more than he wanted to admit. So, Jin threw his body and mind into training. He ran drills with his team, but he also ran them on his own and exercised whenever he could. It was the only way he was able to hold it together. It burned him out enough that he could just collapse into bed at the end of each day without too many thoughts plaguing him.

The inner wall of Fort Blackrock loomed before them. Where Fort Avalon was made up of a few low-profile structures in the mountains, Fort Blackrock was truly a fortress. Set in the Badlands near the Ring of Fire, a series of volcanoes near the Eastern Sea, Fort Blackrock was home to . . . well, Jin wasn't sure, exactly. There wasn't anything out here, but still, the fort was huge. Named for the dark volcanic stone used in some of the architecture, Fort Blackrock had two rings. The outer section was where soldiers trained and sparred and where the garages were. The inner ring was where soldiers lived, worked, and studied. The guards on duty nodded at Jin and the team.

"Join us for lunch?" Rasa asked as they approached the mess hall, a low building near the gates. "We have time before we have to meet Zephyrine."

"I'll just see you at the meeting." Jin needed a shower, and he needed one badly. He also wanted a chance to use more of the numbing salve Eliana had sent him. She'd gotten into the habit of sending him a new jar every few months, and he was eternally grateful.

"You sure?" Dorin asked. "You've got to eat at some point."

"I'll do it later."

Lando watched him for a moment, his lips pressing together. They weren't exactly the best of friends, but the last few months, Lando had started taking more of an interest in Jin. Sometimes that meant teasing him about growing up in Kalama. Sometimes that meant teaching Jin something new about magic. And sometimes it meant Lando checked in on him, like he was now.

But Lando simply shrugged and said, "Just make sure you take care of yourself, alright, kid? I don't need Zephyrine up my ass if you pass out from lack of nutrition."

As his teammates moved on and went to the mess hall, Jin hurried toward the officers' barracks. He had maybe an hour before he needed to meet back up with everyone. Zephyrine was leaving for Fort Avalon soon to meet up with her second team, who were finally coming back from a long-term mission. This would be their last meeting with her for a couple of weeks.

As soon as Jin was in his room, he locked the door behind him and started tearing off his sweat-drenched clothes. Fort Blackrock, though remote, had the added luxury of private bathrooms for the officers, even ones with low ranks like Jin. It wasn't a spacious or opulent space like the bathroom he'd grown up with, but he'd gladly take it. He started the shower, impatient as it heated up to something other than freezing cold.

Jin tried not to look in the mirror often. He tried, but sometimes he failed. He looked so different, had changed so much in just over a year.

Training wasn't just distracting his mind. It was transforming his body, and his once-gangly limbs were getting thicker, harder, stronger with each passing week. Being in the Badlands all summer had tanned his skin past its usual light tawny. Jin didn't mind any of that.

What he hated was how tired he looked. He knew he needed to take better care of himself. Lando was right. Jin could go to bed an hour earlier than he did now, sleep in half an hour later. He could eat on a more regular schedule, and he could eat with his team.

It was just so hard to care when he didn't even know what he was doing any of this for.

The meeting room Zephyrine had taken over at Fort Blackrock was large enough to seat eight, but if the fort's commander was bothered, he didn't say. It seemed, at least to Jin, that whatever Zephyrine needed for her team, she got.

She'd had coffee brought in, and Jin had finished his first cup by the time she got things started.

"So," Zephyrine said from her seat at the head of the table. "You've been here for almost three months. How do you all think it's gone?"

"I think we're working well as a team," Rasa said. "We've started communicating well."

When they weren't sparring, they were pushing their bodies with exercise circuits and even exposure to the desert air. And when they weren't doing that, they were running drills as a team. Sometimes they ran the drills in pairs, sometimes as a triad, and sometimes as all four of them. Zephyrine sometimes oversaw these exercises, but so did some of the trainers at the fort. These drills were never easy: obstacles, battle scenarios, staging ambushes and rescues. Jin had been to the healer more than once in the first few weeks, but with every scenario they ran, the fewer injuries he received. He was getting better at anticipating, at noticing, at control.

"I finally see why you brought the kid to the team," Lando said. Jin fought the urge to roll his eyes. "He's a beast."

"Hm." Zephyrine's gaze flicked from Lando to Jin, then to Dorin. "And what do you think, Dorin?"

"I agree with Rasa and Lando. All four of us have come a long way this summer."

Zephyrine pursed her lips. "Better after . . . ?"

Jin knew what she was asking. Better after losing Neri. One night, after Lando had gone to bed early, Rasa and Dorin had filled Jin in. They all blamed themselves in some way for that loss. Rasa claimed she'd been distracted. Dorin had been jumped by a second person he didn't know was there. Lando had been so focused on getting to their target—whoever they were—that he hadn't noticed Neri in trouble with a third and fourth enemy.

"Better," all three of them agreed.

She nodded, then looked at Jin. "And how do *you* feel?"

Jin swallowed. "Good. I feel good."

"Good," Zephyrine said as she stood, "because you've come the furthest of all. I knew what I saw in you all the way back at Fort Ironwing."

Jin's cheeks heated. He hated thinking about those first few months away from home, but he also hated that Zephyrine was talking about this in front of the others. Could this not be a private conversation?

She fiddled with something at a table on the far wall, her back to the group. "You lacked control, and you lacked discipline, but I knew you had potential. You just needed to learn to harness it."

Jin stole a glance at his teammates. Rasa smiled at him, and Dorin studied him. Lando, even, gave Jin the briefest nod. *Wonderful.* Where was Zephyrine going with this?

She turned, a stack of black cloth in her arms. "And based on what I've seen the last few months, but especially the last few weeks, you've learned how to harness both your power and potential. This sorry lot can barely keep up with you now."

"Getting too old," Dorin joked.

Zephyrine set the stack of cloth in front of Jin. Not just cloth. A uniform? Black pants, black shirt. No insignia, not like the uniforms other soldiers wore. No, this was like what his team and what his commanding officer wore.

"You'll get your body armor when you get back to Fort Avalon next month," Zephyrine said. "Welcome to the team, Jin."

PART 2: BATTLE

CHAPTER 7
SUMMER, YEAR 1014

A year. It had been an entire year since Jin officially became part of Zephyrine's team. Another year of endless training, excursions, and preparations. And now, they finally had a mission.

It couldn't come at a better time. Just days before, Jin had gotten a letter from Eliana informing him that his first niece had been born. Apelo and Thana had welcomed the baby a few weeks prior, just before the summer solstice. They'd named her Velia.

Two years he'd been gone. He'd turned twenty. He'd missed his brother's wedding, his niece's birth, his friends' accomplishments and milestones. Two years and Jin still hadn't been welcomed home by his father. He hadn't received so much as a letter or phone call from the man.

"You ready to go?" Rasa poked her head into Jin's room. "Airship's waiting."

Jin buckled up his knapsack and threw it over one shoulder, then followed Rasa through the quiet halls of Fort Avalon. It had become their home base, where both of Zephyrine's teams stayed when they weren't on missions or off in other parts of Helosia for other training. The fort was quiet now except for the soldiers on duty; the night shift seemed like the worst, especially now. It was nearing three in the morning. A few of those soldiers nodded to Jin and Rasa on their way through the halls, though Jin didn't recognize them.

"So . . . you ready?" Rasa asked as they turned down another near-empty corridor. Even after two years away from home, the empty walls and bare floors seemed almost foreign to Jin. His father's palace had always been opulent . . . over-the-top, even. "Finally going on your first mission."

Was Jin *ready*? He was a strong mage. He'd always been a strong mage—had more raw power than any of his trainers ever had, even as a kid—and with Zephyrine's training program, he'd honed his skills.

He shrugged. "I guess."

"Nothing to guess about when we're out in the field." Rasa's words were gentle, as they often were. She was far gentler with Jin than Dorin and Lando were, and he appreciated her for it. That wasn't to say she went easy on him, but she knew when to push and when to back off.

"I'll stay focused," Jin promised. "You've all beaten that lesson into me."

A grin spread across her pale face. "I suppose we have."

They hurried out of the fort itself and to the airfield just outside the southern gate. A simple gray airship was tethered to a mooring station, its engine already humming. It was small by Helosian military standards. By any standard, really. Jin had been on plenty of airships in his life, and this one's narrow, sleek design was unlike anything he'd seen before. Even the ones usually flying out of Fort Avalon were larger than this.

Their footsteps echoed on the metal stairs leading up to the open door. Once onboard, Jin tried to focus on where Rasa was going. Zephyrine, Lando, and Dorin all stood around a wide table built into the middle of the ship. At the front of the cabin, in the glass-enclosed control room, two pilots were starting them en route to wherever they were going. Zephyrine hadn't told them anything, just that they had to be ready to leave in an hour.

"Get over here, Jin!" Zephyrine called.

He joined the rest of them, throwing his pack next to where Rasa had dropped hers on the ground.

"Now that we're all here," Zephyrine said, "your mission." She gestured to a map spread over the table, one filled with figurines of soldiers, airships, and artillery. "We're going to Delia."

"Delia?" Lando asked. "Why?"

"Things are deteriorating internally for the Delian government," Zephyrine said.

That didn't entirely surprise Jin. The Kingdom of Delia had been unstable since before his birth, several coups having taken place in the last twenty years. Their royal family was extensive, and each member wanted power for themselves.

"What's that got to do with us?" Lando asked.

Zephyrine pointed at the Delian capital on the map. "One of our diplomats and his husband has been taken captive by a rogue faction of the Delian military. We're getting them back."

A rescue mission? Jin wiped his palms on his pants.

"Intelligence says they're being held here." Zephyrine pointed to a spot near the southwestern Delian-Helosian border. The area was mostly forest. "We'll land here"—she pointed again—"late afternoon. Five miles away from the location. It's remote. We can't risk them hearing the ship."

Jin shifted his weight to his left leg. Five miles? That was a long walk. Lando, Rasa, and Dorin said nothing as they studied the map.

"We're keeping this simple," Zephyrine continued. "Get in, get the targets, get out. We'll be on our way home this time tomorrow. Remember the rules."

Lando nodded. "Leave no teammate behind."

They'd been through that rule a dozen times in training sessions.

"Stick to the plan," Dorin said.

Their second rule. Always stick to the plan unless you *had* to change it mid-mission.

"And leave no witnesses," Rasa said with a sigh.

"What?" Jin asked. That one, he had not heard. A whole year he'd been on this team, yet nobody had told him that. His heart pounded. Jin pressed his palms to his pants again.

"People can't know who we are or what we do, kid," Lando said. "We aren't supposed to exist."

Jin understood *that* part. It was why they wore no insignia. No national colors. Their black leather body armor, fatigues, masks, and hoods. They concealed their identities as much as possible and left no sign of which of the five continental countries they might be associated with. They could even be Taipoli or from another part of the world.

Jin understood that killing was part of the job. It certainly would be during war. But leaving *no* witnesses? What was the point of hiding their identities, then, if they were just going to kill everyone anyway? That was . . . brutal. Unthinkable.

Besides, wouldn't the Delians know it was the Helosians coming to rescue *Helosian* diplomats?

"You didn't think to tell me this earlier?" Jin asked past the tightness in his throat. Whether it was disgust or rage, he wasn't sure. Maybe both. "Why are we killing people on a rescue mission?"

Zephyrine crossed her arms. "I ordered the team not to tell you. Didn't want to scare you. None of us like that rule, but it's not on my orders. It comes from higher up the chain."

"From whom, then?" Jin asked. "Whose order is that?" Zephyrine might've been his commanding officer, but Jin was still a prince. Maybe he could talk to whomever was giving out that command.

Dorin swallowed hard. Rasa picked at her cuticles. Even Lando, unflappable as he was, rubbed the back of his neck. A heaviness settled in Jin's belly like a stone.

"Of course," Jin muttered. "My father?"

Zephyrine flipped her braid over her narrow shoulder. "Yes."

Of course. Zephyrine wasn't ranked *that* low. There would be very few people she answered to. The army's generals would hold rank above her . . . and, of course, the emperor.

Jin's arguments would never sway his father. They never had.

"I can't stand him." The admission slipped out before Jin could think twice. He blew out a shaky breath, then said, "I hate him."

There. He might as well tell his team the truth. They could think whatever they wanted.

"Yes, well, none of us are exactly fond of him," Zephyrine said. "But orders are orders. We operate in the shadows, and we do what we must to get our people back. Is that clear?"

As Jin's teammates all murmured their understanding, Jin simply nodded. He didn't know what else he could do. If he didn't follow orders, his team would just have to pick up his slack. Worse, if Jin didn't follow orders, word might somehow get back to his father. Jin doubted Zephyrine would report him, but if his father did find out . . .

What better way to punish Jin than punish Zephyrine and the team? Perhaps Aelius would just transfer him back to Fort Ironwing, but without knowing what the punishment might be, Jin didn't see any other way to protect his team. They didn't deserve to be on the receiving end of Aelius's anger when they were just doing their jobs. Just following orders.

Jin's teammates grabbed their gear and headed to a staircase in the corner that he hadn't noticed before. He picked up his bag and followed. The second level was smaller than anything Jin had seen on an airship before, dark and narrow. His father's airships were all luxury—carpets, expensive decor, better lighting. Not this one. It was bare bones—metal everything, low lights upstairs, and small.

"Take whatever room you want, kid," Lando called over his shoulder. "Except this one." He tapped on the door he was standing in front of. "Get some sleep. It's gonna be a long day."

"Is this something we do often?" Jin asked. "Rescue people, I mean."

Lando shrugged. "Sometimes."

"Can we really leave no witnesses?"

"Look, kid . . ." Lando glanced to where Dorin and Rasa loitered near their doors. "Zephyrine shouldn't have hid that from you. We didn't want to. But you've gotta understand . . . we're just doing our jobs, like it or not."

"I don't blame you," Jin muttered. "It's not your fault."

"No, but when we go out there, it's kill or be killed. The Delians aren't going to look at it any other way. They're probably under orders to do the exact same thing."

Jin didn't like the sound of that at all.

"And I know I give you a hard time, but we don't want you getting into trouble out there." Lando shifted awkwardly as he said it, but Dorin and Rasa both nodded. "Do what you have to."

Adjusting his pack on his shoulder, Jin stared down at the floor. "I don't know if I can." The admission barely left him. But how was he supposed to do that? Take the lives of people just following orders, like he was?

"You have to."

"But what if I can't?"

A ghost of a smile crossed Lando's wide face. "Just pretend it's me. Pretend it's me when I've been giving you too much shit, kid."

"I might have to try that one," Dorin quipped, making Lando laugh.

Jin knew they were trying, but... "I don't hate you enough to pretend to kill you."

"Ah, so you just hate me some, then?" Lando teased.

"It's just part of our job, Jin," Rasa said. "It's awful, but it's true."

All traces of Lando's humor disappeared as he said, "Promise us you'll do what you have to. Promise us you'll survive."

Jin looked at Rasa first, then Dorin, then Lando. They all shared the same hard, uneasy expression. He couldn't remember the last time someone had been worried about him. Astrea, maybe. Eliana, too.

He sucked in one breath, then another, before he finally nodded. "I promise."

The Delian forest was quiet. Sleepy, even, as the sun began to set.

Jin was sandwiched between Rasa and Lando as all five of them crept through the woods. He'd been surprised to see Zephyrine dressed in the same gear as the rest of them—black uniform, black leather body armor, sturdy boots, hood, and mask that covered the bottom half of the face. But she was at the front of the line now, somehow guiding them to the location of their target without a map.

Which diplomat was it that had been given the task of working with the Delian government? Jin's father had dozens of diplomats in cities around the continent. Zephyrine hadn't mentioned their target's name, and Jin hadn't thought to ask. It had to be someone with a high rank to be captured, though. Eliana would probably know; she'd always been better at memorizing people's names and ranks than him.

Jin had tried to make peace with what his team was about to do as soon as Zephyrine had dismissed them after their briefing. He had. They *were* rescuing captured civilians; if they had to take out some Delians, wasn't it worth it? And as Lando said, if it was kill or be killed . . . of course Jin would do what he had to do. At least, he hoped he would. He didn't want to die.

The sun sank lower as Zephyrine's steps finally slowed. The location she had guided them to wasn't at all what Jin had expected. A manor house rose up in the darkness, small by Helosian standards. The green, white, and blue flag of the Delians fluttered from a pole attached to the roof.

The earth under the two guards standing outside the manor's front entrance opened, swallowing them whole. Jin flinched. They hadn't even realized Rasa was there. They hadn't even had a chance to react. They were simply gone.

No witnesses.

As the team started moving again, Jin followed them on instinct and muscle memory, in a formation they'd practiced dozens of times during training. They remained silent, not even whispering a command his way.

A stream of rogue Delian soldiers headed to the front door just as Jin followed Lando inside.

He'd always thought a real fight would be harder, but as he blocked blow after blow from a Delian Fireweaver, Jin found he was barely breaking a sweat. He kicked the woman's legs out from under her. She crashed into the floor hard, her elbow crunching audibly. That would keep her down.

His team had taken out the rest. Six other Delian soldiers lay on the floor in crumpled heaps, dark liquid pooling around them. Jin's stomach lurched as he looked back down at the Fireweaver groaning on the floor.

Yes, he'd tried to make peace with what had to come next. But as he reached for the dagger strapped to his belt, air gusted through the room with such force the woman slammed against the wall behind Jin. She landed with a sickening crack, blood smearing on the taupe wallpaper as she slid down to the floor.

He stared at Zephyrine wide-eyed, but she simply said, "Spread out and find our targets."

Shoving his misgivings deep down, Jin split off with Rasa. They'd done this in drills a hundred times before. Enter a room, one person covering the front and one covering the rear. Check under any furniture and behind any doors before calling it clear. Incapacitate any enemies found.

The first two rooms were clear.

Rasa led the way up a narrow servants' stairwell. After twenty steps, they paused on a landing. To their right was the next set of stairs that would lead them to the next floor, but to their left was a door. Rasa held her fist up. Jin froze. He didn't dare move a muscle as Rasa reached for the brass handle.

Before her fingers tightened around the metal, the door burst open. Rasa stumbled back half a step. Jin threw his hands out. A wall of fire exploded in front of Rasa, so violent it scorched the tapestries hanging on the walls.

Two distinct screams rang out, followed by curses in Delian. Beyond the wall of fire, three Delian soldiers were crammed in the doorway. Two of them cradled hands to their chests.

"Let's get this over with," Rasa said. "You go down, I'll go up."

As Rasa backed toward the ascending stairs, Jin backed toward the descending ones. Every one of Jin's instincts told him not to let the wall of fire drop, but it would just burn the house down eventually. So he snuffed it out.

The Delians charged. Two stormed toward Jin, one his height and one much shorter. Jin shot fire toward the shorter Delian, forcing them back. The taller one rushed forward. Jin sidestepped just as they reached him.

The tall one whirled. Jin grabbed onto the stair's banister, then kicked the Delian square in their midsection. They fell backward, tumbling down the stairs until they crashed onto the stone floor below. They didn't move.

Water soaked Jin's upper arm, followed by the sting of splitting skin. He turned. The short Delian's blue eyes hardened.

Jin's chest heaved. He just had to do it.

Water whips formed in the Delian's hands. They lashed out at Jin. He advanced, fire flaring around his palms. Every time one of their water whips spun out, Jin met it with flames so hot the water simply sizzled into nothing. But he couldn't get close enough.

The Delian backed into the room off the stairs. It was a small, sparsely furnished space. Jin edged closer, desperate for some kind of opening. This was taking too long. They needed to wrap up and find Zephyrine, Dorin, and Lando.

There. The Delian feinted left, but they weren't subtle. Jin grabbed their arm, hauling them off balance as he forced heat out through his palm. The scent of burning flesh clogged the air. Jin slammed the soldier onto the floor. They yanked him down with them.

Jin rolled to the side. The Delian followed, metal glinting in their hand. Jin grabbed his dagger, thrusting up just as the Delian thrust down. Pain flared in his upper arm as blood coated his weapon in his other hand. The Delian toppled over as soon as Jin yanked his dagger back, more blood gushing out of the wound. Coughing, the soldier fell onto the ground and went still.

Jin's heart pounded so wildly he thought it might explode. As he collapsed back on the floor, he stared up at the stone ceiling. Both of his arms hurt; first the water slice, then the dagger. But even without looking at the wounds, he knew they weren't fatal. They just hurt.

His heart hurt, too. *Kill or be killed.* He wasn't supposed to be lying there. Blood leaked down his arms as he pushed himself up. When he was back on his knees, Jin paused. The big Delian was back, blocking the doorway.

Fuck me. Steeling himself, Jin started forward, but the Delian's eyes widened. They stumbled forward and collapsed near their fallen comrade.

"You good?" Rasa asked as she stooped and pulled her weapon out of the Delian's back.

"Yeah," Jin rasped, bile surging up his throat as Rasa wiped the bloody dagger across her thigh. "Fine."

Nobody else came to meet them as they continued ascending the stairs. Would the Delian rogues really only have less than a dozen soldiers guarding their captives? If that was their strategy, they'd never really take over their country's government.

When Jin and Rasa got to the top of the stairwell, she pushed the lone door open. Zephyrine was already inside, her black uniform a stark contrast to the room's mauve wallpaper. Four more Delians lay stone still on the floor, and Zephyrine was untying a brown-haired man strapped to a chair. Another man, a blond, was still tied to another.

"Help me do this," she said.

Jin moved to the back of the chair, summoning a small flame to cut through the thick ropes binding the blond in place. As soon as he was able, the man jumped up.

"Took you long enough," he muttered.

Was he serious?

Jin supposed that was to be expected. People of that rank had been entitled for as long as Jin could remember. At least they'd saved this man. He didn't deserve to die at the hands of rogue Delians, even if he was an ungrateful asshole.

Zephyrine finished untying the brunette, who ran to the blond. Which one of them was the diplomat, Jin wasn't quite sure, but he'd bet money it was the rude one.

"Our ship will be en route now, my lords," Zephyrine said. "I'll go outside with you and wait."

The men started out the main door to the bedroom just as Lando and Dorin yelled their final all clear. Zephyrine looked at Jin, then Rasa, then Jin again. She eyed his arms first, then the rest of his torso. "You're good?"

Jin swallowed hard. "Fine."

"We took care of them," Rasa added. "Three down."

"Good." Zephyrine tilted her head toward the door. "Let's get the fuck out of here."

CHAPTER 8
WINTER, YEAR 1014

That first mission in Delia over the summer had been the first of many. As it turned out, an unstable Delian government gave Emperor Aelius Auris the support he needed to launch a war on the country. That first group of rogue Delians hadn't lasted long, but they hadn't been the only group. The Delian government was facing both a civil war and a war with Helosia.

By some small miracle, Jin was still alive. Five more missions, three semi-close calls, and he was still alive.

And by some greater miracle, he was finally, after two and a half years, back in Kalama.

The last six months had been agonizing. Jin had made it through training thinking that Zephyrine's team had just two rules, dedicated to keeping the team safe. Of course Jin had known missions and war would mean death—would mean killing—but he hadn't been able to get over that third rule. *No witnesses.* Understanding the nature of war and actually living it were two different things. Not just living through the missions, but living with the guilt that never stopped following him.

Jin shoved the thought away as his driver eased the car through the palace's main gates. He'd finally been invited home after two and a half years. His father had invited him home for the winter solstice festival, but why? Why now? Jin had no idea. At least he was finally going to see

Eliana again. He was finally going to meet his baby niece. That was all that mattered.

The long driveway leading to the palace seemed even longer than it used to. The palace, looming in the distance, was bigger than he remembered. So, too, was the observatory tower taller than he remembered. Jin tried not to look at it, but he could barely tear his eyes away from the sight of the gray bricks and dark roof.

He couldn't talk to her. He was just home for two days. He was here for the winter solstice festival, then he had to go back to Fort Avalon. The war with the Delians was just getting started; Jin hadn't had the luxury of visits home even during peacetime. Two days barely gave him time to see his family, let alone anyone else. He wouldn't see Cressida. He certainly couldn't try to talk to Astrea now. Two days wasn't enough time to repair the damage he'd done. She probably wouldn't even want to speak to him.

As the car stopped in front of the palace's front steps, a familiar face opened the door. "Hello, Your Imperial Highness."

Oskar. Still cold, still removed. He didn't even smile. The only change in Oskar was the gray now streaking his dark hair.

Jin slid out of the car, his boots crunching on the gravel driveway. "Hey, Oskar."

"Your family is waiting in the Red Room, Your Imperial Highness. I'll make sure your bags are taken to your apartment."

As Jin climbed the steps to the palace's front entrance, he smoothed the front of his black fatigues. His father probably wouldn't deem it appropriate, but Jin had no need for the formal attire once required at the imperial court. He wouldn't even know where to get it at Fort Avalon. There was a city, Narizon, near the fort; maybe he should've gone into town to find something. *Too late now.*

The halls were quieter than Jin expected. The palace had always seemed loud when he was a child, but compared to the fort, the empty halls were almost eerie. Had his father sent all the courtiers and politicians away just for this occasion?

Jin navigated the palace alone. Oskar didn't escort him. No guards came to meet him. And the ones who were stationed throughout the halls . . . it was almost like they barely recognized him. He'd always hated when they bowed, but now their timing was off, like they only realized who he was too late. That almost felt worse.

Jin forced the thought away as he neared the Red Room's double doors. It was one of the opulent sitting rooms his father used for family gatherings, away from the public areas of the palace that courtiers, diplomats, and senators could also use. This space was just for the immediate Auris family and their handful of cousins, aunts, and uncles on the rare occasion they were invited to the palace. Jin hadn't seen any of their extended family in years, even before leaving for the military.

He sucked in a breath. What was he so afraid of? Jin had been facing life-threatening situations for the last half of the year. Had faced off with countless Delians. Seeing his family was hardly a threat to his life. To his sanity, maybe, but not his life.

Just go in. With one last steadying breath, Jin pushed open the door on the right.

The tinny sound of the radio was the first indication of life inside. Music. They were listening to music.

And his entire family was staring at him. Silent.

Wonderful. He really wished he'd had the foresight to change out of his fatigues.

They took up the two large sofas and a couple of overstuffed chairs in the middle of the room. Apelo and Thana both looked tired but happy. A baby—Velia—was tucked in Apelo's arms, swaddled in so much blanket that Jin couldn't see her face. Kaius stared at Jin, as did their father.

But Eliana jumped up, rushing toward Jin so quickly he could barely catch her as she threw herself into his arms.

"You're home!" she exclaimed, her hold around his neck tightening.

Jin forced himself to breathe as he hugged his sister. "Hey, Ellie."

And then the scene burst to life. Baby Velia let out a squawk of disapproval as Apelo passed her to Thana and got off the sofa to greet Jin. Kaius, usually so callous, also approached. Jin tried to lean into their embraces, their welcomes. He tried.

But his father remained seated, expression unreadable and jaw tight as he stared at Jin.

Aelius was the one who invited Jin home, so why wasn't he happy to see him? Happy to see him alive and well despite what was going on near the Delian border?

This was going to be a long two days.

It wasn't even twenty minutes past breakfast, yet Jin found himself being escorted to his father's office.

He hadn't missed the palace. Jin had only gotten home the night before, but he already wanted to go back to Fort Avalon. The palace was as cold as he remembered. Eliana was the only good thing here. At dinner the night before, Apelo and Thana had also tried to be welcoming. Kaius was a different story, asking endless questions and providing unnecessarily snarky commentary about Jin's military uniform.

Velia had been great. She'd immediately quieted when Thana put her in Jin's arms after dinner, which was apparently a small miracle for the new parents. That, though, had just led to more snark from Kaius.

And now here he was, on his way to talk to his father, who had basically given him the silent treatment since he'd walked into the palace. His closet in his apartment had been cleaned out, just one outfit remaining. A new one, too, that would actually fit his changed body. But based on the expensive fabric and embroidery, he'd assumed that was meant for the festival later that night. Now, he was just in another set of his fatigues. Clean, freshly pressed. Even his boots were polished. Jin was the perfect picture of a soldier as he pushed his shoulders back and waited for Oskar to open his father's office door.

The door opened on silent hinges, and Jin stepped inside.

The image of his father sitting behind his desk, fingers steepled in front of his mouth, used to terrify Jin. That was the look his father always had when Jin was summoned for some kind of punishment or lecture. So why was his father sitting like that now, barely half an hour after their family breakfast? Jin surely couldn't have fucked up in that short time . . . right?

He stopped a few feet from his father's desk and kept his hands clasped behind his back. Yes, this scene might've intimidated Jin once, but compared to what he'd seen the last few months, this was almost pleasant.

"So," Aelius finally said. "You're home."

"That's what you requested, so yes, I'm home."

Aelius sighed. "Must we still do this?"

"Do what?" Jin didn't know where the attitude came from. No, that wasn't true. He did. As he barely looked at his father, all Jin could see was the awful truth. His father didn't care. His father didn't care about much of anything or anyone.

"I thought your time away would've cured you of the attitude," Aelius said. "Has Colonel Kanakos taught you nothing? I expected more from her, considering her record."

Even with that ugly, awful truth settling in Jin's chest, he forced himself to breathe. His attitude might just get Zephyrine in trouble. So, he said, "Sorry, Father. I'm just on edge. I . . . didn't sleep well." Which was true. Jin just wasn't sure his father would find the excuse acceptable. "Colonel Kanakos has been very instructive."

Aelius watched Jin for one heartbeat, two, then nodded. "I've been keeping up with your team's movements." Aelius tapped one finger on a stack of folders sitting in the center of his desk. "You've been doing well."

Doing well. Jin's stomach turned in on itself, threatening to reject the breakfast he'd just eaten. What was that supposed to mean? Doing well, as in he'd managed not to get himself killed? Doing well, as in his whole team was surviving the war? Doing well, as in . . . leaving no witnesses? That was his father's order, after all.

"As I said, Colonel Kanakos has been very instructive. She's good at what she does. I'm lucky to be learning from her."

"Indeed." Aelius leaned back in his chair. "I know you want to ask me something, Varojin. So ask now before I must go to a meeting."

There were a thousand questions he could ask, but only one seemed relevant and remotely innocent. "Why bring me home now? Why now instead of before the war?"

"Everyone deserves a break, do they not?"

Two days at home was hardly a break.

"And I just wanted to ensure we're on the same page, Varojin," Aelius continued. He didn't move a muscle. "I wouldn't want to have to move you back to Fort Ironwing if things stop going so well for you and Colonel Kanakos."

Jin clenched his fists behind his back, muscles straining. *Doing well.* He barely shoved his temper down. *Move you back to Fort Ironwing.*

This was how it had always been with his father. Thinly veiled threats. Control. How could it be no different despite the fact that Jin was now an adult himself? He'd be turning twenty-one in the spring. He wasn't old, but he wasn't the same kid anymore, either. And yet here he was, barely controlling his temper around his father.

Jin didn't want to go back to Fort Ironwing. As much as he hated the war, he actually liked Fort Avalon. He liked the mountains and the cool weather and the quiet. He liked his teammates, and he liked Zephyrine. He couldn't screw this up for himself. So he forced his temper deep, deep down and took another breath.

"Of course, Father."

"You're doing this country a great service, Varojin. You should be proud."

Bile surged up Jin's throat. He forced himself to nod.

"Who knows," Aelius continued as he pushed himself out of his chair, "if things keep going well, maybe you'll be able to come home for the summer solstice, too. I'm sure Eliana would like to see you more."

Don't say it, Jin warned himself. *Do not.*

That was the deal, then? Be a good soldier and fight in the war, and *maybe* he would get to come home to visit his family? What kind of cruel reward was that?

"Of course, Father," Jin heard himself say again.

Reaching for the folders on his desk, the ones full of Jin's mission reports, Aelius smiled. "Good. You're dismissed."

Jin had never left a room so quickly in his life.

The walls seemed to cave in around Jin as he left his father's office. He might as well have been sixteen again, rushing to leave after a particularly brutal lecture or punishment.

Jin didn't understand why he was being punished. Sure, he'd given his father an attitude and spoken out of turn over the years, but were those transgressions really deserving of . . . this? Was Jin really that much of a fuck-up, maybe so much so that he couldn't see it about himself?

He veered down corridor after corridor, barely looking at the faces of guards and courtiers he passed.

No. He'd made his mistakes and his choices, but Jin knew he wasn't *that* much of a fuck-up. But his father always made him feel like one. Always treated him like one.

Doesn't matter, he told himself, just as he'd told himself a thousand times before. His father's opinion would never change. Jin was a fuck-up because his father had fucked up in siring him in the first place. He was the son of the emperor and his mistress, not the emperor and his wife.

Jin's mother had been in his life on and off for years. She'd moved out of the palace when Jin was just three years old, though she'd continued visiting him until she died in a boating accident when he was ten.

As far as Jin was concerned, he was innocent in all of that. He hadn't asked to be born. But nothing was going to change the fact that Jin was only Aelius's bastard. Nothing was going to change the way his father had always disliked him. Nothing he did would ever be enough to change that.

Just do what he wants while you're home and tell Zephyrine tomorrow. That was the plan. And it was a good plan. A simple plan. He could stick with it. He would spend some time outside this morning, get ready for the festival, and go with his family, as was expected. He would play the role of prince as best he could for the night. Then he would return to Fort Avalon and the war, and he wouldn't have to see his father again for a while.

Kalama's chilly winter air cooled Jin's face as soon as he stepped outside. It lacked the same sharpness as that up north, but he would take what he could get.

It took every ounce of control he had not to cut through the gardens and head for the observatory. Its dark roof peeked out from above the trees. It would take no more than ten minutes to get there, five if he wasn't stopped by anyone. He'd always gone to visit Astrea after conversations like that with his father. Had always gone to find his best friend. She was good at listening when he needed her to, and he wished with all his heart he had someone who could listen to him now. But who could he tell?

Not Eliana. Certainly not Kaius. Apelo would just try to find some diplomatic solution, as if that existed. Zephyrine and his teammates knew Jin didn't get along with his father, but he didn't think they could truly understand.

Jin followed the paved garden pathways, pacing back and forth along the same few trails near the palace's side door. He needed to do something. That was one thing he liked about Fort Avalon; there was always something to do. Train with his team. Do chores. Here, in Kalama, Jin had to sit around while everyone else did everything for him.

He'd just started down a path heading east when something—someone—familiar caught his eye. Jin's heart sank.

This was not part of his plan. Seeing Astrea was not part of his plan.

He didn't know whether he wanted to run to her and beg for her forgiveness or run back into the palace and hide. It didn't matter. He couldn't move. His body stayed rooted to the spot. She was headed toward the observatory, her nose buried in a letter as she smiled. Astrea didn't even look up as she walked. Didn't even notice him standing there.

Two and a half years. Jin had grown up, and so had she. Her hair was longer than he remembered, and her body had filled out just like his. Well, not *just* like his. Where he was all hard muscle, Astrea was soft curves. She looked great.

And she looked happy.

Jin's chest heaved. *This is good,* he reasoned. It was what he'd always wanted for her. For her to be happy and safe. And she was. So why did it hurt so much?

Just as Jin had pushed his temper down minutes before in his father's office, Jin pushed that pain down until he couldn't breathe.

Since his garden walk hadn't turned out the way he wanted, Jin had returned to his apartment and taken a long, hot shower. The privacy of his old rooms was one of the few things he'd actually missed about the palace.

He'd just finished getting dressed when a knock sounded on his door. Jin sighed. Who could possibly be coming to get him now? He wasn't scheduled for lunch with his family. He was supposed to have time to himself until they had to go to the festival.

When Jin opened his door, he'd expected to see Kaius or Oskar. Maybe Apelo. But he hadn't expected Eliana to be there with Baby Velia perched on her hip and Thana hovering nervously behind her.

"Um . . ." Jin started, but Eliana pushed her way past him.

"You're not busy, are you?" she asked.

"No." Jin glanced at Thana, who paused at the threshold of his door. "Why? I thought we didn't have to be anywhere until the fifth bell."

"Velia's governess is with the healers downstairs," Eliana said, "and Thana and Apelo need some time to get ready. I thought we could babysit."

"Prince Varojin, if it's too much—" Thana started, but Jin cut his sister-in-law off.

"Just Jin, please," he said.

She smiled weakly, her tan hand pressed to her collarbone. "If it's too much trouble, please don't feel like you have to say yes."

"I've already said yes, so it's happening either way, Thana." Eliana grinned down at Velia, who tugged on a lock of Eliana's wavy hair. "Yes, you want to spend time with Auntie Ellie and Uncle Jin, don't you?"

"We're just right down the hall if you need us . . ." Thana paused, her lips pressing into a thin line. "Please don't hesitate if something goes wrong."

"Bye, Thana!" Eliana said once their sister-in-law finally backed away from Jin's door and started back down the hall. "Well, Vellie, let's go."

"Vellie?" Jin closed his door and followed his sister into his sitting room. "Apelo wasn't calling her that last night."

"That's because it's my nickname for her. Vellie and Ellie, the dynamic duo!" Eliana stuck her tongue out at the baby, who giggled and fisted Eliana's hair again. "Ow!"

After going to his bedroom to get an extra blanket, Jin spread it out on the sitting room floor next to the sofa. Eliana set Velia down on it.

"Do you do this often?" he asked.

"Not by myself, no. I think Thana was worried."

"And she thought *I* was a good choice to help?" Jin didn't actually mind, though. Spending time with Eliana and Velia would be good.

"I think we were her only options. Besides, Vellie's easy."

"I'm pretty sure you only think that because you aren't her parent." Jin knew nothing about children or babies, but caring for them certainly couldn't be easy.

"Just watch her while I call down for coffee, alright?" Without waiting for a response, Eliana scurried to where Jin's phone sat on his desk.

Velia stared up at Jin, her tiny legs spread out in front of her as she absently patted the blanket. He was surprised to see her sitting up like that by herself.

"I know you don't really know me," Jin said, "but I'm glad to see you, Velia."

She smiled up at him and patted the blanket again. He smiled back. Eliana called over her shoulder for him to let Velia practice crawling if she wanted to. Jin hadn't realized she would be able to do that, either. He probably wasn't a good choice for babysitter at all.

"Do you like to crawl?" Jin asked as Velia tipped herself over and giggled.

Velia rolled onto her stomach and crawled away from Jin, looking almost like a tiny soldier as she pulled herself along the blanket and then rug. He jumped up and followed her, picking her up and turning her around to crawl back the other way once she'd gotten too close to the foyer.

"I'll be right back!" Eliana called, and Jin grunted an acknowledgment.

He could do this. He could watch his niece for a few minutes.

Velia was faster than he'd anticipated. Not that he couldn't keep up with her, but he watched her, amazed, as she explored his sitting room. Everything was interesting to her. It was too bad he didn't have any of his toys from his childhood to keep her occupied. After a while, Jin brought her back to the blanket. Velia grabbed onto his hand and pulled on it with all the strength she seemed to be able to muster.

"At least you seem happy to see me," he murmured. "Sorry I don't really know what I'm supposed to do right now." Velia squealed and yanked on his fingers. Jin couldn't help but smile a little.

When Eliana finally returned, she had not just two mugs but also a small stuffed lamb. She set the cups down on coffee table, then offered the toy to Velia. The baby grabbed it, and Eliana smiled back at Jin. "Do you like it?"

"What?"

"Do you like your room?" She gestured vaguely around them.

"Right. That. I can't believe you redecorated it," he said as took in his old sitting room. He actually didn't mind the change. Red was the Auris family color, prevalent in the palace. But Eliana had changed out the bright hues in his childhood rooms to blues, greens, and purples. It was much calmer. It was a welcome change, even if he doubted he'd ever use this apartment much again.

Eliana sat down across from him and picked up her coffee. "Redecorating a room is hardly the same as how much *you've* changed."

He grimaced. "Bad change?"

"No, you just don't look like a kid anymore."

He didn't. That first summer in the Badlands had really started to change him, but so had the endless training since. Jin knew he was still using training as an excuse—a crutch—to avoid everything that hurt. But he also enjoyed the way it helped his mind focus. It helped him stay present. Using his fireweaving every day felt good.

"And Kaius is surely going to hate it," Eliana continued. "Prepare yourself."

"Kaius hates almost everything I do. He didn't seem pleased last night."

Eliana snorted as she reached out and patted Velia's head. She was already growing a head of thick, dark brown hair, the same color as Eliana's and Apelo's. "Anyway, tell me everything," Eliana said. "Your letters rarely go into any detail. What's Fort Avalon like? How are your teammates? Do you like them? Are you used to the northern winters yet? What have you been doing during the war?"

"Everything's fine," Jin said. "I stay busy."

Eliana glared at him. "Fine? Busy?" She scoffed. "You've got to give me more than that. We only have two days and you've been gone for over two years! There must be so much for us to talk about."

What could he tell her? He wasn't sure what Eliana was allowed to know about his team and what they did. Even then, he wasn't sure what she *needed* to know. Eliana may have been eighteen, but she didn't need to hear about the things he'd seen. The things he'd done.

"I spend most of my time training." It wasn't even a lie. He'd spent most of the last two and a half years training. "I have more control over my fireweaving. I've learned how to fight like a non-mage. My team has offered support where we can during the war. I'm sure your life is more exciting than mine."

Eliana studied him in that peculiar way she always had. It was almost like she was a Lightbringer, studying his emotions and the way he was reacting. He knew she wasn't one—she was a Sparkcaster—but she always seemed to be able to call him on his bullshit.

A loud squeal from Velia drew both their attention. She'd tipped over again and rolled onto her back, a grin splitting her face as she chewed on her fingers.

"Is she supposed to do that?" Jin asked.

"She's fine." Eliana frowned. "Are you staying safe?"

"As safe as I can in a war, Ellie."

He didn't know how to do this anymore, talking to his sister. He'd spent most of the family dinner the night before silent, just listening to whatever stories his family wanted to share. He'd heard about Apelo and Thana's wedding, Kaius's upcoming university graduation, and Eliana's selected coursework for when she started at Kalama's university the following spring. But Eliana was the only one to ask about him, and she was only asking now.

It all seemed ridiculous to Jin. Not Eliana wanting to know about his life but being here, in the palace. This wasn't his life anymore. It never really had been. He'd never felt like he fit in here . . . with his half-siblings or with the people who filled his father's court. He didn't care about any of the bullshit. He'd had a bit of a rocky start on Zephyrine's team years ago, but Zephyrine, Rasa, Dorin, and even Lando seemed to understand him better than anyone in the palace. They understood why he didn't talk about what they'd done. They didn't really talk about it, either.

The only way Jin seemed to be able to talk about what he'd seen was writing it down. All those years ago, he'd started writing letters to Astrea to document the things he would've told her if he could've. He'd kept up with the habit even though she was never going to see the damn things. Maybe things would be different if he had the strength to send them to his old friend or tell his sister those very same stories.

Jin blinked. Eliana was studying him again, and he sighed. Could she read his mind?

"I'm sorry, Ellie. It's just . . . strange being back here. It's a little overwhelming."

"I know." She smiled. "But I'm really glad you're home."

Chapter 9
Spring, Year 1015

The Delian island of Ilesouria was usually a destination for people going on holiday. Jin had even been once with his family, invited by the then-king of Delia for a boat race between the two royal courts. But now, he barely recognized it. Its swaying palm trees and tan buildings were a mess of smoke, rubble, and soldiers.

Delians were using the island to launch naval attacks on Helosian trade and civilian vessels. Civilians were supposed to be off-limits. And Jin's team was on Ilesouria for their next assignment: take out Delia's General Basera, the apparent mastermind behind such attacks.

Lando led them past a row of partially destroyed homes, the walls and tiled roofs crumbling. Black smoke rose from within, and the stench of burning flesh was unmissable. Jin swallowed hard but kept following his team as they navigated the island.

"Pick up the pace," Lando said over his shoulder. Though he shared the captain rank with Rasa and Dorin, Lando had become their team leader since the start of the war. "Need to make this quick."

They had just half an hour before Zephyrine and their airship would return to their pickup location. In the distance, on the lower parts of the island, two Helosian battalions were fighting things out with the Delians. Even here, Jin could hear the sounds of battle: clashing elements, gunshots, artillery. He hated those sounds. But Jin's team was supposed to be quick. Efficient. Unnoticed.

Ahead, a small fortress of wind-battered gray brick sat untouched by shelling and fire. Even the palm trees flanking its entrance stood tall and proud, as did the white, green, and blue Delian flag fluttering at the top of the building. No soldiers stood guard. The tall oak double doors were closed.

On Lando's signal, they forged ahead. Skirting the side of the building, they stuck to the shadows, stopping again when they reached the rear entrance. It, too, was unguarded. Jin didn't like that.

Lando entered first, then Rasa, Jin, and Dorin. The distant boom of artillery made Jin flinch. Lando led them down one empty corridor, then another, until they reached what had to be the fort's central room. Twelve Delians loitered around, shoulders and postures tight.

Rasa and Dorin veered right while Jin and Lando went left. The Delians scrambled into action, shouts echoing through the room and magic heavy in the air.

Jin drew his dagger as three Delians circled him. The one to his right lunged forward. Jin spun around her, then rammed his blade through her back. He yanked it back out, letting the blonde fall to the floor. Both of her comrades moved in, water and earth swirling around their hands. The Earthmover charged Jin, slamming into him. With a grunt, Jin shoved the man away. He stumbled back, revealing the glow of water. Not headed for Jin, but . . . a Purifier. The water mage was trying to heal the blonde.

Fire exploded over Jin's palms. He aimed. A fireball shot past the Earthmover, landing square on the Purifier's back. The Earthmover turned. Jin crossed the distance between them in two quick strides, grabbed the man, and rammed his blade into his gut. As he pulled it back out, Jin shoved the man to the ground. The Purifier scrambled to their feet, then stumbled forward. Stone hit them from behind as Lando moved in. And then the Purifier hit the ground with a gut-wrenching crack.

Jin sucked in a heavy breath as Lando nodded at him. He returned the gesture before surveying the room. All twelve Delians were down.

"Split up," Lando said. "You two, go that way. The kid and I will go this way."

The kid. Jin nearly rolled his eyes but instead followed Lando wordlessly to a stairwell on the left side of the fort. He had more important things to worry about than unsuitable nicknames.

Five Delians on the first set of stairs. Lando took out the first, and Jin didn't bother using his fireweaving to take out the second and third. He'd long since learned that a dagger sometimes made things easier. Lando took out the fourth, and Jin took out the fifth. It was barely a fight.

Was this going to be that easy? They hadn't run into such incompetence since that very first mission in Delia to rescue the Helosian diplomat.

The second floor of the fort was quiet. The worn wooden floors didn't even squeak. Jin had expected more Delians, especially considering Basera was around here somewhere. But he and Lando cleared their half of the second floor room by room. Empty.

Were the majority of the soldiers down on the beaches fighting it out with the Helosian army? General Basera was reportedly a powerful Tempest, but to leave a general so unprotected was simply unwise.

Rasa and Dorin met them at the bottom of the stairs that would take them up to the final floor. Lando motioned for them to go upstairs. Jin followed, Rasa behind him and Dorin taking the rear. The intel they had suggested the general would be in the sole room at the top of the fort. The stairs brought them to a small foyer, and sure enough, the door was closed. Two Delians dressed in blue uniforms were stationed outside.

Jin slid past Lando, flames spinning through the air toward the guard on the right. Two icicles shot past Jin, slamming into both guards' chests. They slumped to the floor before Jin's fire even reached them.

Jin forced himself not to look at the bodies and blood as he followed Lando to the door. It never did him any good to look at those he took down. All it did was remind him that they were people too. He didn't need that reminder; it was something he could never forget.

Lando nudged the door open, and the team pushed into the room. A powerful blast of air threw all of them back into the wall. Jin's joints popped with the force of the blow. Wind pummeled into them, so strong that Jin could barely move a muscle. He couldn't even turn his head to see his team, but they were trapped too. They had to be.

They'd been through this in training. It was a drill he'd run with Rasa six times in as many weeks. But he hadn't been trained for the suffocation. The strongest Tempests could pull the air out of someone's lungs; rumor was that Zephyrine could do it.

Jin's lungs burned, begging for breath. A single man stood in the room. Presumably General Basera; he matched the description and single photograph Zephyrine had. Blond, tall, gray eyes, narrow jaw.

Jin pulled on the magic boiling just under his skin as darkness pulled at the edges of his vision. They were supposed to be keeping this efficient. And if Jin wasn't efficient, they might all die here. His chest was impossibly tight.

Despite the wind drying his eyes out, Jin forced them to stay open. He hadn't suffered through those six weeks of drills for this very situation for no reason. One shot. He just needed one shot.

Basera scoffed, his focus shifting to Jin's left, where Lando was. "Just four?" the general muttered in Delian. Then, as Lando coughed, Basera said, "What's the problem, Helosian?"

Jin's flame grew compact. Tight. Dense. A fire bullet. It took every ounce of energy Jin could spare to not let the general's wind extinguish the flame. Jin pushed the compact flame forward, forcing more energy into it as it curved toward Basera.

It pierced the general's upper arm. Jin had been aiming for his neck.

Basera bellowed, stumbling two steps backward and clutching his bleeding arm. The wind stopped. His cursing nearly drowned out the sound of Jin's team gasping for air.

"Fucking Helosians," the general growled, raising his hands again.

Lando surged forward, dagger drawn. One of the wall's bricks shot forward, slamming into the general's head just as Lando stabbed him through the gut. Jin forced himself not to turn away as Basera hit the floor. Blood pooled around his head. Lando stooped, checked for a pulse, then nodded at the team.

Basera was down.

Mission accomplished.

"Nice job, kid," Lando said as he passed Jin and headed for the door.

Jin took the rear on the way back down, trying to steady his breathing. They couldn't have much time left—just five, maybe ten minutes until Zephyrine circled back. If they missed their pickup, they'd have to wait another twenty minutes for her to come back again. That would make them as good as sitting ducks.

They hurried down hallways, a set of worn stairs, and finally, the tall oak doors marking the entrance came into view. Another fifty feet and they'd be outside. Good thing, too, because it had taken a great deal of Jin's energy to fire off that single attack. He didn't usually get tired so quickly. *Skies damned Tempests.*

The earth trembled, then the wall next to Jin exploded. He skidded back, summoning a shield of fire to absorb the worst of the debris. Was the fort being shelled? No. Three flashes of green. Delians.

A red-haired man punched out. More stone soared toward Jin. He forced his shield up higher, then summoned that little bullet again. It went straight through the man's forehead. The Delian fell to the ground.

His two companions rushed Jin. He pulled on his flames and took aim. He faltered as pain blossomed between his shoulder blades. No, not between. To the right.

He looked down. He looked down just long enough to see the tip of a blade sticking out near his collarbone. Long enough to see his fire flicker and die.

Jin looked up. Rasa, stone hovering over her palms. Dorin, water whips already lashing out at the Delians charging Jin from the front. And Lando, the fear in his eyes so real Jin almost didn't believe it.

Then Jin stumbled forward, and everything went dark.

The palace gardens stretched before Jin, the setting sun casting a strange, warm glow over the greenery. The hedge maze on the eastern side of the palace was thicker than he remembered.

"Come find me!"

"Az?" Jin called as he stepped into the maze.

"Who else?" She giggled somewhere in the distance. "Come on!"

Jin sprinted forward. Flowing purple and blue fabric disappeared around the corner of one shrub. He went that way, gravel crunching under his boots. His chest burned as he ran, his lungs impossibly tight.

"Why are you wearing that?" Astrea asked from behind him. "You're not ready for the festival."

Jin looked down at his fatigues, black stained with something dark. He turned, but Astrea was running off again. He sprinted after her.

"Wait, Az!" he called. "Az! I need to talk to you!"

There was so much he needed to say. Why couldn't she wait for him to catch up? His entire body burned. Jin stopped in his tracks, doubled over in agony. He was usually a good runner. What was wrong with him?

"Why'd you stop?" Astrea asked.

Jin's vision blurred as he stumbled to one side. The gardens spun and spun, nothing but a kaleidoscope of colors and shapes. He fell to the ground, but instead of sharp gravel digging into his skin, his fingers dug into soft grass. When Jin opened his eyes again, he wasn't at the palace but rather Crescent Park. A cacophony of laughs and music slammed into him, disorienting.

"Az?" he whispered. Where had she gone? He swore she'd just been right next to him.

A curvy, dark-haired young woman wearing a purple and blue dress disappeared into the crowd. Above the noise, Jin could still hear Astrea call, "Follow me!"

Jin shoved past festivalgoers, each person he passed disappearing like smoke in the wind. He searched frantically, endlessly, for that dark hair again. But he couldn't find her. He tried to follow her voice, but he couldn't find her.

One by one, the crowd vanished, until it was just him standing alone in the middle of the park. The band's instruments were still on stage. The stalls were still filled with food and games, untouched. A cold hand slid over his eyes, blocking his sight.

"Az?"

She giggled. "Took you long enough."

"I'm so sorry," he croaked, chest heaving. Why was it so hard to breathe? "I'm so sorry I didn't write you back. I'm sorry, I—"

Jin couldn't say anything else. He tried, but no words came out. The hand covering his eyes slipped down to his shoulder. Jin's breath quickened. His entire body was on fire.

"I hate you, Varojin Auris," Astrea whispered. *"I never want to see you again."*

Metal sliced his skin as Astrea drove a blade deep into his right shoulder. And when Jin tried to scream, he couldn't make a sound.

"Jin?"

That wasn't Astrea's voice.

"Jin?"

No one else was at the park, who—

"Jin, open your eyes, damn it."

He opened his eyes.

Zephyrine stared down at him, frowning. Jin tried to sit up, but pain shot through his back and his chest.

"Don't try to move," she said. "We did what we could, but Ena is tapped out. She needs to rest before she can finish healing you. Says you're stable. Just don't move."

The hum of engines echoed in Jin's ears. He was on the airship, and he'd never felt pain like this before. It ached and burned and stung and ached some more, radiating out from his right shoulder.

"What happened?" he finally asked. His throat felt like sandpaper.

Jin remembered some of it. Taking out the general. Clearing the fort. No, not clearing the fort. Three, maybe more, Delians had ambushed them. He still didn't know where they'd come from. Even in his cloudy mind, he was sure there'd been no room at that location on the blueprints the team had studied before deploying. He was so sure.

Fuck, his shoulder hurt. Pain pulsed through him again and again and again.

"We'll talk about that later." Zephyrine dropped onto a cot next to him. "I just need you to stay awake. Talk to me. You did good with Basera. Lando filled me in."

Jin didn't care about the general. "How bad was it?"

"Rasa, Dorin, and Lando are fine."

She didn't need to say anything else. He could feel how bad it was, and he'd already been healed. Healing magic couldn't do everything, couldn't fix *everything*, but it wouldn't hurt like this if it hadn't been grave.

"How bad?" he asked again.

"You lost a lot of blood. You could have died," she said simply. "But you won't. Ena just needs a few minutes before she finishes. She'll keep you stable until we get home."

He'd had a few other close calls since the war started, but those were minor in comparison. A blow to the head, a nasty stab to the arm, Basera trying to pull the air from his lungs.

Tears burned Jin's eyes, but he didn't know if they were from the pain or knowing that, indeed, the worst outcome had almost come to pass. Almost.

This was what he got for mouthing off to his father as a teenager? This was his punishment for not being born to the empress but instead to his father's mistress?

War. Death.

That was why Lando had looked terrified. Jin had almost died, and Lando had known it.

Jin didn't know where the rage came from, but it boiled up through his body so fast that his tears spilled. He didn't want to cry in front of Zephyrine, but skies, what would he have missed had the healer not saved him? Eliana's bright future. Little Velia's birthdays. Meeting whatever other nieces and nephews he might someday have. A chance to make things right.

"You kept saying her name," Zephyrine said gently.

"Whose name?" Jin didn't know why he asked. He already knew the answer. He didn't try to wipe away his tears, though. He was sure it would hurt too much to move a muscle. Even taking a simple breath hurt.

"Astrea's."

Jin's eyes fluttered closed. *I hate you, Varojin Auris.* He wasn't asleep anymore, but Dream Astrea's voice ran circles in his head. *I never want to see you again.*

"Did you ever write back to her?" Zephyrine asked.

"No."

"Why not?"

How did he explain this to his commanding officer? How did he explain that this exact situation—and everything that had led up to it—proved that his worst fear would come to life? For months, he'd regretted not trying to find Astrea during the winter solstice festival, but now he was glad.

He blew out a harsh breath. "I knew something like this would happen."

"What are you, a Stargazer?"

Jin glared at Zephyrine. "Not funny," he snapped. She held her hands up. "I knew I would probably die out there someday. I thought it would hurt her less if we weren't friends when it finally happened. And here I am."

Zephyrine watched him for a moment, her stormy eyes unreadable. "That's the stupidest skies damned thing I've ever heard."

"What?" Pain pulsed through him with every beat of his heart, but he focused on Zephyrine's narrow face.

She leaned forward on her knees. "Now that you consider yourself not friends with her anymore, if this Astrea died, would it hurt you any less?"

Jin swallowed. No. It would probably hurt more, knowing he'd never gotten a chance to explain everything to her.

"I didn't think so." Zephyrine set a gentle hand on his forearm, her touch cool despite how his entire body seemed to burn. "Did you do it to protect her or to protect yourself?"

He didn't know. Jin really had thought it was better for her. Part of him still did. But as he looked up at his commanding officer, he wasn't so confident anymore. Maybe he was just a coward.

Jin didn't have a chance to respond. A short, plump woman waltzed into the room. Ena. He'd met her once before when she'd stopped by at Fort Avalon to heal a nasty burn on Dorin's forearm.

"Open your mouth, Your Imperial Highness," she instructed as she opened a small bottle. Her pale cheeks were flushed, and dark circles had made their homes under her blue-gray eyes.

"Why?" Jin asked.

"Sleeping draught."

"Why?" Jin asked again. He didn't want to sleep. What if he dreamed of Astrea again? And besides, he needed to go talk to his team when this was done. He needed to figure out what happened, what he'd missed. What they'd all missed.

"This will make it easier for both of us," Ena said. "Magic will only do so much for you. Your body still needs to rest."

"Do what she says, Jin," Zephyrine said. Her voice was soft. "That's an order."

He didn't want to sleep. He wanted to do something, to figure out what came next. But the longer he was awake, the more he tried to talk with Zephyrine, the more everything hurt. His entire body throbbed in time with his heartbeat, pushing the ache further into his limbs.

Jin swallowed the sleeping draught, welcoming the darkness as it took him again.

CHAPTER 10
WINTER, YEAR 1015

Snow crunched under Jin's boots, the frigid air sharp in his lungs.

Just because his team had a break from the war didn't mean they got a break from training. Zephyrine had forced them on another of her "winter hikes" as she now called them. And the sun, glaring as it was on the white snow blanketing the forest, felt good on Jin's face. He sucked in another deep breath.

"Hey, Jin."

Jin would never get used to Lando using his real name. After what happened on Ilesouria, Lando had made fewer quips about palace life. Fewer implications that Jin might be spoiled. For the better, Jin supposed, though he almost missed his old nickname. Almost.

"Yeah?" Jin asked as the Tephran came up beside him.

"Your sister didn't happen to send you any of that chocolate recently, did she?"

Jin laughed once, his breath fogging in the air in front of him. "She did."

"And did you bring it?"

"Yeah."

"That's why we keep you around." Lando slapped him on the shoulder.

Jin hadn't ever planned on sharing the chocolate Eliana sent him—he had a big sweet tooth himself—but years before, Rasa had sniffed it out on a similar hike in the summer. That had been that. Since then, Jin always brought some with him. It certainly beat Zephyrine's rations.

A small red bird circled their group once before settling in a nearby pine. It was the only sign of life up here except for the five of them. Zephyrine was leading them to a higher elevation than usual, and as they climbed, the winter breeze turned gusty and strong.

"I know I haven't asked," Lando said, "but you doing alright, kid?"

There it was. Maybe Jin hadn't missed the nickname.

Jin forced himself to relax. They were his team. Of course they were trying to check on him. In fact, Jin knew he should be checking in with them to find out how they were doing. He might've been the one to nearly die, but that didn't mean they were alright. He just couldn't find the words. Didn't know what to say.

"Doing fine," he lied as he shoved his hands into his jacket pockets. "Just cold, as always."

He didn't turn to look, but Jin could feel Lando staring at him. Ahead of them, Rasa and Dorin walked side by side. Judging by the tightness in their shoulders, they were listening too. *Wonderful.*

Lando tripped, and Jin hauled the big Tephran back before he fell on his face. Under the snow were all kinds of things that might prove difficult: rocks large and small, tree roots, even ice in some spots.

"Better watch where you're going," Jin said.

Something unreadable, almost soft, flashed across Lando's expression. Then he nodded and adjusted his knapsack. "You're right, kid."

"Can you sorry lot keep up with me or not?" Zephyrine called from a dozen yards ahead. "Pick up the pace unless you want to freeze tonight!"

Lando's large hand landed on Jin's shoulder again. He tilted his head toward Zephyrine and smiled. "Let's go," he said. "I have a feeling she's not exaggerating."

The walls of the fort closed in. Footsteps even though no one seemed to be around. A face cloaked in shadows. A knife through his back.

Hot liquid trickled down his chest, then began to gush. He doubled over, then fell forward as a familiar, feminine voice whispered, "Nice try, Your Imperial Highness."

Jin gasped for air as he sat up. The ground underneath him was cold, freezing even, and the night air nipped at his nose. He lifted a trembling hand to his face, to the sweat beading on his brow.

Not real. It wasn't real.

Death had haunted his dreams for months. Either he was being killed or doing the killing, in waking hours or unconscious ones. He couldn't escape it no matter how hard he tried.

Skies damned Delians. Skies damned Helosian Empire. Skies damned Emperor Aelius Auris.

Jin shimmied out of his sleeping bag and stood, his hands still shaking as he moved away from the camp and toward the edge of the mountain.

Bringing his hands to his mouth, Jin blew into them, forcing his magic out to warm himself up. Skies damned Zephyrine and her skies damned rules. *Fuck the rules.* It had never been particularly challenging for Jin to control his magic in the freezing temperatures—not like other Fireweavers—but the higher they climbed, the more difficult it got. Practicing simply made sense.

"Why are you awake?"

Skies damned Zephyrine.

"Can't sleep," he muttered as she joined him.

Her jacket crinkled as she crossed her arms. "This is the second night in a row."

"Yeah, well." What was he supposed to say?

"Are you reliving it in your dreams?" She kept her voice low as they stared out into the darkness.

He shrugged.

"How long has it been going on?"

"Since Ilesouria."

Sometimes it was that damn Tempest general who showed up in Jin's dreams. Sometimes it was the group of Delians who had ambushed them. Sometimes it was just all of the nameless soldiers Jin and his team killed in Helosia's name. But no matter what, that stabbing pain returned despite his wound being long-since healed. And no matter what, Jin woke up with shaking hands and tears threatening to fall.

It was easy to hide at Fort Avalon since he had his own room. On missions and in moments like this, though? Not so much.

A star shot by overhead, disappearing almost as quickly as it had arrived. In all the years they'd been doing these hikes, in all the years he'd been stationed at Fort Avalon, Jin had never gotten tired of the view of the stars. The purples, blues, and whites. That brilliant, impossible band cutting through the middle of the sky. Part of him still wished Astrea could see this, that he could be the one to show her.

Jin hadn't told Eliana about what happened on Ilesouria. He hadn't told Apelo or Kaius, either. His father certainly had to know at the very least. And even though Jin knew his father wouldn't come to check up on him, some small part of him had hoped that maybe, just maybe, being within an inch of death might've made Aelius give a shit. But it hadn't. He hadn't called. Hadn't written. Hadn't flown out to Fort Avalon. Hadn't bothered to make sure his youngest son was alright.

"You know what helps me when I have dreams like that?" When he didn't answer, Zephyrine continued, "It's a trick my CO taught me and one I've passed on to those three."

Jin glanced back at his teammates. They were all asleep, huddled together near the pathetic campfire Zephyrine allowed. It gave off barely any light and just enough heat to keep them from getting frostbite.

He hadn't thought that they, too, might relive all of the bullshit they'd been through. And they'd been through so much more than him.

"What's the trick?" Jin finally asked as he risked a glance at Zephyrine.

"When it seems particularly difficult to remind myself that it's in the past," Zephyrine said, "I name three things I can see, three I can hear, and three I can smell in the present moment." As he started to protest, she held up a hand. "I know. I also thought it was silly. But it forces your mind to focus on what's actually around you, what's real. You can name more than three if you want, but I find three manageable when I'm . . . upset."

Jin said nothing. How was that simple thing going to trick his mind into realizing he wasn't back on Ilesouria? How was that going to help him accept what he didn't want to accept? What he couldn't accept?

But Zephyrine had been doing this since she was his age, and she was more than a decade older than him. She'd been doing this for a long time. She'd survived. And she seemed to sleep most nights. Maybe it was worth trying.

"I hate this job," Jin muttered. "I hate what we do." He didn't know where the confession came from, but there it was. He hated it.

Deploying into Delia. Mission after mission. Risking his life over and over again, and for what? Jin supposed being away from his father was one benefit. The only real benefit. He missed Eliana, and he missed his niece. He missed Cressida, and he missed Astrea.

"I can't say I'm the biggest fan either," Zephyrine said, "but this team has been good for you. Even if you can't see it. You've come so far. You've gained so much control, so much discipline."

"What good are control and discipline if I still manage to almost get myself killed?"

It was a conversation they'd had before once Jin had recovered his strength. Even with Ena's healing, it had taken days for Jin to be well enough to move out of Fort Avalon's infirmary. Rasa, Lando, Dorin, and even Zephyrine had all said it wasn't his fault. None of them had known where those soldiers had come from. There was no room at that location on the blueprints they'd studied. It had either been outdated intelligence or the Delian Earthmover had tunneled his way under the fort. Lando and Rasa had both insisted that, if that was how the Earthmover got in, they should've noticed. Should've felt the earth rumbling underneath them before the explosion.

That hadn't made Jin feel better. And even though he'd looked back at the blueprints himself one day to confirm he hadn't missed anything, that hadn't made him feel better, either.

"The worst part," Jin said when Zephyrine remained silent, "is that this is all for my father's benefit. His wars. His victories. Filling his coffers. Bolstering his reputation and his fucking ego. And we have to put our fucking lives on the line for it."

"Your father may wear the crown, Jin, but we aren't doing this for him."

"Then who are we doing it for?"

"We're doing it for your sister. For the Helosian people."

Jin rolled his eyes "That's the same thing as doing it for my father."

"Is it?" Zephyrine challenged. She finally turned toward him, arms crossed tightly over her chest. "You think the Delians don't have teams that do the same thing? You think they wouldn't try to force their way to Kalama—possibly trying to get to your sister or brothers or even your niece—if they thought it would end the war? You think Basera was the only one in their military and government who thought it was fine to purposefully target civilians?"

Jin's jaw tightened.

"It's blow for blow against each other, Jin. It's balance. Helosia may have more in numbers, but the Delian military rarely agrees to rules of war. They never have."

"It's still a terrible job," he muttered.

"It is," Zephyrine agreed. "It's a fucking awful job to have. And it's fucking terrible that your father got us into a full-scale war. But we are here when we are needed, and taking out Basera saved so many lives. Civilian lives."

Somewhere deep down, Jin knew that was true. Basera's plans had taken down six Helosian civilian ships in a matter of weeks. Hundreds and hundreds had drowned, including children. Families. His father shouldn't have gotten the country into a war in the first place, but that had crossed a line even his father wouldn't cross.

At least, Jin didn't think his father would cross that line.

"You really believe in what we do?" Jin finally asked.

"I believe we have a role to play. And I believe when your sister is finally named the official heir—when she finally comes to power—maybe we won't have to do this shit anymore."

He eyed Zephyrine. Jin knew there were factions that supported Eliana being named heir over Kaius or Apelo. He just hadn't realized Zephyrine was one of those people. He agreed with her, of course. Eliana was the right choice. Apelo had no interest in ruling the empire, and Kaius would be just like their father.

But to have her admit it now? It wasn't *treason* to have an opinion about which sibling should someday rule, but it would certainly raise some eyebrows back home. Most of the aristocracy supported Kaius being named the official heir.

Jin supposed he hadn't exactly been all that secretive about how much he disliked his father. At least Zephyrine knew Kaius was the wrong choice.

"You really think Eliana should be the heir?" Jin asked.

"I do. So do a lot of people."

"For the record, I agree with you . . . and a lot of people, apparently."

"Never doubted that, Jin. Now go get some sleep." Zephyrine clapped Jin's shoulder once, then walked back to their pathetic camp and slipped back into her sleeping bag.

Jin followed her and settled back into his bag, but he didn't go to sleep. He stared up at the stars, his eyes tracing the constellations he remembered. The Queen. The Dove. The Warrior.

What would Astrea think about this? What would she think if she knew what he'd done? What would Eliana think? Even Cressida—whom he'd never been *that* close with—would surely have something to say about the situation he found himself in.

How long could he go on like this? How much longer would the war with the Delians go on? And when would he finally get to go home again?

CHAPTER 11
SPRING, YEAR 1016

Four missions in three months. It wasn't exactly what Jin was expecting when it came to the Delian War; it was moving more slowly than he'd thought it would. But four missions in three months was still a lot. When his team wasn't out in the field, Zephyrine's other team was.

Jin almost felt guilty about that, but he knew his team wouldn't be at Fort Avalon for long. They never were. Within the next couple of weeks, they'd be sent out again. Assigned a new target, sent in without backup, prepared to lose it all.

With a sigh, Jin pushed his food around on his plate. It was some late-night supper the fort chef had scrounged up for him. He'd been asleep all afternoon, exhausted after another night of not sleeping. His body only seemed to calm down enough to sleep during the day. There was just something about the darkness his mind didn't like.

"What, you don't like the food?" Rasa asked.

Rasa, Dorin, and Jin were the only three in the empty mess hall. Rasa and Dorin had gone out for a hike earlier that afternoon and, apparently, missed the regular supper time as well. The food wasn't bad, just leftover meat, potatoes, and bread. Jin didn't even care what he ate. It wasn't like it mattered. Nothing felt like it mattered anymore.

"No, it's fine," Jin said. He set his fork down. "I don't know what's wrong with me."

"You've been down since Ilesouria," Rasa said. "I know it's hard going back out there after—"

"I'm fine," Jin said quickly. "Just tired, I think. I'm sure other units are more tired than us. At least we get a break."

Soldiers and mages who weren't on Zephyrine's teams had far harsher schedules and deployments. Jin had seen the reports from some of Avalon's commanders. He'd watched soldiers ship out and not return. His privilege—his team's privilege—wasn't lost on him, even if their work was still dangerous.

"We don't expect you to be fine." Dorin sopped up a trail of sauce with his bread. "And you know, just because they're tired doesn't mean we aren't, too."

Jin shrugged, then picked up his fork again. He had no appetite, but he had to feed himself. He needed the energy to train and go out into the field.

"It'd be nice if we at least got something better for dinner," Rasa mumbled. At least she seemed to understand Jin didn't want to talk about it. "Last time I was home, my wife made the best roast." She groaned. "Skies, it was good."

The mess hall doors burst open as Lando kicked his way inside. In his arms was a large crate, glass clinking within. "Oh, good, the kid's here!" he called, voice echoing against the stone walls. "Perfect! I've got a surprise."

"Sounds like beer," Dorin replied over his shoulder.

"Damn." Lando set the box on the table behind Dorin. "Spoiled it already."

"Not exactly hard to guess what's in there," Jin said. "Can't imagine what else it would be."

"Maybe it's wine," Lando said. "Or liquor."

"Definitely beer," Rasa and Dorin said in unison.

"Spoilsports." Lando opened the box and pulled out a tall, dark glass bottle. "It's the good stuff. My brother sent it up, but it took a while to get here."

Jin had never been particularly fond of beer, but he took a bottle when it was offered to him. "Are we allowed? I mean, we're technically on duty."

"*Technically*," Lando drawled, "we're a lot of things. Relax, kid. One or two beers won't change anything, even if we ship out in an hour. It's a long flight to the Delian border."

That it was. Even if they were called up at that exact moment, it would take at least an hour to get on an airship, then another four or five hours to fly to the border. Longer depending on exactly where they were being sent. A couple of beers would be out of all of their systems by then.

Jin twisted the top off his bottle, then took a swig. It was heavy, hoppy, and definitely not his preferred drink. He liked whiskey, and he liked vodka, but this was . . . well, it was alcohol.

"So." Lando dropped down on the bench next to Dorin, directly across the table from Jin. "What has you three looking so glum tonight?"

"Jin's not sleeping," Rasa said, "and I miss my wife's cooking." She stabbed a piece of overcooked meat with her fork. "What's wrong with you, Dorin?"

"Why do you assume something's wrong?" he asked. But when Rasa shot him a glare, he said, "It's what's always wrong. I miss the kids."

"Enough with the sap." Lando took a sip of his beer, then said, "Time to break you sorry lot out of these moods. Let's play Five Fingers."

Dorin groaned, but Rasa dropped her fork onto her plate and raised one hand in front of her. Jin's eyebrows furrowed, but he set his beer down and followed Rasa's lead. After a nudge from Lando, Dorin set his fork down and held his hand up.

It was a game Jin had played before in Kalama, mostly as a child or when some of his peers forced him into games after palace dinner parties. Any time you'd done one of the activities said, you had to put a finger down. The one with the most fingers down at the end of the round had to drink. Playing this game was how he'd gotten drunk for the first time at sixteen.

"I've never been to the imperial palace," Lando said.

"That's just not fair," Jin protested. "I know none of you have been there."

Lando shrugged, to which Dorin and Rasa laughed. With a grunt, Jin put one of his fingers down.

"I've never had the best stroganoff on the planet," Dorin said.

"That's not fair either!" Rasa said. "You know my wife makes the best."

"Yeah, well, you thought the palace one was funny," Jin said. "Put a finger down, Rasa."

She huffed. "Fine. I've never had kids," she said, to which Dorin swore and dropped one of his fingers.

Around and around the table they went until Jin had just one finger still up. And it was Lando's turn to give a prompt. "Well, kid," he said, "it was nice knowing ya. I've never started a fire on Zephyrine's hikes."

With a sigh, Jin grabbed his beer bottle. He took a swig and was about to put it down again, but all three of his teammates protested that he had to drink more. So Jin drank. He downed half the bottle, and only then did Rasa, Dorin, and Lando cheer.

They played three more rounds, and it seemed to Jin that his teammates were out to get him. And to his greater surprise, he wasn't even upset about it. The more beer he drank, the more he actually relaxed. Besides, he'd gotten far drunker other times back home. His entire body buzzed with energy and alcohol, but he still had his wits about him.

After a while, Dorin got bored of the game, so he simply handed out another round of beers. "Tell your brother we said thank you," he said to Lando. "Most appreciated."

"I don't think I've ever seen you drink before, kid," Lando said. "Or do anything fun, really."

"I have fun," he muttered.

"Oh, that's *right*." Dorin grinned. "There was that time a couple of months ago that you spent two nights in town."

Narizon was a mid-sized city a twenty-minute drive from Fort Avalon. Compared to Kalama, with its several million citizens, Narizon was small. But it was large enough that Jin was able to go relatively unnoticed and unrecognized. There was no true anonymity for a prince, though.

When Zephyrine had guaranteed the team three days off, Jin had gone to Narizon with one purpose: a break from Avalon and the war and all of the bad dreams he had. He'd gotten a hotel room by himself but spent most of his time wandering the public parks and picking out new novels at some of the bookstores he found.

"What *did* you do for those two nights, Jin?" Rasa asked. "Or should I ask who?"

Though his teammates chuckled, Jin sighed. Meeting that woman hadn't been the plan. But he'd gone into a bar for a drink one night to try to take his mind off everything, and she'd been the third person to approach him. She'd been the first to actually treat him like he was normal, though. Jin rarely felt pulled enough toward women to actually want to do something with them. Not because he didn't like them or find them attractive. He did. But it was . . . complicated.

Part of that was because Jin didn't know who was drawn toward him for the right reasons. Who was genuinely interested in him as a person, not in trying to use him to gain some perceived political or social favor? And worse, what if someone felt pressured to be with him because of his title and his family? Even if he asked, would potential partners be honest with him? He wasn't sure.

And even still, Jin had asked that woman if she knew who he was. She had. When he asked why she'd come over, she said it was because he looked like he could use a friend. And eventually, she'd gone back to his room with him. It had been her idea.

They'd spent two days and nights together. And while it had been a good distraction at first, all it did was leave Jin feeling even more empty after. As if that were even possible.

Part of him wondered if anyone actually liked casual sex, and the other part wondered if there was just something wrong with him. Everyone in Kalama seemed to like it. And he didn't care what anyone else did. He'd even tried it himself. Tried to fit in. During his teenage years, he'd had trysts with some of the noblewomen his age. Just quick, meaningless kissing and fooling around and, on a few occasions, sex.

Those experiences hadn't exactly been awful, but he just didn't understand the appeal. But was that because of who he was deep down, or was that just how his family's status influenced what others wanted from him? Jin didn't know, nor did it feel all that important to answer the question. It didn't change how he felt or what he wanted.

Every time Rasa and Dorin talked about their wives, Jin got the slightest bit jealous. Not because he was in a rush to be married, but it sounded nice. To be known and loved by someone for who you truly were. *That* was what he wanted. Someday, if he could find it. If he deserved it after everything he'd done during the war.

"Just needed a break from you three," Jin said wryly. "Can't spend all my skies damned time with you."

That earned another round of laughter from his team.

"Look, kid," Lando said, twisting his beer bottle between his palms, "I know I've given you shit over the years, but I'm glad you joined the team. You're a good fit."

That was unexpected. Even Rasa and Dorin cooled their laughter, their faces sobering at Lando's words.

"I understand," Jin said. "I know my father's reputation, and it's well-deserved. I'd be skeptical if our positions were reversed. The emperor's bastard son, shipped off to boot camp before the legal age. It doesn't exactly look good for him or me."

"Well, you're obviously not him," Lando said. "You don't seem to be anything like him based on the rumors about him. And I'm sorry I gave you such a hard time all those years ago."

"Years ago?" Jin said, forcing a laugh into his voice. "You purposefully tried to get me drunk tonight!"

Lando grinned. "I suppose I did."

"But I appreciate you saying that," Jin added quickly. And really, he did. "No hard feelings."

Lando gave a brief nod, then started asking Dorin something about a recent report Zephyrine had given everyone to read. Jin, though, didn't pay attention. Could Lando be right, that Jin wasn't like his father? That had always been one of his biggest fears. He didn't want to be anything like Aelius.

Jin wanted to do something good for the world. He wanted to *be* good. He just had no idea how he was supposed to do that when he was still fighting his father's war.

Chapter 12
Summer, Year 1016

The war with the Delians was almost over. In the last six months, Jin's team had been on ten missions. The first few months after the incident with Basera had been especially hard on Jin, but now he was back in the strange routine that was war. And now it was almost over. Almost.

They had one more target to take out, and they were going to need help. Zephyrine's second team was going with them.

"This," Zephyrine said, gesturing at the map laid out on the table in the middle of the airship cabin, "is General Vaiss's camp." It was right near the Helosian border, Jin realized. Literally within a few hundred feet of their country. Bold. "We need to take him out and recover some of our people. A dozen of our people, actually."

"Where's he holding 'em?" asked Tanas Trialis, a Tidebacker and leader of the second team. He ran his hand over his face. A handful of sunspots covered his deep bronze cheeks. "Seems like an awfully big camp for the nine of us."

"Aw, c'mon, Tanas," said Anka Koen, the other group's Tempest. She was a waif of a woman with wheat blonde hair and skin. She wasn't much taller than Rasa, who was short by any standard. "If any nine people can do it, it's us."

Tanas merely grunted as he pushed a few coiled black curls out of his face. His stormy blue eyes flicked from Zephyrine to the map and back again.

Despite having been under Zephyrine's command for four years, Jin didn't know her second team well. They'd trained together a few times, but seeing as they were Zephyrine's *only* two teams, they often worked opposite schedules. They'd also worked separate missions throughout the war to cover more ground.

Even before the war, Jin hadn't seen much of them. He'd been so busy trying to keep up with his own team's drills and training. Besides, that was right after Rasa, Dorin, and Lando had lost Neri. They'd been informally sidelined, and Zephyrine's second team had picked up the slack.

But Zephyrine trusted these people. That was good enough for Jin.

"Reconnaissance teams say the Helosians are being held here, near the camp's rear exit," Zephyrine said. Jin followed her finger along the map. "We'll approach from the right, as there's more tree coverage. With the shift change near dusk, we should have no issue getting in."

"How are we splitting this up, Zephyrine?" Lando asked, his jaw flexing as he crossed his arms. Tanas assumed an identical posture.

"Intel says Vaiss is planning to use his airships to bomb Sapoi in the coming days, a last-ditch effort to turn the tides of the war. Anka and Bel will come with me to take out the ships," Zephyrine said, nodding to the pair.

Anka's gray eyes were kind as she smiled at the group. Bel Nasikus, the other team's Metalli, had a Kalamian look to them, with tan skin and wavy brown hair that matched nearly half the population of the capital. They were closer to Dorin's height, and while everyone else's armor was leather and largely unadorned, Bel's had tiny pieces of metal woven in. A rifle was also strapped to their back.

"Tanas and Sanne will go with Rasa to get our people back," Zephyrine continued.

Sanne Gellia, the group's Sparkcaster, tossed her long blonde braid over her shoulder. Her pale, narrow nose lifted into the air. "Easy."

"Which leaves me, Dorin, and Jin to go after Vaiss," Lando said. "Easy." Sanne laughed.

"Vaiss is a Stormchaser. Remember how you took Basera out." Zephyrine glanced at Jin. He simply nodded. They'd need to keep this quick and efficient. "Now, we've got another hour before we arrive at the landing site. Let's talk layout and strategy."

If someone had told Jin two years ago, when the war first started, that his team would be able to take out an entire Delian camp, he would've scoffed. But now, Jin knew exactly what they were capable of. They'd taken out smaller camps on their own, just the four of them. And with Zephyrine and her other team here, Jin was sure they would succeed.

Jin watched his steps as he crept through the darkening forest. Lando and Dorin were right beside him, their footsteps almost silent despite the thick brush and slightly muddy ground underfoot. Jin strained to make out the rest of the team's dark shapes.

The tree line thinned, giving way to a crowd of white tents and a hastily erected log wall. Night was always a good time to approach a camp. Shift changes combined with the start of soldiers drinking typically made for disorganization on the Delians' part. They did the same thing to Helosian camps; Zephyrine had been right about this being blow for blow. The Delians had taken out two Helosian camps in the last two weeks. And now, Jin listened carefully. The commotion of the shift change had begun.

At the head of the group, Zephyrine paused near the camp's rear entrance. She held her fist up, a signal to wait. Everyone huddled in the shadows of the perimeter wall as a soft, warm rain began to fall. Jin held his breath under his mask, straining to listen for anything beyond the chatter of bored Delian foot soldiers.

Warm firelight glowed from just within the camp, casting shadows on the ground beyond the fence. When Zephyrine turned, Jin saw the warning in her eyes. *Heads down, move fast, take out your targets.* Bel and Anka moved into position next to her. Tanas and Sanne joined Rasa. Zephyrine held her hand up, then tilted her head toward the camp.

One heartbeat passed, then another, then another. Zephyrine whispered something to Lando, and he nodded. The rowdy cheers of the Delians inside the camp broke up the pitter patter of the rain.

Zephyrine signaled for them to go, then darted into the camp. Everyone followed.

Row after row of white tents spread out before them, making two neat columns on either side of the narrow road that cut through the middle of the camp. At least the map had been right about that part.

Just ahead of them was a group of soldiers—sixteen, based on Jin's quick count—with their backs to the exit. *Fools,* he thought. This was the problem with the Delian army. They had egos that didn't suit their talents. He couldn't count how many silly mistakes the Delians had made over the last two years.

Zephyrine skidded to a stop and flung her arms out in front of her. The soldiers sank to the ground, choking for only a few moments before they were gone. Jin's heart thundered in his ears. That was quick, efficient. Brutal. She'd pulled the air right out of their lungs. Jin suppressed a shiver; he'd gotten firsthand experience with that just a year before from General Basera. To do that to sixteen people at once, and so quickly . . . he'd always known Zephyrine was strong, but that was exceptional.

"Go," Zephyrine whispered to the rest of them. "Make it quick." Then she, Bel, and Anka split off to the left at the next break in the tents.

The plan was for Dorin, Lando, and Jin to make a beeline for the general's tent as the others fanned out and did what they needed to do. Once they took out Vaiss, they'd take out any Delians who resisted and radio for the rest of the nearby Helosian troops to come and collect anyone who surrendered. That was the one good thing about missions like this. Jin's team was rarely alone now and just had to to take out camp leadership. Helosian troops would come in and deal with the rest. His father, apparently, saw some use in not eliminating *all* witnesses.

They followed the exact course they'd plotted through the drawing of the camp just an hour before. They passed the tent with the captives as Rasa, Lars, and Anka slipped inside. With the shouts of Delians already ongoing from the shift change and dinner hour, the added noise of his teammates taking out the Delians guarding the prisoners didn't seem to draw any attention.

"To the right," Lando whispered as they came to the next break in the Delian tents. "Make it quick."

A group of four Delians were seated around a low card table, their attention stuck on their game as they jeered and jostled each other. The rain had stopped, and they didn't seem to be bothered by their slightly damp playing cards or muddy ground.

Fire bullets sparked over Jin's right hand. Dorin did the same with his water. Four shots. That was all they'd have time for . . . and all they needed. The four Delians slumped over their game without so much as a shout.

Four lives gone.

They moved on, repeating the exercise at each break in the tents, taking down whoever they could. Quick. Efficient. They barely had time to hide the bodies. Jin stopped counting; it did no good to count how many lives he was taking.

"Gotta move faster," Lando whispered as he finished shoving a dead Delian into a nearby tent. "Keep up with me."

The closer they got to the center of the camp, the quieter it became. The rain returned, harder this time but no worse than summer showers in Kalama. Jin blinked past the raindrops stuck in his eyelashes. The general's tent was easy to pick out among the rest. It was larger and taller, and the green, blue, and white Delian flag fluttered high above it.

"Let's go," Lando said. "Backup'll be here soon."

Jin sucked in a breath. Six guards were stationed outside the general's tent, each one of their blue uniforms stained with mud. Jin took the three on the right; Lando and Dorin took the three on the left. They barely put up a fight. Thunder crashed overhead, rattling Jin to his core.

Lando signaled for time, then motioned for them to move. The wind picked up as they slipped in through the tent's flap. Inside was dark; only a few candles lit up the sparse space. A single person was hunched over the table in the middle of the room, his back to the door.

That had to be General Vaiss.

Lando moved first, dagger drawn. That was *not* the plan. They'd agreed to move in as a unit, using their magic to control him. That was what they always did when going up against powerful mages. But . . . maybe taking Vaiss out without a fight was best. Jin inched forward, warm magic surging just under his skin.

Thunder crashed again as the howling wind pushed against the tent's sturdy frame. Vaiss's hand hung loose by his side, his fingers twitching. *Stormchaser.* Of course. The storm had moved in too quickly. Summer weather was volatile on the southern part of the continent, but not like this. Never like this. *Shit.*

Lando angled his long dagger toward Vaiss. Jin pulled on his fire as Dorin started forward, water swirling around his hands.

Metal flashed. Lando's legs faltered as a sword pierced his torso and came straight out his back. Vaiss pulled the weapon out with a sickening squelch. Lando barely made a sound as his knees hit the muddy ground. Dorin froze. Jin froze.

Vaiss turned and wiped his blade on his white uniform. Lando's blood smeared across the thick cloth, the red so bright even in the darkness of the tent. "Nice try."

No. Blood leaked out of Lando's gut. *No.* More blood bubbled from his mouth, spilling down the sides of his face and neck. *No.*

Mud squelched. Jin looked up. Vaiss stalked toward him. The storm outside raged so hard the tent began to shake. It sounded like a freight train was coming—a tornado? More of Vaiss's magic?

Jin looked at Lando again. His green eyes were wide open, frozen. His body convulsed once more, then stilled.

He was gone.

No.

Jin stared at Lando's body, unmoving, covered in blood and rain and mud.

Pain flared in Jin's chest, white-hot and angry. His fucking father. Fucking Basera and Vaiss and all the others they'd taken out these last two years. Why did these people insist on fighting? Zephyrine said it was about balance, but balancing what? The death tolls on each side? One country trying to overtake another? Was that really worth . . . this?

Jin had told Zephyrine he hated this job. And he *hated* it. He hated everything about it. This wasn't fair. It wasn't fair to anyone. It wasn't fair to the Delians or the Helosians or Lando. It wasn't fair to Jin or Dorin or Rasa. It wasn't fair to any of them being forced out here for . . . for nothing more than a few extra miles of border and some despot's pride.

Jin's magic strained against his skin, pushing and pushing. Even the flames in the room seemed drawn to him, their energy calling to him. He breathed in, welcoming them. They grew with his anger, burning brighter and brighter. Flames spiked over his palms.

His skin burned. His lungs screamed. Too much. There was too much—

Fire burst out from Jin with an ear-shattering boom, knocking Vaiss back. The man screamed. The stench of burned flesh hung heavy in the air as the storm suddenly died off to little more than a sprinkle of rain. Jin's fire kept reaching, pushing.

The tent was gone, nothing but a smoldering mix of fabric and wood. Gone, too, was the furniture from the general's tent. The neighboring tents in every direction. The bodies of the guards they'd just taken down. Gone, gone, gone.

Lando. Dorin. *Fuck, fuck, fuck.*

A shield of water swirled around where Dorin had crouched next to Lando, their bodies safe but obscured by the miniature waves. Jin hadn't even thought about them. Hadn't even seen them. This wasn't his training. He was supposed to be watching them. They were supposed to stick to the plan.

He rushed forward, reaching for his teammates. Wind knocked him back, sending Jin sprawling. Rolling to his feet, Jin pulled on his fire again. Vaiss was standing despite the blood oozing from his blistered skin. Gone was whatever minor advantage his team had with the weather and shift change. Jin had ruined that. He had to make this quick so they could find Zephyrine.

Fire whips formed in his hands. He lashed out at Vaiss just as Dorin's water and ice blasted into the general. The wind kicked up again, then died as Vaiss stumbled over the ruins of his tent, cursing. Jin was on Vaiss in a heartbeat, maybe two. Flames coated his fists as he pummeled the general.

This was the opposite of quick. What was he doing? Some faraway part of Jin's mind knew that none of this was his training. He knew better. He needed to just take out his dagger and get this over with. Just like Lando was going to do.

Jin reached for the weapon, but it wasn't in its sheath.

A sharp sting pulled across his thigh. When had Vaiss managed to grab Jin's weapon?

Fire burned in Jin's veins. He pulled on it, forcing it not into bullets but the shape of a dagger. Then he plunged it down, down, down. It burned through Vaiss's armor, his uniform, his skin, as it pushed toward his heart.

Vaiss screamed. He screamed so loud Jin was sure it was going to make his eardrums bleed.

And then it stopped.

Jin's chest heaved as he pushed off the dead general. He stumbled back, surveying the damage again and looking for any other Delians. His body ached. His head swam. Too much. He'd used too much magic, and now he could see why.

He'd thought it was just the tents that were gone, but a radius of a couple hundred feet was simply . . . destroyed. Tents, furniture, weapons racks, all obliterated. Nearby soldiers burned, some alive and others not.

Jin stumbled backward again.

Dorin hunched over Vaiss, checking that the general was really dead. Jin tripped over himself as he lunged for Lando's body and dropped to his knees. What had once been muddy earth had dried, scorched by Jin's flames. The rain began to slow.

This wasn't supposed to happen. Two years they'd been in this stupid fucking war. They'd been training together for longer than that. Why?

Why hadn't Jin moved faster? Done something to prevent this? Why hadn't Lando stuck to the plan? They were supposed to stick to the plan.

Jin knew he had to move. He had to find Zephyrine or Rasa. He should be covering Dorin. Every bit of training screamed at him to move, to cover the teammate who was still alive. They'd run countless drills for this scenario. He couldn't just sit here in the open, but his body wouldn't move.

Something near the camp exploded. Jin flinched. One of the Delian airships went up in flames, as did the one next to it, and the next three in the line of airships. The final one lifted off the ground, then exploded mid-air. A white-haired woman jumped from the wreckage, cushioned by a vortex of air. Zephyrine.

Jin tried to force himself to his feet. Someone was shouting for him. Rasa. Rasa was sprinting toward them, shouting something.

"I'm sorry," he said as she dropped down next to him. "I tried, I didn't mean—"

"Not your fault," Rasa said, her usually soft voice so, so hard. "Not your fault. Come on. We've got company."

Dorin was back on his feet, a dozen water whips lashing out as more Delians stormed into the area. Rasa slammed her hands onto the dusty ground. The earth trembled, cracking and splitting into a chasm right under the Delians' feet. Dorin's water pushed the rest of the nearby soldiers into the hole.

"Come on." Rasa grabbed Jin's forearm. "We'll get him home, but you have to move. We can't carry both of you."

That got Jin moving. The earth under Lando's body raised up, a makeshift stretcher that Rasa pushed along with her magic. Dorin covered the front and Jin took up the rear. Zephyrine, Bel, and Anka sprinted toward them as the airships continued to burn and smoke. No Delians chased them. And in the distance, a familiar rumble of tank engines and shouts in Helosian told Jin that backup had arrived.

Their job was done. They'd weakened the camp. They'd taken out Vaiss.

But at what cost?

"You did good." Zephyrine placed a hand on Jin's shoulder, but he shrugged it off.

The hum of airship engines rattled Jin's bones. He was tired. So fucking tired. They were en route to Fort Avalon, far away from the remnants of the Delian camp. Jin knew, somewhere in his mind, that they'd done what they had to do. They'd stopped the Delian attack on another civilian target. Likely saved thousands of lives. Vaiss was dead. The center of the fucking camp was destroyed.

And that was Jin's fault.

Zephyrine didn't see it as a fault at all.

"Lando knew the risks, Jin."

He said nothing.

Dorin had filled in the rest of the team—including Anka, Sanne, Bel, and Tanas—when they'd gotten back to the safety of their airship. Jin had listened as Dorin described everything in precise detail, everything except for the explosion Jin had somehow created. Because that was exactly what it had been. It hadn't been his fire. It had been an explosion. Dorin made up something about a combination of wind and fire; Jin didn't really listen. He'd been too busy trying to figure out why Dorin didn't tell the truth.

The one thing everyone else agreed upon, though? That Lando had miscalculated. He'd been rushing.

Now it was just Zephyrine, Rasa, Dorin, and Jin, all squished together in Zephyrine's makeshift office on board the airship. The space barely accommodated the four of them and the narrow table she used as a desk. There wouldn't have been any room for Lando had he been with them. Tears burned the back of Jin's throat.

"Lando also should've known that storm was Vaiss, not nature," Rasa said gently. It was the second time she'd said it. "He was a great mage, but he didn't always think. This isn't the first time he deviated from the plan."

"But I should've done something," Jin said. "I realized—"

"It sounds to me like you realized the storm wasn't natural right when the rest of us did," Zephyrine said. "*I* should've realized it sooner."

"I blew the fucking camp to the void!" Jin slammed his fist on the metal table, forcing his tears back. "I fucking lost it, Zephyrine. That was me, all me, not what Dorin said."

"You did what you had to do," Zephyrine said. As if the truth were that simple.

She hadn't *seen* that . . . that bomb he set off. Hadn't seen that he *was* the bomb. She hadn't *seen* what he did to Vaiss. She hadn't heard the man's screams as Jin had shoved a blade made of pure fire into his heart.

Yes, he'd killed before. For two years, he'd fought and killed and barely survived. But *that?* That wasn't who Jin was. That couldn't be who Jin was.

He was not a monster.

He couldn't become a monster. He could not lose control like that again.

He would *never* lose control like that again. Jin wasn't sure exactly how he'd generated that much power, but he would not do it again. He would follow his training. He would stay in control.

"Vaiss was going to kill you if you didn't do something, Jin," Dorin said. It was the first time he'd spoken in ten minutes. "You saw what he could do. Probably would've wiped out half of his own forces and our entire team with that storm if you hadn't stopped him."

Maybe. Maybe that was true, but it didn't make Jin feel any better.

"Losing Lando hurts," Zephyrine said. "It will never not hurt. He mourned Neri for years and blamed himself even though it wasn't his fault. We all still mourn Neri, just like we will always mourn Lando. But I don't want you to think that you fucked up. You didn't, Jin. You can do everything right, can do everything by your training and instinct, and you can still lose."

That didn't seem fair. What was it all for, then, if they could still lose? Could still lose one of their own?

"Just like none of you did anything wrong on Ilesouria," Zephyrine said gently, "and you still almost lost."

But they hadn't lost then. Jin hadn't died. Lando had.

"Did you know you could do that?" Dorin asked, his gaze trained on Jin.

"No." Jin shook his head. "No, I didn't. I didn't know it was possible. Did I hurt you?"

"Don't think so," Dorin said with a shrug. But his body told a different story. Tiny cuts marred his skin, as did a few minor burns. Even his leather armor had a few scorch marks on it. It could've been far worse considering Jin hadn't even given Dorin a warning. Hadn't been able to give him one. "I've never seen anything like that before."

"Nor have I," Zephyrine said, "but mages discover new techniques all the time, especially strong ones." Jin refused to look at her as she repeated, "You did what you had to do, Jin. You did good."

Silence settled over the room. Jin scrubbed at his face, but all he did was smear blood and dirt there. He pulled his hands away.

"When we write our reports, there will be no mention of what Jin did." Zephyrine looked each of them in the eye. "What happened will never be discussed outside of this team. As far as anyone else will be concerned, Jin is a strong Fireweaver, which they already know. And that's *all* they're going to know, including the emperor."

Jin was the strongest Fireweaver by far at Fort Avalon. Though he'd never heard of a Fireweaver setting themselves off like that, Dorin's explanation of Vaiss's wind and Jin's fire mixing might be believable. The only true witness to what had happened was Dorin.

While the thought of asking his team to lie to his father made Jin sick, he also instantly knew the truth Zephyrine was dancing around. If his father *ever* found out what Jin could do, how strong he was, Aelius would want to use it to his advantage. And that simply couldn't happen.

"Whatever you need us to do," Rasa said, and Dorin echoed his agreement.

Zephyrine nodded. "Dismissed. Get some sleep. We'll be home in a few hours."

By the time they arrived at Fort Avalon, all Jin wanted to do was go to his quarters and sleep. But sleep still meant seeing Ilesouria, and he was sure he'd see Lando and Vaiss now, too.

After cleaning the blood and sweat off himself, Jin returned to his room and sat at his small desk. It probably looked silly, him hunched over it. He didn't care. He needed to do something.

The empty paper in front of him almost mocked him. It had been a few months since he'd written one of these letters to Astrea. He hadn't written to her since before the night Lando brought in beers to get Jin and the others drunk. This used to be easier. He used to tell her everything. Then he'd started telling these pieces of paper everything. Then he'd almost died, and it had become nearly impossible.

He forced out a breath and picked up his pen. He could do this. It was just words.

Dear Az,

These last four years have been hard. Hard doesn't seem like the right word. It's not strong enough, but it's the only one I can think to use. I imagine that if I were at home and struggling to figure that out, you'd have suggestions for me. You always were better at that than I was.

You wouldn't believe what I've seen the last two years at war. I'm lucky that my team only deploys when we're needed, but we usually go once a month now. Things picked up after Ilesouria. I made a full recovery. That's what the healers say, anyway.

My heart hurts, Az. It hurts all the time. I never wanted this to be my life. I never thought it would be my life. Never. I never liked the palace, but I hate this. I hate the war, and I hate who I've become.

Remember how, in one of your letters to me years ago, you hoped I made new friends? Well, I did, and I lost one of them today. Lando. I told you about him. A few days ago, he was giving me a hard time for sleeping in late. And now he's gone. I don't know what to do. Dorin and I were supposed to be covering him. We're a team, and we failed him.

*You would be so ashamed of me, Az. All of the things I've
done since the war started . . . none of that compares to what
happened with Lando. And I know that war means death,
and sometimes it means taking a life to save your own, but
I just can't believe I would*

Jin's hands began to shake so badly that his words became illegible. Tears dropped onto the page one by one, muddying the ink that had yet to dry.

Zephyrine had once asked Jin if he'd been protecting Astrea or himself when he broke off that friendship. He'd thought he was protecting her from the pain of losing him to the war. He'd later thought that maybe he was just a coward. But *this* was it, the truth. Astrea might be sad if he died at war, but she would be so ashamed of him now. To know what he'd done. What he'd become capable of. What he'd probably always been capable of. How he'd failed not just Astrea but another friend, too.

What good was he? All Jin did was hurt people.

Eliana would be ashamed. So would Cressida. Even Kaius might have a certain level of distaste for the situation, and hardly anything fazed Kaius.

Jin set his pen down, then picked up the paper in one trembling hand. With the other, he summoned a small flame, so gentle compared to the one he'd generated at that Delian camp. And then he willed the fire forward until it licked the corner of the paper.

He didn't put the flames out until the letter was nothing but a pile of ash. Jin considered burning the rest of the letters he'd written to Astrea over the years, but that would require digging them out of his wardrobe. Exhaustion tugged at the corners of his mind.

Later. Jin would deal with all of that later.

For now, he would sleep. Even if Basera, Vaiss, and Lando haunted his dreams. It was the least he deserved.

CHAPTER 13
WINTER, YEAR 1016

Jin stared down at the palace gardens. He was back for the winter solstice festival and some dinner party his father was throwing. It was his first time back in two years.

The palace was just as cold as he remembered.

The war with Delia was over, thanks in large part to that skies forsaken mission to take out Vaiss. He was one of the last Delian military leaders unwilling to sign a treaty, and with him gone, Jin's team had brought them all one step closer to the end of the war.

Now the treaty was signed and fighting had officially stopped, so the winter festival promised to be an even bigger party this year than any Jin could remember before. The entire capital buzzed with excitement, as did the palace. The senators and courtiers in the palace halls gossiped and quietly cheered. Banners with the Auris family crest and Helosian flag hung from the palace's rafters and even the columns outside. Everyone was elated that not only was the war over, but Helosia had won. Control over Ilesouria and its surrounding islands was the only concession, but to Emperor Aelius, a win was still a win.

Jin didn't feel much like celebrating. It didn't feel like a win at all.

He was home for a whole five days this time, and he'd spent the first day here in his old apartment. That was how he planned to spend most of the second day, too.

Except being inside the palace was like being in a cage. He spent most of his time outdoors up at Fort Avalon—training with his team, training some of the younger soldiers, doing chores for Zephyrine, anything to keep himself busy. And now, he needed that fresh air. Going to the gardens was a risk. He might run into some obnoxious courtiers or old friends.

It was a risk worth taking. Staring at these stupid walls was going to make him lose his mind.

Jin slipped out of his apartment and wove through the upper halls until he found one of the less used staircases near the back of the palace. He made his way downstairs and outside without being seen by anyone except a handful of guards.

He should've asked Eliana to go with him, but she was mad at him. He'd stopped writing to her that summer after losing Lando. Jin hadn't been able to bring himself to put words to paper after that failed attempt at writing something to Astrea. He hadn't told his baby sister about what had happened—not about his magic or losing Lando—and he didn't think he could.

Eliana couldn't know any of it. Not the lie and certainly not the truth. What would she think of him? And, perhaps worse, what would she say to their father if she knew the reality of Jin's life now? Though he'd warned her years ago about not mouthing off to their father, Eliana had shared in some of her letters that she disagreed with decisions he was making. Eliana often disagreed with their father. Knowing Jin's reality would just give her more reason to disobey, and if she disobeyed, she might not be considered for the role of heir anymore.

Jin didn't know how long he spent wandering the gardens. He walked the same path over and over again along the western side of the palace, around to the northern side, and back again. The only thing he avoided was going too close to the observatory. He'd thought about going to a spot he used to play in with Eliana, Cressida, and Astrea when they were children, but that seemed like a bigger risk. He had no idea if any of them still went there.

Eventually, Jin found himself sitting on a low wall on the northern side of the palace, one that overlooked the green-blue stretch of Tinale Bay. Kalama was abuzz below: colorful sailboats docking in the harbor and steam-powered shipping vessels blowing their horns as they made their way out to sea, cars winding their way through the streets, airships angling toward the airfield on the far side of the city.

Rasa was down there somewhere with her wife, Coral. Dorin was supposed to attend the festival with his wife and children. Zephyrine had arranged for the two families to be brought to the capital just for the event.

What about Lando's family? Jin knew he had a brother, but Lando had never mentioned any other family or friends.

"Eliana told me she'd seen you moping around somewhere back here."

Jin turned in time to see Kaius picking his way through the overgrown section of garden, his nose wrinkling as a branch snagged his red satin shirt.

"What do you want, Kaius?" Jin muttered.

"She wanted me to check on you."

Eliana and Kaius never agreed on anything. The odds of Eliana asking Kaius to do that were very low.

"Well, you've checked. I'm here. I'll be back inside in time for dinner. Tell Ellie I'm fine."

"Oh, you're fine?" Kaius laughed, a dark sound. "You've really got the whole brooding soldier bit down now, brother."

Jin's jaw tightened. "Did you just come out here to antagonize me?"

"Believe it or not, no." Kaius brushed off the wall, double-checking the spot before he sat down. He remained an arm's length away. "I know you didn't tell Eliana about what happened during the war."

"And how do *you* know what happened? We haven't exactly been pen pals."

"Because Father gets reports, and as his heir, he's been allowing me to read them."

Jin forced his expression to remain neutral, but his pulse jumped. "He named you as heir?"

"It's just a matter of time until he does." Kaius waved a hand.

So that's a no, Jin thought.

"I'm truly sorry you lost . . . what was his name? Lando?" Kaius continued. "I imagine that was difficult."

Jin's jaw tightened again. *Great.* He'd always assumed his father knew about his team's missions, but Jin had never considered that Kaius might become privy to that information. How much, exactly, did Kaius know?

Once things had settled after Lando's loss, Jin and his remaining teammates had gone back to their training routine. Jin had barely been able to practice his fireweaving at first, too ashamed of what had happened on that mission. But his magic had called to him, and that pull toward his fire had been too strong to ignore.

Jin still didn't know how he'd created that explosion. He simply had. He'd lost control . . . but it had been more than that. He'd been able to recreate the dagger. That was easy. Zephyrine had asked Jin twice in the last two months to try to recreate that bomb, but he couldn't do it. He'd wanted to do it, just once, to figure out how to avoid ever doing it again.

But not knowing? That was scarier than being able to do it on command.

"I have to say, though, I was surprised by how many kills you've made over the last couple of years," Kaius continued when Jin said nothing. "I never would've thought you had it in you."

"Yeah, well." Jin shrugged.

"The gentle Varojin, a fucking war hero."

Jin scoffed, keeping his gaze trained on the ships far below them. "That hardly makes me a hero. You learn how to survive when you're thrown into the middle of a battlefield by your own father."

Kaius clicked his tongue. "He wouldn't have sent you there in the first place if you had shown him even a shred of respect."

Respect. On that skies forsaken day Jin had first left Kalama, his father had used the same word. Respect.

Aelius Auris thought respect and unquestioning loyalty were the same things. Do what you're told, don't ask questions, don't push.

But that wasn't respect.

Jin mouthing off hadn't been respectful, either, but he'd been pushed too far by both his father and Kaius over the years. He'd gotten so sick of their bullshit, just like he was already sick of Kaius's bullshit again. Jin had a thousand things he could say to Kaius, but none of them would be productive.

Perhaps Zephyrine was right. Perhaps he had learned some control after all.

"Is that all you came out here for?" Jin asked. "I told you I'd come inside in time for dinner."

"No. I thought you could probably use a distraction from all this brooding."

"And what distraction might that be?" Jin asked with a sigh.

"We're in Kalama. You can take your pick."

Jin simply stared at his brother. Kaius rolled his eyes.

"Right. You've been gone far too long." Kaius pointed down at the city far below. "The theater. A concert. Shopping."

Jin crossed his arms over his chest. "No, thank you."

"Gambling?" Kaius offered. "Alcohol. Sex. I mean, you can't have any of that up at Fort Avalon, and I know some very good clubs and some very interested young women. They have a real thing for soldiers."

That was the last thing Jin wanted. None of it would help him forget, and that was all he wanted. To forget the last four and a half years.

He glanced back toward the palace, back toward the observatory.

"Oh, don't tell me you're still stuck on her."

"What?"

"She's not here. You don't have to pretend you don't know what I'm talking about." When Jin still said nothing, Kaius huffed. "You cannot still be stuck on the Stargazer's niece."

"I'm not stuck on anyone," Jin muttered.

They hadn't spoken in years, and besides, he'd been such an asshole. A bad friend. He doubted he even had a right to put Astrea's name on those letters he was never going to send, the ones he still wrote despite that. She had a life of her own now, one that didn't include him. And that was *good*. He wasn't going to fuck that up for her.

Looking at the observatory was just instinct. Memory.

Jin shoved to his feet. "Fine, Kaius, you win," he said, forcing himself not to look at the observatory again. "Show me one of these spots you like in the city."

"First, you have to change," Kaius said, upper lip curling as he motioned at Jin's black fatigues. "You cannot go out looking like that."

"Whatever."

Jin didn't care what he had to wear. Anything would be better than sitting in this stupid palace compound for a minute longer, even going out with his brother.

Anything would be better than the numbness that had seemed to take over his entire body for these last six months.

Club Pyre was the last place Jin wanted to be. Agreeing to Kaius's outing had been that latest mistake in Jin's very long line of mistakes.

"Oh, come on," Kaius drawled as he shoved a glass of whiskey toward Jin. "Have another drink."

"I've already had two," Jin muttered. "I don't need another."

Upon arriving at the club, Kaius had immediately been escorted to a booth at the far end of the room. It was roped off, spacious, and obviously reserved. The booth gave Jin the perfect vantage point to watch the entire club and its occupants dressed in their silks and jewels. The big band's music echoed in Jin's ears. A haze of blue lotus smoke filled the air, dimming the bright gold, red, and white decor.

Kaius scoffed and nudged the crystal glass closer. "Just drink."

Jin picked up the glass and took a sip. "Happy?" he asked.

"Impossible," Kaius muttered, but his attention was already shifting to the crowd around them.

Oskar and another guard, a young man named Sav, stood at attention just inside the velvet ropes creating a perimeter around their booth. Jin wasn't sure why they needed two guards with them; not only was Kaius a well-trained Sparkcaster, but Jin could probably take out the entire club if he needed to.

He tipped back the rest of the whiskey.

"There you go," Kaius said. "See? It's fun." Jin said nothing, and Kaius scoffed. "First you didn't like The Aura, and now you don't like Club Pyre, either? You're making this difficult on purpose, aren't you? These are two of the best clubs in town. Where else am I supposed to take you?"

"I'm not making it difficult."

When a nearby woman shrieked, Jin flinched. Years ago, he'd been used to crowds like this thanks to functions at the palace and even a few trips to nightclubs just before that fateful eighteenth birthday. Zephyrine had also invited him to go to a place called the Whiskey Dream, a club her friend owned, before they went back to Fort Avalon. He hadn't yet decided whether he was going with her or not.

"Do you know how annoying you are?" Kaius snapped as he flagged down a waiter in a revealing outfit made of glittering gold fabric. "I invited you out of the kindness of my heart, to help my poor younger brother get his mind off his troubles, and you are taking up this *entire* booth"—he motioned to the black leather seats— "with your pouting."

"I'm not pouting."

Kaius rolled his eyes. "Varojin. Look at yourself."

Jaw tightening, Jin spared a glance down at his black slacks and crimson shirt. He was sure Eliana had been the one behind the few court-appropriate—and club-appropriate—outfits in his closet. The silky shirt wrinkled where he folded his arms over his chest.

Jin forced himself to unwind his arms and loosen his jaw. As much as he was loath to admit it, Kaius was right. He was pouting. And this was not about pouting. It was about . . . distraction.

"Fine," Jin said. "Give me another shot."

One vodka shot turned into two turned into three. Tension melted from Jin's body with every extra ounce of alcohol. He was at the precipice of drunkenness, that euphoric state where his entire body felt warm. Cozy, almost, despite the chaos of the club around them. He could breathe for the first time all day. He relaxed into his seat and sighed.

"Sav," Kaius called out to his fair-haired guard, "open the gates. We're ready."

"Certainly, Your Imperial Highness."

"What the fuck does that mean?" Jin asked as he accepted a fourth shot from his brother.

"I told you these girls have a real thing for soldiers, didn't I?" Kaius replied, sliding out of his seat at the edge of the booth. "Drink your shot."

"Kai—" Jin started, but Kaius was already walking toward where Sav and Oskar stood. Where people were beginning to draw near.

Oh, this night was definitely going on Jin's long list of recent mistakes. He tipped his shot back and settled in.

Skies, Jin was drunk. Drunker than he'd been in . . . well, he couldn't remember. Couldn't remember much of anything, really. Couldn't even remember how many shots he'd done, but as Kaius slid another to him, Jin drank it.

Warmth pooled in Jin's veins as he sank deeper into the booth. The band's music pulsed in his ears, disorienting and overwhelming. His head was far past swimming. Lando might even be proud. He'd always tried getting Jin to loosen up.

But as Kaius welcomed a pair of young women into the booth, Jin sighed. It was the fourth such pair, dressed to the nines in dazzling beaded dresses and sparkling jewels. Jin didn't recognize either of them from court. The first, with dark brown skin and tightly coiled hair, had a thick Tornamian accent. The other, whom Kaius pushed toward Jin, had bright red hair and pale skin covered in freckles.

Kaius whispered something to the redhead, who giggled as she scooted closer to Jin. Then Kaius shouted to a waiter, "Another round!"

Jin tilted his head back against the seat, letting the alcohol already in his system wash over him again and again. He may as well have been liquid himself with the way his whole body finally relaxed.

A hand on his shoulder didn't even make him tense. He forced his eyes open, only to find the redhead moving closer to him. Her gaze was trained on him, and her hand didn't move.

"Your Imperial Highness," she said as she leaned toward his ear, her accent distinctly Kalamian. "I'm Minerva, but my friends call me Minnie."

"Minnie." Jin turned the name over in his cloudy mind. He definitely didn't know this woman, but she looked to be around his age. "My friends call me Jin."

"Is that what I should call you, Your Imperial Highness?" She batted her eyelashes. In the darkness of the club, Jin couldn't quite make out her eye color. Blue or green? Impossible to tell.

"If you want."

Smiling, Minnie passed him one of the vodka shots Kaius sent their way. Jin barely even registered the slight burn of alcohol as it rushed down his throat. Six? Was that his sixth shot? Seventh? He should've kept count.

Minnie scooted closer, her hand brushing the side of Jin's thigh. A few bracelets on her arm clinked together. "Prince Kaius said you've been on some very important missions recently. That you helped end the war."

"Don't believe everything you hear."

"Oh, you're being humble! My father's a newly elected senator, and he was telling me—"

Jin huffed. "Can we not talk about all that? The war, I mean."

"You don't want to talk?" she asked, and he shook his head. "Maybe we can do something else."

As Minnie leaned in, Jin leaned away from her. "That's not what I meant."

"And why not? You don't think I'm pretty?"

"What?" he asked. "No, it's not that—"

"Don't be a prude, Varojin," Kaius called over his shoulder.

Jin wasn't being a *prude*. Skies. But he didn't even know this woman. She didn't even know him. He was pretty sure he'd had enough to drink, but anything was better than sitting around and having Kaius judge him, so Jin said, "Let's go get a drink."

Minnie squealed, then said something about going to the bar. Jin climbed out of the booth and followed her through the crowd, trying to keep his eyes trained on that green dress and red hair. The room swayed with every step. *Too much*, he told himself. The team would never let him live this down. Lando certainly wouldn't if he were there.

He found his way to the bar, then found Minnie. *Senator's daughter* . . . Which senator? Jin almost asked but stopped himself. What did it matter?

Minnie passed him a drink, some cocktail made with amber liquor and topped with a slice of orange. "To the end of the war and your homecoming," she said, raising her glass for a toast. "And to a fun night," she added with a wink.

Jin wrinkled his nose but clinked his glass with hers. None of these people knew. All around him, these people were happy the war was over, but they didn't know the toll it had taken on everyone actually on the battlefield. None of them knew that Lando was dead or that Jin had barely made it out alive. None of them would probably even care.

No. No pouting. Jin could almost hear Kaius scolding him. Lando would probably scold him, too. Lando was always trying to make the most out of a bad situation.

"So . . ." Jin glanced down at Minnie, who had inched closer to him. She wasn't even half an arm's length away. "Is this what you always order?" He gestured to the cocktail. It wasn't very good.

"No, but I heard you like whiskey."

Jin frowned. Was there even whiskey in it? He couldn't tell. "I do."

Minnie laughed and leaned closer to him. Her hand brushed his. "You need to loosen up!"

"It's just loud," he lied as he leaned toward her. "Hard to focus."

With a final chug, Minnie finished her drink. "Should we rejoin your brother?"

The crowd shifted, giving Jin a brief glimpse of their booth. It looked like Kaius had cozied up with that Tornamian woman. More than cozied up. Skies, Jin did not want to go back over there. He grabbed Minnie's hand. "Maybe let's not . . ."

Minnie smiled. "Upstairs is quieter anyway. Shall we?"

Quiet. Quiet sounded perfect, especially with the way his head was thundering in time with his heart and the band's drums. Jin hadn't even realized there was an upstairs to the club.

Minnie laced her fingers with his as she led him past throngs of club-goers until finally, she pulled him down a dark hallway. It was quieter already. Jin's shoulders dropped as they climbed the stairs at the far end of the hall.

Upstairs was cool and dark, and though they could still hear the music, it was only a fraction as loud. Minnie led him to a sofa, and they both dropped onto it. Drapes surrounded them, creating a little alcove. Was the whole second floor like this? Who else might be up there? Jin's muscles flexed, like his body wanted him to go check and shout the 'all clear' he'd so often called to Lando, Dorin, and Rasa. *Not a mission.*

"I didn't realize you were so tense," Minnie said.

"Not used to all this."

"Prince Kaius did tell me you don't get out a lot."

Jin frowned. When had Kaius told this stranger that? *Why* would Kaius tell her that? Did he know her?

"In fact," Minnie continued, "he told me you don't get to do much of anything fun where you're stationed. Is that true?"

"True enough, I guess."

"I've heard that from a lot of soldiers, actually." Minnie leaned in. Jin leaned back, away from her. And she laughed. "Relax. Your shoulders are practically up to your ears."

Were they? Jin sucked in a deep breath, then pushed his shoulders down again. What was wrong with him? He'd just been melting into a puddle in that booth. Now, it was like his body couldn't decide what it wanted, to relax or to fight. And his head wouldn't stop pounding.

"I'm always looking for a good time," Minnie said as she leaned toward him again, "and *you* seem like you're in desperate need of one. What do you say? Let me show you how to have fun here in the city."

Jin's muddled mind was still trying to process her offer when Minnie pressed her mouth to his. And for a moment, Jin melted into the sofa and the kiss. *No pouting.* As Minnie kissed his neck, Jin considered finding a hotel room for the night and taking her to it. *Distraction.* Wasn't that why he was there?

But as her hands began wandering from his chest toward his belt, he stiffened. "Wait—"

"We'll go slow," she whispered against his mouth as she moved her hands higher again. Then Minnie climbed into his lap, straddling him.

Somewhere past the haze, Jin knew he was going to regret this if he did it, just like he'd regretted it with that woman from Narizon. Even if Minnie seemed very enthusiastic. Even though she smelled nice, like jasmine and honey. Even if he was lonely and just wanted to feel *something* besides—

An awful screech echoed through the club. Jin jumped out of his skin, nearly sending Minnie tumbling to the floor. She caught herself on his shoulders and cleared her throat. Jin's pulse skittered as the screech came again. What was that? It sounded almost like metal on metal . . . like when

Zephyrine had taken out those airships at the Delian border camp. He tensed again.

Minnie laughed and ran a gentle hand through his hair. "Relax, it's just the microphones on the fritz. Happens all the time. New tech. You know how it is."

"Microphones?" Jin asked, trying to force himself to breathe.

"Surely you know what *those* are."

He swallowed thickly. "Yeah. Of course. But listen . . ."

She shook her head. "Just relax," she said for what felt like the thousandth time. "Consider this a thank you."

"What?"

Her lips were just inches from his as she whispered, "A thank you for your service in the war, Your Imperial Highness."

Jin grabbed Minnie by her shoulders as heat rushed through him. "No."

She swallowed hard. "What do you mean no? Don't you want to—"

"No," Jin repeated. "No . . . I . . . I need some air."

"I can come with you."

"No," he said again. No, he was better off alone.

Minnie deflated, but she climbed off his lap. As soon as he was free, Jin bolted up, making his head and stomach spin unpleasantly. He headed downstairs. The oppressive noise of the crowd returned, and those skies forsaken microphones screeched again. Someone shouted an apology for the delay in the band's performance.

Jin headed for the front doors, ignoring the hostess calling after him. He burst out into the cool winter night, then sucked in one deep breath, then another. Above, in the cloudless sky, he could barely make out the brilliant band he always stared at up in the mountains. A few streets over, an engine misfired. Jin flinched. His whole body may as well have been on fire. He couldn't breathe, even out here.

Too much. He'd drank too much. Had tried to do too much. He moved a little ways down the sidewalk and leaned his forehead against the cool brick wall of the building. All he wanted to do was leave. Go back to the palace, spend the next few days alone. *Don't be a prude. Relax. For your service in the war, Your Imperial Highness.*

Skies, Jin just wanted to get away from the noise, the people, the bullshit. He hated this place.

"Varojin?"

Jin looked up. Kaius stood a few feet away, Minnie holding onto one arm while the Tornamian woman held onto the other. Oskar and Sav were waiting near a black car idling at the curb.

"What, Kaius?" Jin asked.

"Why'd you run off like that? Minnie said you were having a nice time."

Minnie flashed a smile. Jin said nothing.

Kaius rolled his eyes. "I should've known this was a mistake."

"I'm just tired and drunk," Jin lied. "This is a lot . . . after being away for so long."

"You always manage to spoil things." Kaius rolled his eyes again. "I'm taking Minnie and Leyla to a hotel for the night. I'll be back at the palace tomorrow afternoon."

Jin blinked. "You're taking . . ."

"You could join us, if you wanted, Your Imperial Highness," Minnie said. "We could get two rooms . . . or just the one."

Jin hadn't really been interested in Minnie, but to have her jump at the opportunity to leave with Kaius . . . to have Kaius willing to take her home after . . . to *suggest* . . . It just made Jin's stomach churn. And the worst part? He wasn't even sure he was surprised.

"I'll find my own way home," Jin muttered.

Kaius led the girls to the car, and soon, they'd all climbed into a shiny black car and sped away into the night.

Jin slumped against the wall again. He didn't just want to leave the club. He wanted to go back to Fort Avalon, back to his team, to the few people in the world who actually gave a damn about him. But he couldn't go yet. And so with one last deep breath, he headed up the street and started back toward his father's palace. All he had to do was make it a few more days.

CHAPTER 14
SPRING, YEAR 1017

Chunks of rock flew through the training center's air, the atmosphere thick with humidity and magic. Jin leaned against the low wall surrounding the training ring, watching the intricate earthmoving dance Rasa was performing with the newest member of their team, Adi Kuwat.

Like Rasa, Adi was an Earthmover, and though he was a decade younger than her, he was stronger. One thing Jin had noticed about many of the soldiers stationed at Fort Avalon was that no matter their magical affinity, they didn't seem to think outside the box. Earthmovers liked large rocks, Fireweavers liked large flames, and so forth. Jin understood the appeal. Of course he did. There was nothing like embracing the full strength of your magic. But there was something to be said for the smaller, subtler things too. And Adi understood that after just a couple of months on their team.

Rasa and Adi had been sparring for a good ten minutes, but finally, Adi had the older Earthmover pinned back against the wall of Fort Avalon's indoor training center. An onslaught of spring rain had forced them inside for once, and the dry dirt floor of the training center was far easier to practice on than mud. Pools of water lined the far end of the gym, and a few fire-lit lamps flickered nearby. The strongest Tidebackers and Fireweavers didn't need those resources, but having one's element nearby was useful in some drills.

"Showoff!" Rasa called as she grinned.

With a flick of his wrists, Adi's rocks keeping Rasa pinned dropped to the ground. Sweat poured off his dark brown skin. "I'm not showing off," he said, but Jin knew that smile. That dimple in his right cheek. Adi was definitely showing off.

Adi had just turned twenty-two, but that was older than Jin had been when he'd joined the team. Jin had been the exception. And though he was about to turn twenty-three—which hardly made him old—Jin still hated that Adi was going to lose his youth to Emperor Aelius's skies forsaken army.

So far, Jin enjoyed Adi's company. He was funny and kind. But it pained Jin to know that Adi was only there because Lando was gone. How had he been gone for nearly a year? The rest of the team had barely talked about that day. Jin didn't think he could, even though part of him wanted to.

"You're not getting any younger out there, Rasa!" Dorin called from next to Jin.

Rasa flipped him the middle finger before shouting, "You're not either, old man!"

Dorin laughed, then clapped a hand on Jin's shoulder. "Looks like you're not the kid on the team anymore."

"And Rasa's right," Jin quipped. "Neither of you are getting any younger."

It was a conversation both Rasa and Dorin had brought up several times since Adi had joined the team. Always in private, never when the kid was around. Sometimes with Zephyrine. They'd been on her team for many years, had joined when they were close to Jin and Adi's current ages. They were tired.

Jin understood. He, too, was tired, and he'd only been working under Zephyrine for half that time.

"Yeah, well." Dorin shrugged.

"You still thinking about retiring?" Jin kept his focus on Rasa and Adi as they discussed something in the middle of the sparring ring.

"More time with the family would be nice." Dorin sighed. "Missed the baby's first steps."

"I'm sorry." Jin wasn't a father, but he'd missed his niece Velia's major firsts. Missing that as a parent had to be a million times harder. "But Meri's doing well?"

Jin also couldn't imagine having a wife and having a job like this. Rasa was in the same position as Dorin; she and her wife had been married for most of Rasa's tenure on the team. They didn't have children yet, but Rasa had recently mentioned wanting to settle down eventually. None of them could keep this up forever.

"Meri's great," Dorin said. "But I know she'd like me home. Her sister and brother-in-law help out, but she's got all three children now. That's a lot of responsibility I've left her with."

"Have you talked to Zephyrine about it?"

"She's looking into options for me."

"Well, I hope she figures something out."

Dorin laughed. "Trying to get rid of me?"

"I wouldn't dream of it."

Dorin chuckled again, then took a few steps forward toward the edge of the ring. "You two need to get cleaned up! We're leaving in an hour."

"Coming!" Rasa called back.

They were due to go on one of their excursions in the mountains again, Adi's first since joining the team. It wouldn't be as bad as Jin's first had been since it was spring, but the night air still held some bite.

Jin didn't wait for the rest of his team. They didn't need him standing watch to ensure they were on time. After saying a quick goodbye to Dorin, Jin headed out of the training center. The rain had finally stopped, and now the late afternoon sun filtered through the last of the storm clouds.

Jin was glad to be back in Fort Avalon. His last trip home to Kalama had been just five days, but that was five days too many. Seeing Eliana—and apologizing for not writing to her more regularly—had been good. Following Kaius's suggestion to spend a night on the town had been a mistake. Not only the debacle at the club but all that alcohol. Jin had returned to the palace only to stay up half the night vomiting.

And beyond Kaius's bullshit that night, Jin's trip home had been filled with familial obligations. Another winter festival celebration, plus attending one of his father's infamous dinner parties. Jin hadn't been to one of those in years. They hadn't changed, nor had the guests. It might've been more tolerable if he'd had a few drinks, but after his hangover from the night at the club, Jin hadn't dared have even one cocktail.

As soon as Jin got to his quarters, he pulled out his knapsack. He always kept it packed with his gear, but he slipped an extra bar of the chocolate Eliana had sent into one of the front pockets. Zephyrine pretended not to approve, but Rasa and Dorin always wanted Jin to bring it. Lando had loved it, too.

Jin shouldered his pack and headed out the door. He didn't want to be late.

"How do you manage to do this in winter?" Adi asked as he ran a hand over his short, dark, coiled hair.

Jin had just started their fire for the night, and Zephyrine was busy searching through her pack for something. Around them, the forest had grown quiet, and the sun had finally set. The air was crisp but hardly cold.

"You get used to losing all of the feeling in your body eventually," Jin said as he crouched in front of the flames. When they started jumping too high, he forced them back down with his fireweaving. "And just when you're sure you're going to die from exposure, the morning finally comes, and you start the process all over again. Besides, I still think it's better than the swimming drills she puts us through."

"Sounds awful," Adi muttered.

"It's not as bad as he makes it sound," Zephyrine said. "He's survived every drill and every hike."

"Barely." Jin stood and scooped his bag off the ground. "Just like I barely survive on those rations."

"A soldier must learn to survive on the bare minimum," Zephyrine said simply.

Jin had learned to do that, all right. Not that he'd ever needed that training; they were almost always in and out of their missions in one day, maybe two. Whether they were rescuing Helosians or sent in to take out Delian military leadership, the war had never taken their team too far away from the Helosian border.

"Don't worry," Rasa said as she joined them. She dropped her pack to the ground and waited until Zephyrine was a dozen paces away from the fire. "Jin's sister always sends chocolate for us to take on these excursions. Makes the jerky a little more bearable."

Adi's thick eyebrows shot up. "Chocolate? Really? From the palace?"

"From her favorite shop in the city," Jin corrected.

"Wow." Adi shook his head. "My little sister's never going to believe this when I tell her."

"How old is she?" Rasa asked.

"Eighteen. She just enrolled in university in Kalama."

Rasa nodded. "Any other siblings?"

"No, it's just me and Noemi."

She wasn't in much of a different position than Eliana, then. Jin's sister had started her second year at Kalama's university.

"And your parents?" Rasa asked.

When Adi hesitated, Jin looked up. In the few months of knowing Adi, he'd never seemed to frown. Not even when he was being sent to the healers after a particularly brutal drill. Adi loved to joke and laugh no matter the circumstances.

"It's just me and my sister," Adi finally said. "Our grandmother and father both passed a few years ago."

Rasa nodded again. "It's just me and my wife. And my mother-in-law."

"How does your wife deal with you being away most of the year?"

"It's hard," Rasa said. "But she understands why I do what I do."

"Serving the empire?" Adi asked.

Rasa glanced at Jin. Once Jin had found out where Zephyrine's real loyalties lay—with what the Kalamian newspapers had recently nick-named 'the rebels' for their ideas about changing some of the imperial government's policies—he'd found out everyone else on the team agreed with their CO. But he hadn't learned that on his first excursion with them. It had taken several years for them to trust him with that. Which was understandable, given who he was.

And he appreciated that they'd trusted him with that over time. He knew that must've been hard, admitting that to one of Emperor Aelius's children. Jin was just glad they were all on the same page.

"Serving those who want to do right by the Helosian people," Rasa finally said.

Adi's gaze flicked to Jin, a slow horror spreading across his face. "Jin . . . I'm sure she didn't—"

"Relax, Adi," Jin said quickly. "Nobody here is particularly fond of my father or his policies. I don't consider it treason to question my father's . . . well, everything he does." He met Adi's two-toned eyes—one was forest green, the other brown—and held his stare. "Is that going to be a problem for you?"

"No! No problem." Adi sighed as his entire body relaxed. "I'm . . . relieved to hear it, actually. I didn't know what to expect. My last unit was, well . . ." He paused. "Patriotic? Enthusiastic? Never said anything bad, ever, about Helosia."

"We're unexpected, I'm sure," Rasa said.

Adi nodded, but his attention stayed on Jin. "So, why are you here and not in Kalama?"

It was Rasa's turn to raise her eyebrows. Jin didn't mind the question, though. It was nice to be around someone who wasn't treading on eggshells just because of that heavy, invisible crown Jin wore. Even after all these years, and even after trusting Jin to know their politics, Rasa and Dorin skirted the issue of Jin's family. Even Lando had skirted it despite his jokes.

"My father shipped me off when I was eighteen," Jin said. Adi stared at him, mouth open slightly. "Zephyrine plucked my sorry, angry ass out of the slush pile at Fort Ironwing not long after. I don't think landing here was what my father intended."

"Then what did he intend?" Adi asked. If he was fazed by Jin's description of the emperor, he no longer showed it. "I'd think a prince would be given special treatment."

Jin laughed. He couldn't help it. *Special treatment. What a joke.* "I think my father saw two outcomes," he said. "I would either learn whatever lesson he was trying to teach me, or I would die in the process and wouldn't be his problem anymore."

"That's bleak," Adi murmured.

Jin shrugged. "It's reality." One he'd finally accepted.

He couldn't change his father's opinion. Jin was sure the only thing that *would* change it was if Aelius knew how strong Jin's magic truly was. How he was a monster, just like Aelius. And that was never going to happen. So it was what it was. Jin could live with that.

"I don't think I've ever heard you talk about your father so much." Rasa plopped onto the ground in front of the fire. There was no malice behind her words.

"That's because none of you have ever asked." There was no malice behind Jin's words, either. "Adi asked me a question, so I gave him my answer." Jin reached into the front pocket of his pack and pulled out a rectangle wrapped in gold foil, then tossed it to Adi. "And for that, he also gets as much chocolate as he wants."

"Hey!" Rasa exclaimed. "I would've started asking you more questions years ago if I'd known there was a reward involved."

"Well," Jin conceded, "it's not like I've ever asked many questions of you or Dorin, either."

"No one ever asks me anything." Dorin dropped a bundle of kindling on the ground near Jin, then circled to the empty side of the fire. "Why does Adi get chocolate first?"

"Apparently we were supposed to ask Jin about himself for that honor," Rasa said. "Seems he's talkative now."

"Five fucking years and you finally want to chat?" Dorin quipped. "Took you long enough."

Jin had never been one for small talk with his teammates. He'd enjoyed their company over the years, but he'd always preferred to simply listen and watch. Him getting roped into that drinking game that Lando had proposed was one of the few times Jin had ever shared much about himself.

And lately, he'd been wishing that he'd opened up more to his team over the years. That he'd been willing to share. That he and Lando could've talked more before, well . . . Jin couldn't change the past, but he could start now. If that meant telling Adi about himself, and if that meant Dorin giving him shit, that was fine. It was better than keeping himself entirely closed off.

"Never had much to say," Jin retorted.

"Enough of all this," Zephyrine said as she sat on the ground next to Dorin. "There's a much better question you should be asking."

"And what's that?" Rasa asked.

Zephyrine smiled and stretched her hand out. "Why isn't the highest-ranking officer here getting the first round of sweets?"

CHAPTER 15
SUMMER, YEAR 1017

Fort Avalon was a flurry of activity despite the heavy, oppressive sun beating down outside. Jin didn't see what the fuss was all about.

It was just his father visiting.

Of course, Jin understood why *other* people would be rushing around to prepare for the emperor's arrival. But as far as he was concerned, his father was just like any other person with a lick of power in Helosia: entitled, overbearing, and annoying.

Which was why it was no surprise to him that Aelius's airship had radioed into the fort just a few hours prior, giving the base's leadership no time at all to prepare. Apparently his father wasn't staying long, but he hadn't been by in years and wanted to pay a visit to the remote fort while he was in the area.

Jin knew this was no coincidence. This wasn't about checking on imperial assets.

This was about checking on *him*.

I suppose I am an imperial asset, Jin thought as he fiddled with the sleeves of his fatigues. Every fucking person in this fort was basically owned by the government.

The worst part about all of this was that nobody would let Jin himself help prepare the base for the visit. Most of them had reverted back to using his old title, his imperial one. That didn't belong to him, not anymore. It never really had.

"Jin!" Adi called as he ran toward Jin. "Zephyrine wants us all up in her office right now."

Jin followed Adi from the mess hall through the fort, past soldiers young and middle-aged, until they finally reached Zephyrine's office. The five of them barely fit in the space; it was a good thing Zephyrine's other team had been sent to Fort Ironwing for the summer to train some of the newest conscripts.

"Close the door behind you," Zephyrine said as Jin and Adi stepped into the room.

"What's this about, Zephyrine?" Rasa asked. She leaned against the wall behind Zephyrine's desk, hands clasped in front of her.

"Emperor Auris is coming here today," Zephyrine said. "He'll be here any minute."

"And?" Dorin asked. "We knew that."

"And I know none of you are as dumb as you like to pretend you are," she said. "You know this isn't about him visiting the fort for administrative purposes."

Everyone's attention landed on Jin. He sighed. "No, it's not."

"Do you know what he wants?" Zephyrine asked.

"No. I haven't spoken with him since the last winter festival." And even then, Jin had barely spoken to his father. The handful of visits Jin had back to Kalama in the last five years had involved as little interaction with his father as possible. Just a few greetings and dinner conversations and little else.

"While the emperor is here," Zephyrine said, "a few changes need to be made."

"I don't like the sound of that," Dorin muttered, but one look from Zephyrine shut him up.

"Rank and surname only while he's here, for starters," she continued. "Lieutenant Kuwat"—she nodded at Adi—"Captains Tysias and Foscari"—she motioned to Dorin and Rasa, respectively—"and of course, Colonel Kanakos."

"And what about Jin?" Rasa asked.

"His Imperial Highness."

Jin sighed. "Is this really necessary?"

"Yes, it's necessary."

"It's ridiculous. That's not who I am."

Zephyrine ignored him. "If the emperor asks to see us, we'll cooperate. If not, stay out of his way."

"Anything else?" Rasa asked.

"No. Dismissed. Except for you, Jin."

Jin waited until Dorin had shut the door behind the rest of them before he spoke again. "What does my father want?"

"All I've been told was to prepare for two meetings." Zephyrine shrugged one shoulder. "One between him and myself, and one between you and him. He wants to meet you right here in my office."

"Wonderful," Jin muttered as his pulse skittered. What the fuck would his father want to speak with him about now? And Zephyrine on the same day? Was this some kind of transfer?

Jin didn't like the job during wartime, but he liked it now that there was peace. He liked being here, so many hundreds of miles away from the palace. He liked working with Adi, Rasa, and Dorin. He liked running drills and refining his fireweaving techniques. It kept him distracted, kept him grounded when the nightmares and memories became too much.

"Do not say anything to give him reason to take you home," Zephyrine said, voice low.

Did she fear the same thing as Jin, then?

He nodded. "I'll try not to say anything at all."

"Alright. Well." Zephyrine stood. "I'll be meeting him in one of the war rooms. Assuming he's not spending the night here for some reason, I'll find you and the team later. Make yourself comfortable."

When Zephyrine slipped out of the room and closed the door behind herself, Jin didn't make himself comfortable. He started pacing as much as he could in the small office.

This was how it always was when he was around his father. Always guessing at what the man's true intentions—true motives—might be. Always guessing about what he wanted because even when he was in the room, Aelius Auris was rarely straightforward or honest.

And this was how it always was—time left passing with no idea of when the esteemed emperor might actually show up to a meeting *he'd* asked for.

Jin kept his eyes trained on the clock. Twenty minutes passed first, then thirty. An hour went by, then another.

Was he supposed to sit there all day?

Jin was tempted to simply leave and let his father find him whenever he was ready, but that was like teasing a hungry dog with a treat. His father would be looking for a reason to send Jin away from this place he'd started to think of as home and the people he thought of as friends. Anything to punish Jin, whether that meant dragging him back to Kalama or sending him to a different fort.

He'd finally settled in the chair behind Zephyrine's desk when the door swung open. Jin didn't jump to his feet like most people would when Emperor Aelius Auris entered a room. Instead, as his father stepped into Zephyrine's office, Jin counted to twenty in his head.

Aelius looked the same as he always did. Tan skin and coiffed hair. A crisp, freshly pressed suit. Hints of maroon and gold woven into the details of his outfit. The hard edge to his posture.

"Varojin."

"Father." Jin finally stood.

One of the guards in the hallway outside closed the door. It wasn't exactly privacy, but it would have to do.

"I was surprised to hear you were coming all the way up here," Jin said. "Seems like it's awfully far out of your way."

"I had business with your commanding officer."

Jin kept his face calm, but inside, his mind screamed. Had his father taken out some perceived slight on Jin's part on Zephyrine instead? Had he somehow found out that Jin's team wasn't exactly loyal to the crown in the way he'd expect them to be? Had he found out that they'd fudged the reports about what happened on the day of Lando's death?

"I'm sure she'll want to tell you herself, so act surprised when she speaks with you," Aelius continued. Jin braced himself. "I've personally seen to her promotion."

"Her promotion?"

"To general."

"General?" Jin echoed. His father had . . . promoted Zephyrine? He wasn't punishing her?

"I'd been pushing for this to happen for months, but it seems I have to do things myself if I want them done in a timely manner," Aelius said. "Yes, Lady Kanakos has been promoted for her outstanding service during the Delian War."

"And you had to come all the way out here to tell her the good news?" Jin asked. He'd promised Zephyrine he wouldn't say anything to upset his father, but that question made Aelius's jaw tighten.

"I came to meet your entire team, Varojin. Is it unacceptable for me to meet one of the teams that helped end the last war?"

Aelius had never cared about this team before. He'd never cared about Jin. He hadn't even called when Jin nearly lost his life two years before on Ilesouria. He hadn't written to ask about Jin's condition or flown out to visit him then. If there was any time for the emperor to leave his palace, to check on his youngest son, it was then. Not now.

Besides, the war had ended a year ago. So what did his father really want?

"I know you were angry when I sent you to Fort Ironwing, Varojin," Aelius continued. "It was because you needed to learn respect. Control. Discipline. That's what it takes to be an Auris, to be a true Fireweaver. I'm sure you see that now."

Jin said nothing. Control and discipline were vital to any Fireweaver, but for an Auris? It almost made him laugh.

"And you've made the Auris family proud. I've read every report on your progress from these last five years. Every training report, every mission debrief." Aelius smiled. "Dozens of missions, some of the most crucial in our entire military operation. *You* helped us win the war when you took out that general last summer."

Jin's stomach sank.

"You took out that general on Ilesouria, and you helped destroy that Delian camp in just minutes. Minutes! You've proven just how strong your Auris blood is, how strong your magic is. Perhaps even stronger than mine."

Jin's chest tightened as his father smiled again. Did he know? Did Aelius know the truth about that day with Vaiss and Lando? No, Jin didn't think so. It wouldn't unfold like this.

"Now I see what I couldn't before."

"And what is that?" Jin heard himself ask. He still hadn't moved from his position behind Zephyrine's desk, as if the furniture would somehow shield him from whatever blow his father was about to deliver.

"I thought I had four children, and that one of them needed some firm guidance," Aelius said. "But I don't just have four children. I have three heirs and one weapon. What more could a father ask for?"

Jin's entire body burned. A weapon?

That was what Aelius saw when he looked at Jin?

Not a soldier. Not an officer. Not a prince. Not even a son.

A weapon.

Fire sparked in Jin's veins. He forced his magic down, down, down. Three things he could see. *Lamp. Bookcase. Pens.* Three he could hear. *Shouts outside. Footsteps in the hallway. My heart.* Three he could smell. *Laundry soap. Cold coffee. Cologne.*

He would never be his father's weapon. Not any more than he had to be. And though he'd already sworn to never lose control again like he had the day Lando died, Jin doubled down on that promise to himself. He wouldn't. He couldn't.

Aelius moved around the desk. He clapped one hand on Jin's shoulder and smiled again. "I'm so proud of you, Varojin."

PART 3: WEAPON

CHAPTER 16
WINTER, EARLY YEAR 1018

"Watch it, Adi." Jin stuck his arm out, stopping the younger Earthmover from taking another step. They were in the middle of Posan, a territory sandwiched between Zaikudo and Delia. It was freezing here, as cold as the Macadian Mountains, and the sun was setting quickly.

It had taken them days to get here, hiking all the way from the northern edge of Corsyca. They couldn't fuck this up now.

Jin's team had been ordered to enter Posan and gather intelligence, nothing more. Delia and Zaikud were fighting over the territory, and Emperor Aelius wanted information on what, exactly, the two armies were doing up here in the north. Jin's team wasn't specialized in gathering intelligence, but Aelius had insisted they deploy regardless.

It was the first Zaikudi camp they'd found. The intelligence briefings they'd received prior to deployment had apparently been outdated; the first two camps hadn't been in their designated locations. But finally, ahead, was the third Zaikudi camp. Exactly where it was supposed to be.

It was also Jin's first time as mission lead. It was odd, not taking orders from Rasa or Dorin. It was even stranger barking orders at Adi; this was his first mission. But Zephyrine had entrusted the task to Jin.

It had only been a year and a half since they lost Lando, and they hadn't deployed since the end of the war. There hadn't been a need. In that time, Dorin had started making more and more mistakes in training, even in drills he'd run hundreds and hundreds of times. His temper had gotten shorter. Dorin just hadn't been quite the same since that skies forsaken mission. Jin suspected that was at least part of the reason the older Tidebacker hadn't been put in charge.

"Binoculars in my pack," Jin said, voice low.

Adi circled behind Jin. Strange, too, was seeing his team's typical black uniforms swapped out for white. Even their knapsacks were white, meant to blend into the snow. Adi fished a pair of binoculars out and handed them to Jin.

Jin peered through the device. He ignored the cold metal against his skin as he tried piecing together what he could see of the Zaikudi camp. Their fires burned bright in the growing darkness. Several airships were on the far side of the camp; frost and snow glistened on their metallic bodies. There had to be at least thirty tents, probably more. That was more than there were supposed to be. Hopefully Rasa and Dorin had a better view and could confirm.

"Let's go back to our meeting point," Jin said as he tucked the binoculars into Adi's pack. "Can't see much from down here."

Rocky ridges stretched down their right, and behind that, mountains rose up into the dusky sky. The Zaikudi probably thought their backs were safe being backed up to mountains. And they were. Technically. Jin's team wasn't there to do anything except watch.

Snow began falling faster as Jin and Adi picked their way back through the dark forest, then started up a path obscured by a particularly thick copse of trees. The snow had only started falling about an hour before, making for an easy enough, if not freezing, walk. By the time they reached their destination, Adi was shivering. Even Jin's fireweaving wasn't helping him much. So when they entered the opening of the small cave Rasa had found that morning, Jin let out a relieved sigh. It wasn't warm by any stretch of the imagination, but it was far warmer than the winter night outside.

"This seems useless," Adi said as they dropped their packs on the ground. He brushed snow off his coat. "Are these missions always so fruitless?"

"Sometimes, but we learned something."

"What's that?"

"That our old intel is outdated already."

"And you think this won't be by the time we get back to Zephyrine?" Adi muttered. "It'll be days."

Jin's team wasn't the only one out here, but Adi had a point. "It's not a perfect system," Jin conceded. "But we do our best. Every time we come out here, we just have to do our best."

Jin was, finally, starting to understand that lesson himself. Every close encounter he'd had during the war, almost losing his life, losing Lando . . . that was all his team had been doing. They'd done the best they could in those moments, whether making judgment calls or going off intel other teams had gathered. That was just the way it was.

Footsteps crunching in the snow outside made Jin and Adi tense, but two figures clad in white and covered in snow slipped into the cave's opening.

"Just us," Rasa said as she pulled off her hood and mask. Her light hair was a mess, static clinging to it in the dry air. "You got anything?"

"No," Adi mumbled.

Rasa glanced at Jin, who simply shrugged. He'd been that way once, too: on edge and easily frustrated. Adi was going to have to learn, just like the rest of them.

"Any guess on how many were in the camp?" Jin asked as Dorin started placing kindling on the ground. "And how many airships? I counted five."

"Ten airships." Dorin moved a few of the sticks around, frowning. "Two rows of five."

"Damn." Jin hadn't been able to see that from his angle.

"I'd guess it's a battalion," Rasa said. "Three hundred, maybe more? Has to be a decently large force for that many airships."

"Any way to get confirmation?" Jin squatted down in front of his pack and pulled out a small notebook. Folded up inside was a map Zephyrine had given him before they left. The first two camps were marked off as dismantled, but he started jotting down what they knew near the third.

"I was thinking we might be able to climb up a little higher here and get a view from above," Rasa said. She joined him on the ground and pointed to the rough location of their cave on the map. "Just up here. There should be enough cover."

Unless the Zaikudi were incompetent or overly confident, they'd be keeping an eye on the mountains. Still, they needed more information if they were going to call this mission any kind of success.

"We'll be right back," Jin called to the other two. "Stay here and stay together."

After putting the map away and shouldering his knapsack, Jin shot a small flame to the kindling Dorin had set up, forcing its energy to stay low. Then he followed Rasa back out into the snow. They walked north for a few minutes, squinting against the wind and snow.

This was not good. It was impossible to know how long the weather would continue like this, but Jin doubted it would let up anytime soon. If they were lucky, they wouldn't have too many snow drifts to contend with in the morning.

"There," she said, stopping and pointing above them.

The rocks jutted high up, but they were almost unnatural in shape. It could've been the work of an Earthmover long ago. Despite the low light and snowstorm moving in, Jin could see enough erosion to suggest the rock had been that way for a long time. That same unnatural shape also had plenty of angles to hide behind.

"Worth a try," Jin said.

"Worth trying to Earthmove right now?" Rasa asked. "To get up."

"No." They were some distance from the Zaikudi camp, but even with the howling wind, Jin didn't want to risk it. Someone would feel the earth shaking. "We'll climb."

Rasa went first, charting a path for them both. Jin had climbed plenty of rocks and mountains, though rarely in the snow, and he nearly fell twice on his way up. When they were finally at the top, both Jin and Rasa crouched low.

"Well?" she asked as Jin pulled the binoculars out of her pack.

"Give me a minute."

Dots of orange far below broke up the blur of white and gray. The binoculars weren't that strong, but being up here gave him a much better overview of the camp, even in the darkness.

"I think you're right that it's a battalion." Jin handed the binoculars to Rasa. There were dozens and dozens of figures milling around the camp below, and Jin was confident dozens more were secure inside the tents. "I thought it was supposed to be smaller than that."

"Maybe they combined with one of the other camps that weren't where we thought they'd be."

"Maybe." That was logical, but why? Well, Jin's job wasn't to figure out the *why* right now. It was simply to figure out the *where* and the *how many*. "We'll come back here in the morning, then move on."

After returning the binoculars to Rasa's knapsack, they began their climb down. That was far more difficult than climbing up. Jin banged his elbow so hard trying to stop his own fall that he was sure he'd bruised the bone.

When they got back to the cave, Jin lowered the flames on the campfire again with a twitch of his gloved fingers.

"Hey!" Dorin called. "I was just getting warm."

"Too bright," Jin said. "Someone's going to see it from a mile away."

"Nobody's going to be up here," Dorin said. "It's a fucking blizzard out there. Will be, anyway. We'll be lucky if we don't get snowed in tonight."

Jin shook the snow off himself. "*We're* up here. I'm not taking that risk. Just get in your sleeping bag if you want to warm up."

"The kid gets one shot as team lead and thinks he knows everything," Dorin muttered.

"And how many shots have *you* had as team lead?" Rasa quipped. "Oh, that's what I thought. None. Jin's right."

"Thank you." Jin paused as he surveyed the cave. Adi's pack was on the ground near the fire, but the Earthmover himself was nowhere to be seen. "Where's Adi?"

"Sent him out for a walk about five minutes ago," Dorin said. "Kid was getting frustrated."

"First, stop calling us both kids," Jin said. Rasa snorted. "And second, why the fuck would you send him out there by himself?"

"You've seen how frustrated he is," Dorin snapped. "He needs a few minutes to cool down."

Jin ground his teeth together. They weren't supposed to split up except in very limited circumstances. Dorin *knew* that. Probably knew that better than Jin did considering he'd been on the team longer. They especially weren't supposed to send one of their own out into a snow storm in the middle of the night behind enemy lines. In fact, Jin had given them both a direct order to stay put and stay together.

Tugging his hood and mask back on, Jin started toward the cave's opening.

"Where are you going?" Dorin called.

"Fixing your mistake," Jin snapped as he stepped back out into the snow and wind. "Stay here."

Where would Adi have gone? He couldn't have gotten far in these conditions. Adi obviously hadn't gone north; that was where Jin and Rasa had just come from. They would've seen him. East was just more fucking rocks, and Jin doubted Adi was climbing them. He was frustrated, not a fool. South?

Jin started south, back toward the slope they'd used to get up to their cave in the first place. Nothing looked out of place, though, and there was no sign of Adi. It would've been easier if Jin could've called out for him, but on the off chance that someone else was out here, Jin didn't want to give his position away. That was also why he didn't give himself more light.

Now what? Adi would freeze if he didn't get back inside soon.

Jin might not freeze thanks to his fireweaving, but he wasn't sure Adi would find his way back to the cave. The wind had picked up, whipping snow around Jin in a dizzying pattern. *Shit.*

Maybe Rasa and Dorin could help him. They weren't supposed to split up without specific circumstances, and yet he'd split the team up even more. *Fuck.* What was wrong with him?

Jin had just started back toward their camp when the earth rumbled. Further south. The earth rumbled again, followed by shouts in Zaikudi.

That was not a coincidence.

Jin skidded down the slope and stopping just in time to move into a thicket of trees to his right. Adi fought three Zaikudi by himself—at least, Jin thought they were Zaikudi based on their dark uniforms. Adi was strong, but his steps faltered as wind gusted and howled. Then he went down, and the Zaikudi hauled his unconscious form away. West. Toward their camp.

Fuck.

Jin sprinted back uphill, scrambling every time he hit an especially slippery spot. Even stumbling through the storm, he managed to find his way back to the cave. "Adi," Jin said between heavy gasps. "They took him."

Rasa rolled to her feet and pulled her gear back on.

Dorin, though, was slow. "What do you mean they took him?" he asked, hands still held out by the fire.

"The fucking Zaikudi, Dorin," Jin snapped. "What's wrong with you? Move your ass."

Dorin's eyes widened, but he simply tugged his body armor on. They knew what this meant. It didn't need to be said. Rule number one: Leave no one behind. Rule number two: No witnesses.

But how were three of them—four if they could get Adi out first—supposed to take down an entire battalion?

And how the fuck were they supposed to do it without somehow pointing back to Helosia?

They didn't even know enough about the camp to know where the Zaikudi would take Adi. Where would they take a prisoner with no markings on his gear? Adi's pack was still in the cave, so at least they couldn't open it and find anything written in Helosian. And Adi could speak all of the main languages on the continent, just like the rest of them. That was required to even be considered for Zephyrine's teams, and he'd been studying hard the last few months with tutors at Fort Avalon.

"Hide Adi's pack," Jin ordered. Rasa nodded, and with a shake of her palm, pulled the cold rock of the cave over Adi's bag.

We will figure this out, Jin told himself as he extinguished the fire and led his team outside. *We will figure it out.* They had to figure it out. He would not leave Adi behind. He would not lose another teammate.

They retraced Jin's path down toward the flat grounds of the clearing, Jin melting snow as they went and forcing Rasa and Dorin to keep up with his pace. They would figure this out, but they didn't have much time.

"We start at the rear of the camp," Jin whispered when they stopped several dozen yards from the first tent. "Stick together. Do not get split up. We take out who we can, then find Adi and get the fuck out of here."

"And then?" Rasa asked.

"And then we're going home."

"We're supposed to be here for another three days," Dorin said.

"They've probably already radioed to any of the other camps that might be on our route," Jin said. "Mission's over. Now come on."

He started moving again, and as snow crunched behind him, he knew Rasa and Dorin had followed. Dorin took out the two guards stationed at the rear of the camp, thick icicles straight to the heart. They dropped without a sound, the snow turning red under them.

Right near those dead guards was a tent. Jin pulled his dagger out of his sheath and lifted one of the tent's flaps with just the point of the weapon. Inside, four soldiers were asleep in their cots. He couldn't see the other side of the tent, but his best guess was that there were eight total.

Jin hated what he was about to do. He signaled for Rasa and Dorin to move in with him anyway. The best thing they could do was make this quick, quiet. And they did. There had actually been nine sleeping soldiers in the tent, but now they'd never wake up.

They forged ahead, encountering little resistance from the sleepy Zaikudi at the rear of the camp. It was too easy. Jin headed for the next tent. Three soldiers stepped out. At first, the soldiers just looked confused, but then one opened his mouth to shout. An icicle through the throat stopped the man before he made a sound, red blood leaking out of his mouth and down his neck.

The other two soldiers watched in horror, frozen. Jin grabbed one, and Rasa and Dorin grabbed the second. They shoved them into the tent. Jin was worried they'd shout, too, but the two Zaikudi just stared up at Jin's team.

"Have you seen a man dressed like me being brought to the camp?" Jin asked in Zaikud.

They continued to stare. *Skies fucking damn it.*

"I asked you a question," Jin growled. "Have you seen him or not?"

One shook his head, but the woman nodded. "I think they took him to the infirmary," she whispered.

"And where is that?"

"Two rows up."

Why would they have taken Adi to the infirmary? Had they hurt him more than Jin realized? He supposed they would need Adi alive and well to interrogate him, but it still seemed . . . off. The infirmary?

"Why?" Jin asked.

"I don't know."

Of course. Their uniforms only had the sword insignia stitched over their hearts. They weren't even mages. They were just foot soldiers and wouldn't know much. They didn't even look much older than Adi or himself.

Jin huffed. He never should've let this happen.

"Now," he said, hating how steady his voice was.

Dorin said nothing as he flicked his wrist. Thick icicles shot forward, piercing the Zaikudi through the hearts. They slumped to the ground.

Swallowing hard, Jin headed back outside. They skirted the side of the camp this time, moving up the two rows to the infirmary unnoticed. The camp had grown quieter. Some quiet would be expected; it was late, and soldiers had to sleep at some point. But it was quieter than Jin would've expected with a mystery captive in their midst.

Something wasn't right.

Jin signaled for Dorin and Rasa to stop. They did, their gazes questioning. Did they not feel it too?

"Something's not right," Jin whispered in Zaikud. He'd never quite been able to get rid of his accent when he spoke the northern language, but at least nobody nearby would hear Helosian.

"Isn't that the infirmary?" Dorin replied as he nodded toward one of the tents in front of them. "Let's go."

"No."

"I said let's go."

Jin grabbed Dorin's arm. "And *I* said no." He didn't know what right he had to command Dorin, but Zephyrine had put him in charge for a reason. She must have.

Dorin glared at him, his blue eyes cold. Jin was about to bark out another order when an earthen wall appeared behind Dorin.

"Get the fuck down," Rasa hissed.

Too late. A Zaikudi squad was on them, calling out in accented Helosian. "What the fuck are you doing in Posan?" one of them yelled.

"We need to hurry," Rasa whispered, her hands stretched out wide. Her wall rumbled but didn't break.

"I know." If the Zaikudi even suspected they were Helosian, they'd be sending warnings out soon. They might even reach out to the Delians. It didn't matter how the Zaikudi had figured it out. Jin could not let Helosia get dragged into this war just because of his—because of Dorin's—mistake. He should've been keeping a closer eye on his entire team. "On your mark, Rasa."

As Rasa lowered her hands, her wall broke. Three Zaikudi advanced, all Tidebackers relying on the snow and ice around them. Dorin yanked control of the element away from them. Whatever he couldn't grab, Rasa blocked with shield after shield and Jin boiled away with his fire.

Those first three Zaikudi were barely down when more soldiers moved in. Skies, Jin wished Zephyrine were there. Having a Tempest around to simply suffocate most of these soldiers would've made this so much faster. A dozen soldiers surrounded them now, some mages but most not.

"We need to find him!" Jin shouted in Delian as he shot off two fire bullets.

Maybe Adi really was in the infirmary. Some of the Zaikudi were loitering near the infirmary tent's opening. Guarding it.

Rasa must have seen it, too, because she opened a portal in the ground, the churning earth sucking in half a dozen Zaikudi en route to the tent.

"Go," she said, also in Delian. "Dorin and I will cover."

"Stay on me."

They moved as a triangle, Jin in front and Dorin and Rasa covering his back on both sides. The crowd of Zaikudi soldiers was thinning, but Jin knew this wouldn't last long. Even if there wasn't an entire battalion here like Jin and Rasa had first estimated, this was nowhere near the number of soldiers that would be at a camp this size. They'd taken down maybe three dozen since sneaking in. More would surely come.

The infirmary guards moved toward Jin as a solid unit, an Earthmover and a Fireweaver. Jin went for the Fireweaver, blocking blow after blow but unable to get his own shot off. Behind Jin, Dorin and Rasa both grunted. Metal clashed with metal.

A rock slammed into Jin's shoulder. He stumbled right into the other Fireweaver's grasp. They burned through Jin's jacket, scorching his skin. Swearing, Jin wrenched his arm free and shoved his dagger through the man's midsection. An icicle through the Earthmover's throat let Jin push forward again.

Inside the tent was quiet. Still. Only the wind howled outside, shaking the thick canvas walls. Adi sat strapped to a chair, and two Zaikudi officers flanked either side of him. One of them, a man with tan skin and reddish hair, crossed his arms over his chest. The other, a woman with taupe skin and dark brown hair, crossed her arms behind her back.

"Tell me," the man said in heavily accented Helosian, "what is the son of Emperor Auris doing here in Posan?"

Jin racked his brain. How would this man know who Jin was? No one had seen them until they'd gotten into the camp. No one had ever known who Jin was before, not through the entire war with the Delians.

His eyes, maybe? Something about the Auris eyes was unique, even if they surely weren't the only family in the world with golden irises.

"I don't speak Helosian," Jin said in Delian. It felt pointless now, desperate, but he had to try. They had to try everything. "I just want my man back."

"Fine, we'll do this your way," the Zaikudi officer replied, matching Jin's language change. "Tell us why you're here and you can have him back."

A few wounds and burns marred Adi's dark brown skin, one particularly nasty one cutting from his forehead through his right eyebrow. A trail of dried blood ran down his cheek. Adi gave the smallest shake of his head.

"What do you think we're doing here?" Jin asked in Delian. "This is war. We're doing reconnaissance."

Growing up in the imperial palace in Kalama, Jin had learned that the truth could still obscure one's real motives. He'd hated that about the court, but now, he was glad he had practice for so many years.

"Reconnaissance." The man nodded, but he moved behind Adi and rested his large hands on Adi's shoulders. Adi flinched. "I suppose I can't be surprised. We have teams doing the same."

Behind Jin, Rasa and Dorin shifted. What was he supposed to do now? Jin was fairly certain the Zaikudi officer wasn't buying any of this. Even if he did, they couldn't let the camp stand.

Even if they got Adi out of here in one piece, how were they going to take down this entire camp? How would they ensure rumor about their presence—Varojin Auris's presence—didn't get leaked?

Jin hated what he needed to do.

He needed that skies damned bomb of his, the one he'd somehow set off when Lando had died. He still didn't know how to do it, though. Not really. He'd tried a dozen times to lose control during training. He'd been angry that day during the war. So Jin had thought of his father and all the little nasty ways Kaius had made his life miserable over the years. He'd tried having the team hurl insults at him. He'd tried everything any of them could think of to provoke his anger. But he'd never been able to recreate that moment.

"This is the part where you offer to trade me some of your prisoners for this young man," the Zaikudi officer said. "If you do have anyone to trade, that is."

Jin said nothing.

"Unless I was right, and it really is the Helosian emperor's bastard standing here in my camp." As Adi tensed, the Zaikudi officer smiled. "So I was right. Your reputation precedes you, Prince Varojin."

Jin still said nothing. Behind him, Rasa and Dorin shifted again.

"I was being honest when I said I just want my man back," he said in Helosian. "That's it."

"And I was being honest when I said we had our own teams doing reconnaissance during the war," the man replied. "During the Delian-Helosian War. We thought it was just a rumor, that our teams had been mistaken, yet here you are."

Rasa could open the earth below them, but that might suck Adi in with the Zaikudi officers. Dorin might be able to freeze them, but they had no idea what magical affinities these two had, if any. Jin couldn't make out their eye colors in the darkness of the tent to even hazard a guess.

"I always thought this day might come," the man continued. "My scouts stumbling upon your comrade here was just a happy accident. Tell me, how is your sister doing? And your niece? She's turning, what, four years old soon?"

Who the fuck was this man? Zephyrine hadn't given them any names during their intelligence briefing. But this man had to be high up the Zaikudi chain of command if he knew about Jin's involvement in the war.

"I'll make you a deal, Prince Varojin. You come with me, and I'll let your friend here go."

"No."

"You drive a hard bargain." The man chuckled. "Fine. How about you come with me and I'll call off my people in Kalama keeping an eye on your siblings and niece?"

Jin wasn't naive enough to think the continental powers didn't spy on each other, even in times of peace. But how close were they to his family?

"Maybe I haven't made myself clear." The man's magic burst to life in the small tent, wind knocking Jin, Rasa, and Dorin back.

The woman stepped back as the man pulled the air out of Adi's lungs, the magic almost imperceptible in the dim light. But Adi gasped, his head tilting back with the force of the officer's magical pull.

"Like Vaiss," Dorin whispered from behind. "Come on, Jin."

Jin pulled and pulled on the fire simmering within him, on the anger and fear bubbling under the surface. Anger at himself, at Dorin, at this man. At his father.

Power surged through his body, warm and familiar.

Fear for Adi, for his team, for Eliana and Velia, for innocent Helosians who might get swept up in another war.

That day Lando died.

Something in Jin ignited, a torrent of magic and heat and pain. His insides burned, but it almost felt . . . right. Like somehow, he was still in control. Like all of that energy he kept in a cage deep within himself was now bursting at the seams.

His father had said being a Fireweaver was about control and discipline. And it was. Fireweaving took immense control and precision. Losing control of oneself could mean losing control of the flames.

But maybe this wasn't about completely losing control. Maybe this was about a different kind of discipline, a different power. One Jin *could* control.

"Cover Adi and Rasa," Jin hissed.

Dorin had one shot to get this right. Jin had one shot. Their timing had to be perfect. And Adi was just about out of time anyway.

Jin swore he'd never use this magic again. As soon as his father had called him a weapon, Jin had made that promise to himself.

But he couldn't let Adi die. He couldn't let Adi's sister be alone in the world. He couldn't lose another friend.

And he couldn't let Helosia get dragged into this. This wasn't about his father. This was about all the people his father had forced into his armies, and it was about their families. This was about all the bullshit they'd been through the last few years fighting the Delians. Jin couldn't let that happen again because of *his* mistake. *His* failure.

His magic pushed and strained against that invisible cage. It begged to be released. Unleashed. It burned in his veins, screaming and pushing. It demanded to be let out. To be used.

And so Jin let it out.

Fire exploded around him, vaporizing the tent. Shockwaves rippled out, so heavy that the Zaikudi officers were thrown back, back, back. The ground rocked and shook. Jin strained as he held onto those flames. His muscles seized with the effort. His fists clenched. The tents around them caught fire, flames and smoke swirling with the snow and wind.

His fire tried to keep pushing out, but Jin pulled back on that power. Just a trickle of magic remained within him, faint. With great effort, he reined it all back, and the flames died. His shoulders sagged, and he started to turn toward his team. More shockwaves rocked the ground. Jin stumbled once, then again, as something exploded nearby. He caught himself before falling onto the scorched ground, then sucked in a deep breath. Adi, Rasa, and Dorin were where Jin expected to find them. Encircled in shields of water and stone. Safe.

The shields dropped.

"Fuck," Adi hissed as Jin ran to him and sliced through the bindings still holding him to a chair. Adi coughed again, a harsh, painful sound. He cleared his throat. "What the fuck—"

"Talk later," Jin said. "Come on."

Jin didn't want to look around. He didn't want to see the destruction his careful control had wrought. But he had to. Rasa and Dorin scrambled to check that the Zaikudi officers were dead. Both pulled out their daggers. Jin sucked in a shuddering breath as he turned away from them.

This was worse than during the war. Despite Jin's control of the flames, it was worse than that day with Vaiss.

So many of the soldiers here weren't mages, that much was becoming clear. That was why the ground had shaken so much. It wasn't just Jin's magical explosion. His flames had reached munitions stockpiles. Gasoline supplies for the vehicles here. Fires had broken out all around the camp, black smoke rising into the cloud-filled sky. Something under the airships exploded, and several caught fire. Distant shouts in Zaikudi signaled the soldiers' confusion.

"We need to go." Jin's energy was sapped. His legs and arms trembled. But he had to keep going. "I just need to check one thing first."

"What could you possibly have to check?" Rasa asked as she brushed snow from her hood and sheathed her dagger.

"Officer's tent."

Jin headed for the center of camp, where the tent had once stood. He'd spotted it while on those mountains with Rasa earlier in the night. Though it was no longer standing, remnants of slightly more luxurious furniture remained. But all of the papers and files Jin had been worried he might find were just blackened scraps now.

Good. Whoever that man was, if he'd heard rumors or read reports about Jin's activities, any evidence that might have been in this camp was gone. It was likely the Zaikudi government had files with that information, and Jin guessed the Delians did, too. He couldn't do anything about that.

A scrap of green, blue, and white fabric caught Jin's eye. He stooped, then pushed a few pieces of splintered wood off the cloth. It was the remnants of a Delian flag, mostly untouched by the destruction. Probably some kind of sick trophy the camp's leader had kept after a battle. Jin had seen Helosian officers do the same during the last war.

This was how they got away with it. They could pin this on the Delians right now. No reason for Helosians to do this.

Besides, it was all they had.

Jin shivered as he draped the flag over a pile of wood, then pinned down its edges with large pieces of debris. Hopefully it would survive the storm. Hopefully it was enough.

"Back to the cave," Jin said as he rejoined his team. "Get Adi's stuff. Then we're going home."

His team asked no more questions as they hurried through the destruction and headed back into the snowy night. They said nothing, didn't even try to deal with the survivors still shouting about Delians and putting out the fires. Witnesses didn't matter. The camp was too far gone to mobilize. Their leadership was dead. The Delian flag was set. If Helosia was accused, bureaucrats and military leadership would have to talk their way out of the situation.

"When we get back to Fort Avalon," Jin said once they reached the cave, "I don't want a word of this spoken to anyone besides Zephyrine. And no reports."

Adi said nothing, his face ashen.

"Why?" Dorin asked. "We did what we had to do."

"I just did something I promised myself I would never do again, Dorin," Jin snapped.

"But you can—"

"When my father came to visit the fort a few months ago, do you know what he said to me?" Jin's team remained quiet, stone still. "He said he had three heirs and a weapon. And that was based on the reports we *faked* last time."

"*You* did that?" Adi asked.

Right. Adi had been covered in two shields, so opaque he wouldn't have been able to see what was going on.

"A lot of it. And my father does not need to know this. He cannot know this."

Jin could only imagine what his father would want him to do if he knew that. If he knew Jin could cripple an entire fucking battalion like that, that Jin *could* control flames that strong . . .

"Is that an order as team lead or imperial prince?" Dorin asked.

It took every ounce of control Jin had not to lash out at Dorin. If he hadn't sent Adi out on his own, if Dorin had stuck with the plan and their team rules, maybe none of this would have happened.

But it had happened. And now Jin was cleaning up the mess. If throwing his stupid title around was going to help him do it, then he would use it all skies damned day.

He looked at Dorin. "Both."

Dorin huffed, then took a few steps toward the mouth of the cave. *Fine*, Jin thought. *Let him be angry with me.* Jin was angry too.

"Can you even walk after that?" Rasa asked after getting Adi's pack back out of the cave floor where she'd hidden it. "Maybe we need to camp for the night."

"No camping." Jin was exhausted; it took so much out of him to do that. Just the smallest trickle of fire still burned within him. His magic would replenish with time and rest, two things they didn't really have. "We get as far away as we can from here before we stop. Got it?"

"Got it," the team echoed.

And with that, Jin led them back into the cold, stormy night.

CHAPTER 17
SPRING, YEAR 1018

Springtime at Fort Avalon was beautiful. Bright green foliage had returned to the trees. Large flowers bloomed on shrubs lining the fort's walls, the petals in every color imaginable. And Jin hated it.

He sneezed, then sneezed again, as he walked with Adi toward the fort's garage. He'd never had much of an issue with allergies in Kalama, but up here in the mountains, everything seemed to generate more pollen.

"You good?" Adi asked.

"Fine." Jin squeezed his eyes shut, shook his head once, then huffed. "It'll be over in a couple of weeks."

The one good thing was that Fort Avalon was quieter than usual. Perhaps everyone else had been driven inside by the pollen and the slight chill in the air. Adi, though, needed to go back to the garage. He'd left something there during daily rounds and swore he needed it.

"You really don't mind coming with me?" Adi asked as they headed down the long, winding path toward the garages.

"No," Jin said. "Better than sitting around and staring at Dorin and Rasa."

During peacetime, there wasn't that much for their team to do. Sometimes they were deployed to rescue people, but after what happened in Posan, neither of Zephyrine's teams had been sent out on missions. There'd been no whisper of Helosians possibly taking out that Zaikudi camp, no accusations from the other governments. The last few months had been quiet, filled with nothing but chores and drills.

Adi snorted. "No kidding. But hey, if you want something to do, you could come to the kitchen with me. Chef's letting me go there unsupervised in the evenings now."

"Unsupervised, huh?" Jin asked.

Over the year since Adi had joined their team, Jin had gotten to know him well. Though Jin had grown fond of Dorin, Rasa, and Lando, he just hadn't ever clicked with them the same way he was clicking with Adi.

Adi was easy to talk to. He seemed to understand Jin on a level no one had since . . .

Since he'd still been friends with Astrea.

Jin didn't have to explain himself to Adi, nor did Adi expect him to chat when he didn't want to. They got on well, meshing far more quickly as partners than Jin had with anyone else on the team. It still took some work, but now they ran drills together as if they'd worked together for many years. It had taken years for Jin to get that synergy with even Rasa; he'd gotten it with Adi in a mere twelve months.

Jin had also learned that Adi was good at a variety of tasks and had a wide range of interests. He liked to cook. He could sew, at least enough to mend holes in their fatigues and hem Rasa's pants that proved too long. He'd learned how to fly an airship, apparently, before being transferred to Jin's team. And Adi was also handy in the garage; he'd fixed up a few trucks with engine issues in the last month. He also shared Jin's growing interest in motorcycles, and they'd started riding them together on the long stretch of road to Narizon when they had the chance. It was fun, getting to leave the fort and everything behind for a little while.

"Finally, right? I've only been using the facilities for a year," Adi said. They passed a private, who scurried by with little more than a quick salute. "I miss my kitchen back home."

"You like to cook that much?" Jin asked. He'd never had to learn the skill. Growing up at the palace, everything was prepared for him. And at Forts Ironwing and Avalon, there had always been a crew in the mess hall that prepared meals.

"It's great," Adi said. "Just you and the ingredients, something simple but important to accomplish. *And* it's a delicious result at the end. I love it. I used to cook with my father and grandmother all the time."

"You make it sound fun."

"That's because it is. You should come with me tomorrow."

"Oh, I don't know . . ."

"Why not?" Adi asked. "You just said it sounded fun."

"I said you make it sound fun," Jin corrected. "I don't know the first thing about kitchens."

"I'll teach you," Adi offered. "It's the least I can do, considering what you've done for me the last year. What you did on our last mission."

Jin frowned. He thought they'd been over this already. Well, they *had* been over it already. They'd already had this conversation a few times, and it always resulted in the same thing: Adi apologizing for ever listening to Dorin in the first place. And Jin had already forgiven Adi. He didn't think there was much to forgive. If he'd been in Adi's position—new to the team, on his first mission, and frustrated—he probably would've listened to Dorin too.

"You know I don't expect anything, Adi. It's what teammates and friends do for each other. I know you'd do the same for me."

"Then let this teammate and friend teach you something new. I've learned so much from you three over the last year. Come on."

"Well . . ." Jin's only duty the next day was leading a few fireweaving lessons in the morning. What harm would it be to try something new? "Sure, I guess. If you don't mind."

"Great!" Adi grinned, a contagious gesture. Jin smiled back. "Now, let me just grab my mail and we can get you back inside and away from all these flowers."

"My one true weakness," Jin quipped as he followed Adi the last few steps toward the garage. "I'll wait out here."

Two of the garage bay doors were open, though the other five were closed. Warm lights spilled onto the road in front of them, and the soft sounds of a radio filtered outside. Someone was certainly in there. Adi disappeared inside and around a corner.

Jin didn't mind the garage, not at all. He'd always liked driving, and he'd even started learning how to ride a motorcycle about half a year before. It was all a good distraction, and as Zephyrine said, could be valuable someday. She also wanted him to learn to pilot an airship 'just in case,' but Jin had yet to begin that endeavor.

Jin walked the same few steps back and forth, back and forth. He hadn't trained at all that day, instead spending half the afternoon asleep since he was off duty. Sleeping during the day was still sometimes easier for him than at night. It had been almost two years since Lando had died, but Jin still saw that awful day in his dreams. He saw Ilesouria, too, and countless other missions they'd been on. Sunlight streaming through his windows somehow kept the worst of it all at bay.

Adi may have been keeping up appearances around almost everyone at the fort, but in the last few weeks, he'd confided in Jin that he was struggling, too. Struggling with sleeping and keeping the memories away. Adi hadn't been to war, but he'd been to Posan. That was enough.

Jin nodded at a few younger soldiers who saluted him as they scurried past. He didn't love the gesture; it reminded him too much of the palace guards back in Kalama and how they always stood at attention whenever an Auris family member entered the room.

A startled yelp echoed inside the garage, then Adi backed out of the bay, a few envelopes clutched in one hand.

"What's wrong?" Jin asked, his muscles tensing.

Adi pointed. And there, strolling out of the garage, was a large orange cat. It stared up at Adi with wide green eyes.

Jin relaxed. "Really?"

"He wouldn't let me take my mail!"

"A *cat* wouldn't let you take your mail?"

Adi shoved his hand toward Jin. Sure enough, several long, narrow cuts marred Adi's skin. "See?" he said. "I told you. And it *hissed*."

"The cat did this to you when you tried to collect your mail?"

The cat sat back on its haunches, the end of its tail flicking as it watched Adi.

"Yes," Adi said. "What's he got against me? Animals usually love me!"

"Well, let's leave him to whatever mail-guarding duties he thinks he has, alright? This pollen's giving me a headache."

"Yeah," Adi muttered. He shook his head as they started back toward the officers' quarters on the far side of the fort. "Damn cat. Nearly took my hand off."

"A few scratches hardly count as taking your hand off."

"That's what you think." Adi shook his head again. "Mark my words, Jin, I'm going to get that cat to like me."

"Good luck."

As they started back up the hill toward the proper fort, Jin peeked up at the stars again. With the fort's dim outdoor lights, he could still see most of the brilliant night sky. It wasn't the same beautiful sight as up in the mountains, but it was nice. He searched the stars, straining until he found the Warrior and Queen constellations.

"Which one's your favorite?" Adi asked.

"Huh?" Jin shook his head as he focused on the road again.

Adi gestured up at the sky. "Which constellation?"

"The Warrior."

"That's a bit on the nose, isn't it?" Adi teased.

"That was the last one my best friend showed me before . . . before I left Kalama. I mean, she used to be my best friend . . ." Jin hesitated. He couldn't remember the last time he'd talked about Astrea.

"When was the last time you saw her?" Adi asked.

"We haven't spoken in years." Jin hadn't received a single letter from Astrea since that last one so many years before, nor had he tried to reach out to her. The last letter he'd written to 'her' was one about Posan months before. "Do you miss anyone back home?"

"Oh, plenty of people, but mostly just Noemi," Adi said. He shared stories of their misadventures often, and Jin had gotten the sense that Noemi was the less adventurous of the two siblings. Adi was usually up for anything. "Some old friends from school, too, and family friends." Adi sighed. "Does it ever get easier, being so far away from everyone?"

"You're asking the wrong person." Jin kicked at a small rock, watching as it skidded across the worn path. "I don't really miss anyone besides my sister and niece."

"And this mysterious best friend."

"And her," Jin agreed. Even after all this time, Jin missed Astrea. He regretted never saying goodbye to her, but what was he supposed to do now? Too many years had passed. Too much had happened.

Jin heard the smile in Adi's voice as he asked, "Does she have a name?"

"Astrea." Jin shoved his hands in his pockets. "Her uncle is my father's Stargazer and tutored me and my siblings in Novarian for years. We practically grew up together. We did everything together."

"Why'd you lose touch, then?"

Jin grunted.

"That's not an answer," Adi said.

No, it wasn't, and Jin didn't want to give one. Zephyrine had already made it clear that Jin had made a mistake. He knew he'd made one. He didn't need Adi judging him for it. But as he snuck a glance at his friend, Jin muttered a curse. Maybe it was the kindness in his dual-colored eyes or the openness of his expression, but something about Adi just felt safe.

"You'll think I'm an ass," Jin said.

"Try me."

As they rounded the next corner up the hill to return to the fort, Jin paused. With just the light of the stars and nearby flickering gas lamp, Jin started to explain to Adi how he'd left without saying goodbye. But then a familiar voice called out to them.

"There you two are!" Rasa yelled.

She strutted toward them, Dorin not far behind. Part of Jin was relieved to see the pair; it would spare him telling Adi the worst of the story. But part of him also regretted the interruption. Talking about Astrea even for a few moments made him feel . . . lighter.

"What do you want?" Jin asked once Rasa and Dorin were just a few feet away. He doubted there was a mission; Zephyrine would've been searching for them had that been the case.

"What's with the attitude?" Dorin retorted.

"His allergies," Adi said. Dorin smirked.

"We want to hike up to an old spot tomorrow," Rasa said. "Thought you two would want to go with us."

"When?" Jin asked. "I'm teaching fireweaving classes in the morning."

"We'll leave after that if you want to join us," Rasa said. "It's only a couple of miles from the fort."

Jin liked hiking. He'd never been until he'd arrived at Fort Avalon—there was no place to hike in Kalama—but now, he liked going when he had the chance. The southern Macadian Mountains offered great views, and he knew the terrain like the back of his hand after all these years. Something about the quiet of the forest and pushing his body made Jin feel at peace. Being out there was one of the few times Jin ever felt that way anymore. Watching the ocean from his bedroom growing up had resulted in a similar effect, but the ocean was hundreds of miles away.

"How long do you plan on being gone?" Jin asked. Just minutes before, they'd planned to start Jin on cooking lessons, but Adi had said they couldn't use the kitchen until the evening anyway.

"Just a few hours," Dorin said. "Should be back around dinner."

"Adi?" Rasa asked.

The Earthmover smiled. "A hike sounds fun. Where should we meet you?"

"Just meet here," Rasa said. "We'll plan everything else."

By the time Jin met up with Rasa, Dorin, and Adi the next day, it looked like they were en route to some kind of picnic. Both Dorin and Rasa had packs full of food and drinks. They hadn't struck him as the type for springtime picnics, but what did he know?

It was an hour into their hike before they were even close to what Dorin and Rasa promised was worth their time. The hike wasn't particularly difficult, not compared to the ones Zephyrine still made them go on several times a year. The incline wasn't awful, and there was even a fairly well-worn path for them to follow. Jin may have known this part of the Macadian Mountains very well, but the overgrown brush and fauna hid the entrance to this path. At least Rasa and Dorin seemed to know where they were going.

After climbing up several rocky outcroppings, Dorin turned right at a fork in the path. "Just up here!" he called over his shoulder.

As Jin skirted around a particularly unruly bush, he knew exactly why Dorin and Rasa had wanted to come all the way up there. Stretching out before them was a view that rivaled those higher up in the mountains. Fort Avalon was situated just at the base of the range, nestled right in the valley below. Mountains stretched to their left and right, and in front of them was a panoramic view of the valley.

"Wow!" Adi exclaimed as he nudged Jin to keep moving forward.

"It's beautiful at night or first thing in the morning," Rasa said.

"You've been holding out on us," Jin quipped. "How long have you known about this?"

Dorin cleared his throat before setting his pack on a large, flat rock nearby. "This, uh . . . Rasa?"

"Lando found this spot," Rasa said. She half-turned to look out over the landscape. "Neri and Lando found it."

"Oh, fuck, Rasa, I'm—" Jin started.

"It's alright," she said, smiling as she faced them again. "Lando always wanted to bring you up here. Just never made time, I guess."

"Who's Neri?" Adi asked.

Jin still knew almost nothing about Neri, the Fireweaver he'd been brought in to replace. The team never had talked about him much.

Rasa's lips pressed into a thin line. "Neri was our Fireweaver before Jin."

"I'm so sorry," Adi said quickly. "I didn't realize—"

"You two have got to stop apologizing," Dorin called over his shoulder. "Rasa and I wanted to bring you here for a reason."

He pulled a few bottles out his pack, then passed them out. As Jin took his, he turned the bottle over and examined the label. It was the same beer Lando had given them years ago, back when the war was still on. When they'd played that game and gotten Jin drunk on purpose.

"Where'd you get this?" Jin asked.

Things had been awkward between him and Dorin the last few months. Jin was trying to cut him some slack. Getting cocky—or perhaps indifferent—and making a mistake like that wasn't easy to own up to. Jin was also trying not to forget exactly what had led to that situation. He shouldn't have had to order Dorin not to send Adi out on his own, nor should Dorin have disobeyed the order. That should never have been a concern in the first place. Dorin knew the rules.

"Remember a few weeks ago when I went home for some leave time?" Dorin asked, and Jin nodded. Both Rasa and Dorin had made trips back to see their families in the last few months. "I was able to track some down."

"It was Lando's favorite," Rasa explained to Adi. "And we've been putting this off for far too long."

"Putting what off?" Adi asked.

"We did this with Lando when we lost Neri," Rasa said, "and now it's time we do it for Lando."

Dorin twisted the cap off his bottle, then Rasa did, too. Jin and Adi followed suit. "Lando, you skies damned bastard." He tilted his face toward the sky. "Brothers-in-arms for nearly a decade, and you go and do something reckless." He shook his head, then smiled. "I hope, wherever you are now, that you've finally found some peace. Who knows, maybe you're with Neri causing trouble just like you two used to."

Jin swallowed hard. This was what they wanted to do? Send Lando off after nearly two years? They'd never had a proper funeral for him; his body had been sent back to his family, and then they'd all just seemed to . . . avoid this. Avoid the topic of Lando at all. They'd hardly talked about him since that awful day. Rasa and Dorin hadn't wanted to talk about it, and Jin hadn't been capable.

And it wasn't that Jin didn't want to partake now. The fact that Rasa and Dorin had decided to bring not just Jin but Adi here meant a lot. But he had no idea what to say.

"Lando," Rasa said, "you never did tell me what kept you tied to this team for so long despite how much you disliked the work. But I like to think it was because you hated the thought of leaving Dorin and I . . . and Jin once he came along." She smiled. Jin's eyes stung. "I miss you, old friend. Nothing's ever going to change that."

"Lando . . ." Jin stared down at the bottle in his hands. "I know I was probably the last person you wanted to see join the team all those years ago. I mean, you were always right. I was just a kid. But I'm glad we had time together. And I'm . . ." Jin blew out a harsh breath. "I'm sorry I couldn't do more that day. And I'm really sorry you had such horrible taste in beer."

At that, both Rasa and Dorin laughed. "Fuck," Dorin said, "Jin's right. You really did have bad taste in beer, Lando."

Rasa smiled through her tears as she looked at Adi. "You don't have to say anything if you don't want to. I know you didn't know him, but we thought it'd be good for you to see this place."

"No," Adi said quickly. "No, I have something I want to say." He pushed his shoulders back. "Lando, I know we never got to meet, and as much as I like these three, I'm sorry that your absence is the reason I'm here. But, uh . . ." Adi smiled. "I promise I'll do my best to watch out for them. And I'll definitely take over providing the drink of choice for the team."

Dorin raised his bottle first, then they all did. And when Dorin took a drink, they all did. Jin had to suppress a cough, but Adi's shocked expression made him laugh.

"Okay," Adi choked out, "wow, you really weren't joking about him having bad taste in beer. This tastes like ass."

"It's better when it's cold," Rasa said with a grin. "Or at least, that's what Lando always tried to convince us."

Jin pivoted to look out over the valley again. He was honored that Rasa and Dorin would bring him and Adi to this old spot. Neri and Lando's spot. The team's spot before they'd started losing people. Jin hoped that, with the Helosian borders quiet, they wouldn't have to come here for this reason for a long time. Or ever.

"While we're here," Dorin said, his voice softer than Jin had ever heard it, "I wanted to apologize to both of you." Jin glanced over his shoulder to find Dorin motioning to him and Adi. "And you too, Rasa. Honestly. I shouldn't have done what I did in Posan that night."

"Oh, Dorin, that's alright—" Adi started, but Rasa held up a hand.

"Took you long enough," Rasa snapped. Her pale cheeks flushed. "What were you fucking thinking, Dorin?"

"I wasn't," Dorin said. "I knew better, but I just . . . I don't know. I was wrong that night. That's all I can tell you. I keep thinking back and trying to figure out why I put us in that position. I just . . ." He sighed. "I'm sorry. My mind hasn't felt right since . . ." He shook his head. "I could've gotten Adi and the rest of us killed."

"Yes, you could've," Jin said. Next to him, Adi shifted. "That mission could've dragged us into another war. There are far bigger consequences than just us dying."

"I know," Dorin gritted out. "I know that. I've thought about it every skies damned day for the last few months."

"Are you even fit for missions right now?" Rasa asked. "Do we need to talk to Zephyrine?"

"I'm fine if we're needed," Dorin said. "I talked to Meri, and I talked to Zephyrine again. I don't know when it'll happen, but I'd like to transfer when the opportunity arises. I miss my kids. I miss my wife. And I think I've given all I can to this team."

When Dorin's youngest child had been born the year before, he'd mentioned Zephyrine was looking into alternatives for him. How had nothing come up yet? Jin didn't know how the military decided what positions were open or needed at different bases—he'd never needed to know in the last six years.

Besides, he understood why his teammates were there. It wasn't because they believed in serving the emperor. It was dangerous work they did, but it paid very well. It wouldn't be easy for Dorin to walk away from that much money for his family no matter how much he missed them. Adi was able to pay his sister's university tuition in full. Rasa was able to support her wife's business and her mother-in-law, who needed regular healing treatments.

"If that's what you want," Rasa said, "we'll support you."

Dorin nudged a rock with the tip of his boot. "You won't hate me for leaving?"

"No," Jin said. "Do what's best for you and the family. That's all we really have at the end of the day, and if you want to be closer to them, then you should try to make that happen."

Jin's family may have been less than ideal, but he'd seen what real family could look like. He'd seen the way Astrea got on with Saros, Cressida, and her parents. They weren't exactly a traditional family unit, but even when Jin was a kid, he'd known that was alright. The Sovnas and Nikaphoroses were a family, one that took care of each other and made sacrifices for each other.

Maybe this team was, too, in a way. Adi was more of a brother to Jin than Apelo or Kaius ever had been. He missed Eliana, yes, and she'd been a good sister, but so had Zephyrine and Rasa. Dorin and Lando had been good to Jin, too, even if Dorin had gotten reckless and Lando had teased Jin endlessly in his early years.

"Thank you," Dorin said quietly. "And Adi, I really am sorry. Missions don't usually go that way, and that was my fault. I put you at the most risk out of all of us."

Adi smiled. It wasn't his usual grin. It was gentle, if not a little sad. "I appreciate that, but you've got to stop beating yourself up over it. People make mistakes. I wasn't exactly faultless that day."

Dorin nodded. "Thanks, kid."

"Enough of that," Rasa said. "Lando hated depressing talk like this, and we're here for him today."

"What was Lando like?" Adi asked. "Besides the horrible taste in drinks."

"We might be here a while," Rasa said with a smile. "We've got plenty of stories about him and Neri both."

Chapter 18
Summer, Year 1018

Jin was officially done with boats. He'd had enough time on the sea to last him a lifetime. Air travel was definitely the way to go.

"You're still looking a little green," Adi said as they passed through the eastern gates of Fort Avalon.

Their airship had just landed, bringing them home after a very long standoff in southern Helosian waters. Pirates had started targeting Helosian merchant and civilian ships, and Jin's team had been brought in to retake an entire merchant fleet from a band of pirates.

"I'll feel better when I've been on solid ground for an entire day."

"Welcome back." Zephyrine stood just outside the building where all of them had quarters. Despite her arms crossed over her chest, she smiled as they formed a loose circle around her. "I'm glad you've all returned safe and sound."

Though Zephyrine had gone on a handful of missions in Jin's first years on the team, her promotion meant she was spending less and less time in the field. It was usually just the four of them now—Jin, Adi, Rasa, and Dorin.

Zephyrine had changed since Jin had told her exactly what happened in Posan. She was worried about the fact that certain parties seemed to be aware of his movements. She'd also agreed with his decision to withhold certain details from all reports and had followed up Jin's command with one of her own. No one on the team was to breathe a word of Jin's ability outside of that very office.

Jin followed his team to one of the meeting rooms Zephyrine often used for their debriefs. He sat next to Adi and tried to focus on the fact that the ground under him was solid. No swaying. No waves. Just good old-fashioned stone and earth.

"Now that you're all home, I have some news to share with you," Zephyrine said.

"No debrief?" Rasa asked.

"I'll read Jin's report later."

Following the incident in Posan, Zephyrine had alternated who was in charge on missions. Jin would've thought it made sense for Rasa or Dorin to lead; they were, after all, captains, a higher rank. But Zephyrine continued to put Rasa or Jin in charge, and it wasn't lost on Jin that it frustrated Dorin.

"What's the news?" Adi asked.

"I'm retiring."

Zephyrine said it so casually, so calmly, like it should've been obvious. Jin stared at their commanding officer, trying to find the humor behind her expression or voice. It wasn't there.

"Retiring?" Rasa asked. "From the team?"

"From everything," Zephyrine said. "I've been asked to return to my civilian station. I'll be joining the emperor's council."

"Congratulations," Jin said. Being appointed to the council was no small accomplishment. It was the greatest honor a noble family could receive. It was a massive promotion, even compared to her earning the rank of general. "When do you go to Kalama?"

"In a few days, and you're all going with me."

"We're going to Kalama?" Adi perked up in his seat. "Do we have leave time?"

Zephyrine smiled. "I've already called your sister at the university. She knows you're going to be in town."

"And the rest of us?" Dorin asked, glancing at Jin.

"I expect all four of you to be at my retirement party," she said. "And then you have a few days in the city to yourselves. I think you've all earned a break."

"Not to be the spoilsport," Jin said, "but if you're leaving, who's going to take over your position?" Whoever it was, Jin needed to be able to trust them as much as he trusted Zephyrine. Very few people would have the same outlook on the Posan incident as her.

Zephyrine's gaze swept over the team before it settled on Rasa. "I was thinking Captain Foscari would make a fine choice."

"What about the team?" Dorin asked.

"There are going to be some other changes around here," Zephyrine said. "Rasa will take over my spot. Jin will become the permanent team lead, and the four of you will continue serving as needed for the time being. But you will also begin training others."

Jin's stomach tightened. Being the permanent team lead meant Zephyrine believed in him despite everything that had happened in Posan. And training others? What, his father wanted more teams like this? He supposed Emperor Aelius would want that considering what he thought Jin was responsible for. Of course he'd be trying to create more teams, especially now that they were at peace. That meant there was actually time to train them.

"I've barely completed my own training," Adi said. "Am I really fit for that?"

"You're a talented mage, Adi," Zephyrine said. "There's a lot you can teach others. But that's all to be figured out in the coming days. I'll meet with you, Rasa, and then the whole team to discuss what comes next. In the meantime, go get some rest. You've earned it."

It had taken days for the news to truly sink in for Jin. Zephyrine was leaving her post to move back to Kalama. Jin was taking on a permanent leadership role on his team. And Rasa was moving on—sort of. All things considered, Dorin seemed to be taking the news well.

Jin didn't know what he was going to do without Zephyrine. She'd taught him so much over the years. Six years prior, almost to the day, she'd offered him that mysterious opportunity. She'd seen him at his worst, and she'd certainly seen him at his weakest since then. But she still believed in him.

"You're looking pensive," Adi said as he joined Jin at the edge of the crowd of party guests.

They were in the palace gardens, dressed up for the ridiculous retirement party being thrown in Zephyrine's honor. Jin had half expected it to be more strict, more proper, but this was Kalama. These were nobles and aristocrats. A party was still a party, even if it was for a woman retiring after years of war and trauma and bloodshed. That didn't matter to any of these people. They were there to schmooze and have a good time.

"I'm never comfortable being home, Adi," Jin said.

"You're welcome to come into the city with me later if you'd like to get away. You could meet my sister. She did warn me, though, that there will be graduation celebrations this weekend. Apparently things get a bit wild down there."

Jin stifled a sigh. He knew about that. Eliana had warned him that she wouldn't be able to stay for Zephyrine's entire party because she was attending Astrea's graduation. Astrea was graduating that very same weekend with not one but two degrees. Skies, he'd missed so much over the years. But he was so glad that Astrea had found her own path. A safe path. One that was far, far away from his.

"I think I'll stay here, but I would love to meet her before we go back north," Jin said. "I promised my brother I'd spend some time with him and my nieces."

Apelo and Thana had another baby just after the winter solstice, right around when Jin was in Posan with his team. Another little girl, Nina. Both Nina and Velia were currently with their governess in the palace, and Apelo and Thana were speaking with Zephyrine on the far side of the party.

"I should probably go see him, actually. I haven't said hello yet."

"You good on your own?" Adi asked.

"I'll be fine. Maybe you can sneak out of here early to visit your sister."

"You think so? I don't want to disappoint Zephyrine."

"Just make sure you say goodbye again before we head back north. I'm going to visit her one last time the morning before we fly out, and you're welcome to go with me."

Adi grinned. "I suppose a few extra hours with Noemi wouldn't hurt."

"Go," Jin said. "If anyone asks, I'll cover for you."

As Adi snuck off, Jin turned back to the party. He was glad Adi would get to spend some time with his sister. The longer Adi was on the team and the more Jin got to know him, the more he realized they were alike. Not just in their interests but their lives. Both of Adi's parents were dead, and while Jin's father was alive, both his mother and stepmother were gone. They were both older brothers who felt perhaps a bit too responsible for their younger sisters. And neither of them enjoyed the job they had.

It was good being able to relate to someone. It was nice having someone close to his age around, too. Jin couldn't relate to Dorin's family and marital problems, nor did Rasa or Dorin really understand what it was like to be in Jin's shoes.

Jin made his way through the throngs of nobility, senators, and high-ranking military personnel, managing to dodge most attempts at conversation with a few polite smiles and excuses. The sooner he could get out of these gardens, the better.

"Oh, Varojin!" Thana called as he walked toward them. It was odd, hearing his sister-in-law use his full name, but it had taken almost a full hour of convincing the last time he'd seen her to do just that. She'd been trying to call him by his title before. "There you are."

"Here I am," Jin said, forcing a smile as he joined the trio. "I was actually looking for you both"—he nodded at Apelo—"and I was thinking I might go visit the girls, if the general is alright with me leaving early?"

Zephyrine smiled. "You don't have to ask my permission to see your family. Or for anything, for that matter."

"Old habits." Jin shrugged.

"I suppose that would be alright," Thana said, her brown eyes sparkling in the setting sun. "Apelo, my love, perhaps you'd like to join your brother?"

Apelo seemed surprised by the suggestion, his thick brown eyebrows rising as he swallowed the last of his drink. "Yes, I suppose I could do that," he said. "General Kanakos, it was lovely seeing you. Thank you for watching out for my brother all these years. It means the world to us."

"Of course," Zephyrine said. "It's my honor to have worked with one of the Auris siblings, and I look forward to getting to know the rest of you when I start on the council, Your Imperial Highness."

Jin almost laughed. So much spectacle, and for what? Zephyrine didn't like this bullshit either, but he supposed they both had a different role to play in Kalama.

"I'll stop by your home with the team before we go back north," Jin said to her. "We'll see you in a couple of days, General."

"See you then, Your Imperial Highness."

Apelo said his goodbyes, then joined Jin as they walked toward the palace. The sun was just starting to set behind the building, the sky a brilliant mix of oranges, pinks, and purples.

"Just don't get them all wound up before they need to go to bed," Apelo said as they walked through the quiet halls of the palace. A few servants scurried by with more platters of food. "Thana will kill me if Velia doesn't sleep well tonight."

"Has she not been sleeping well?" Jin asked.

"No, but the healer says she's fine. She's just an active child."

"Ellie was like that too," Jin said.

"Oh, I remember."

Apelo had always been a mystery to Jin. Though he was only older than Jin by a handful of years, Apelo had been the most removed of his three siblings. It was like he'd always known he wasn't going to be their father's pick for heir. That, just like Jin, he wouldn't *really* be considered for the role. Apelo didn't bend to their father's will like Kaius, though he also didn't push against it like Jin. And while Eliana, Kaius, and Jin had all inherited some kind of magic, Apelo was no mage. That wouldn't do for the next Helosian ruler.

They'd never connected much as brothers, but at least as Jin got older, Apelo seemed open to some kind of relationship.

"Velia asks about you all the time, you know," Apelo said as they reached the second floor. "She always wants to know when her Uncle Jin is going to come home next."

"I'm surprised she remembers much of me at all." Jin had only seen Velia a few times, but he'd been able to speak with her on the phone over the years, too, and he made sure Eliana always sent an extra birthday gift to their niece on his behalf.

"We all wonder when you're going to come home, to be honest," Apelo said. "I still can't believe he sent you away at eighteen. He should've waited."

Jin shrugged. "It is what it is."

"Is it, though?" Apelo asked. He stopped when they reached a far corner of the third floor, close to his old apartment. Apelo lowered his voice as he said, "I've read some of the reports, Jin. I know what happened on Ilesouria."

"You didn't tell Ellie, did you?"

"No." Apelo sighed. "But I can't believe you didn't tell us."

"It is what it is," Jin said again. Then, he asked, "Does Father know?"

"Of course."

"And?"

"And nothing. You know how he is."

"And how is that?" Jin snapped. He didn't mean for it to be so harsh, but this was exactly the problem. Eliana could see through their father's bullshit. Kaius fed into it. But Apelo didn't seem to care one way or another.

"He just *is*. He's always been harsh on us."

Jin didn't want to fight with his brother. It wasn't worth it. Apelo was never going to pick a side; he was fine staying in the middle of it all, telling people whatever it was he thought they wanted to hear. He'd even advised Jin to do that once, just before Jin turned eighteen. *Maybe I should have listened to him.*

The door behind Apelo burst open. A squealing, giggling little form wearing purple striped pajamas ran into the hallway.

"Princess Velia!" a woman called. "Oh!" A plump older woman dressed in a simple cream blouse and maroon skirt stopped short. "Your Imperial Highnesses, I'm so sorry, but she heard you—"

Jin stooped and opened his arms just in time for Velia to launch herself into them.

"Uncle Jin!"

"Velia!" he exclaimed as he hoisted her up. "Are you misbehaving?"

"No," she said, but a sly smile pulled at her lips. Velia was the spitting image of Apelo: dark brown hair, tan skin, golden eyes. She was exactly what an Auris was—in Jin's father's mind—supposed to be. "Look what I can do." A tiny flame burst to life over her palm. "I'm just like you!"

Exactly what an Auris is supposed to be. Jin's heart squeezed. What would Velia's future hold with a pushover for a father and a dictator for a grandfather?

"Would you look at that?" he asked, forcing himself to smile. "You *are* just like me. Do you like fireweaving?"

"I do, but . . ."

"But?" he asked.

"Mama doesn't want me to."

"Because it's dangerous?" he asked, and she nodded. "You should listen to her and your mage teachers. You must be very careful with your magic."

"Okay."

"Velia, my sweet pea," Apelo said, "I know you're excited to see Uncle Jin, but it's almost bedtime."

"Will you read me a story?" Velia asked, her Auris eyes wide and bright as she stared up at Jin. "I'm only allowed one story before bed, and I haven't had it yet."

"If that's alright with your father," Jin said.

Apelo glanced at the governess, who was practically cowering near the door. "As a special treat," he said, "Uncle Jin can read you your story, but you must go to bed after. Promise?"

"I promise," Velia said, throwing her arms around Jin's neck.

"Maybe I can finally meet your baby sister," Jin said as he carried Velia into Apelo's old apartment. "I've heard she's very cute."

"Not as cute as me," Velia said as Jin lowered her to the ground. When her feet hit the floor, she took off into the sitting room. "Did you know this used to be Papa's bedroom?"

"I did," Jin said as he sat on the sofa. "Did you know my old room is around here too? Has Aunt Ellie shown it to you?"

"No, she didn't."

"Maybe I can show you tomorrow." Velia nodded eagerly, and Jin laughed. "Will you sit with me before we read your story?"

The governess walked past them both and went into Apelo's old bedroom. Apelo followed her, then returned to the sitting room with a quiet bundle in his arms. When he offered the baby to Jin, Jin couldn't help but smile. Nina was so tiny. Her cheeks were fat and rosy, and her eyes were closed. She slept soundly, apparently undisturbed by Jin's visit.

"She's beautiful," he said, looking up at Apelo. And there it was, that hint of pride and peace on his older brother. Even if Apelo wouldn't truly acknowledge how bad their father was, he seemed to really care about his two children. He was already a better father than Aelius had ever been. "And so quiet."

"I have to be really quiet when Nina is sleeping," Velia whispered as she scooted toward Jin. "*Really* quiet."

"And you're doing a good job," Jin whispered back. "Did you know I met you when you were this tiny?"

"Really?" Velia asked. "I don't remember that."

"Nobody remembers being a baby."

Velia's face scrunched. "Oh."

Jin didn't know what it was about that, but it made him laugh. Velia simply hopped off the sofa and walked toward a stack of books on the floor.

"I don't want to wake her," Jin said as he handed Nina back to Apelo. "But thank you for letting me see her."

"Just the first of many visits, I'm sure," Apelo said, half-smiling as he cradled his baby to his chest. "It's good that you're coming home more often."

Jin knew this was a rare occasion; he was only here because Zephyrine was retiring. And Zephyrine was only getting a retirement party like this because she was about to join the council. And Jin had the sneaking suspicion that Zephyrine was only invited to the council because of her role as his commanding officer. In Emperor Aelius's eyes, Zephyrine had done what no one else could. She had broken Jin.

Except she hadn't. She'd taught him how to harness his power, how to gain control, how to think, how to respond. But his father didn't need to know that. He could believe whatever he wanted.

"Can we read this?" Velia asked as she set a book on the sofa next to Jin. Apelo walked back toward the bedroom.

Jin picked up the book. "*The Little Warrior*," he read aloud. "This is what you want me to read?" It was a fairytale that he'd heard as a child, one about a young Fireweaver who had to save his town from a monster. "It's not too scary?"

"It's my favorite," Velia said as she climbed back onto the sofa next to him.

"Oh?"

"It's about a Fireweaver like you," she said as she pulled the book from his hands and opened to the first page.

"Like me?" Jin asked, swallowing hard.

"He's brave like you," Velia said matter-of-factly. "And he helps people. Mama says that's your job, helping save people from scary monsters."

Jin swallowed again. He wasn't so sure about that. After what had happened with General Vaiss first, and then again in Posan, Jin thought *he* might actually be the monster.

"Well," he said instead, "I also liked this story when I was little. You're sure this is the one you want me to read? Your father said you only get one."

"I'm sure," Velia said as she settled in next to him. "I'm ready."

Jin chuckled. Apelo returned, then sat down in one of the adjacent armchairs. Behind him, Jin heard more footsteps heading toward the bathroom. The governess, probably getting Velia's things ready for the night.

Velia insisted on holding the book as Jin read to her, surprisingly silent even as she pointed to the different pictures that went with the story. By the time Jin was done reading, Velia was slumped against his side, fast asleep.

"I'll take her," Jin said when the governess swooped in to reach for her. "In the bedroom?"

"Come with me," Apelo said, then nodded at the governess. She backed off with a small curtsy.

Jin carefully lifted Velia from the sofa, then followed Apelo into the adjoining bedroom. One small bed and one bassinet had replaced Apelo's old bedroom furniture. The bassinet was quiet, Nina's little blanket holding her snug. Apelo peeled back the blankets on Velia's bed, and Jin set his niece down gently.

Kalama was barely home, but it would be nice to do this more often, to actually see his family and get to know his nieces. How nice it would be to read them bedtime stories every night they were in the capital and play in the gardens with them, to teach them what he could about fireweaving.

"She's going to insist you take her to your old room tomorrow, you know," Apelo said as he shut the bedroom door and they re-entered the sitting room. "I hope you're prepared."

"I'm happy to spend time with her. It's nice."

"She talks about you all the time."

"I hope Thana isn't filling her head with too many stories about what I do," Jin said. The governess had made herself scarce. "I don't want Velia to think I'm something I'm not."

"She thinks you're a hero, Jin. How is that a bad thing?"

Jin wanted to argue. If Apelo had read the files, as he claimed, surely he knew at least some of what Jin had seen. Some of what he'd done.

"So, tomorrow," he said instead. "What time should I come by?"

"After breakfast?"

Jin nodded. "I'll see you four then."

"Are you not going back to the party?" Apelo asked.

"No, I think I'm just going to go to bed. We had a long flight back to the city."

"Well, get some rest. Trust me, you're going to need it if you're spending the day with Velia."

Jin parted ways with his brother and retreated to his old bedroom. He shucked off his formal attire, changing instead into one of the well-worn sets of fatigues he always wore at Fort Avalon. He was tired, but he wouldn't be able to sleep now. If he stayed on the western side of the palace compound, away from the party and away from the observatory, he could work off his stress in peace.

And he did just that, pushing his body well past the tenth evening bell. Finally, he was so tired he could barely walk. That was when he dragged himself back to his old apartment, took a shower, and collapsed into bed.

CHAPTER 19
SPRING, YEAR 1019

Another fucking war. Why did his father keep getting the country into more wars?

Jin stared down at the file Rasa had given him, identical to the ones she'd handed to Adi and Dorin. They were in their new meeting room at Fort Ironwing, a simple, utilitarian space with Rasa's desk in one corner and a round table on the other side of the room. Their team had been moved there a couple of months prior to start training more specialized teams. So far, nearly sixty recruits had flunked out of training. Worse, though, was what was in the file in Jin's hand.

Four hundred dead in one day in one attack in northern Corsyca. Three hundred more wounded near the border. That didn't account for the thousand casualties they'd had the week before. And as far as he knew, Zaikud and Delia weren't faring any better.

What was the point? Corsyca was a small territory bordering Helosia, Delia, and Zaikud. It had barely any natural resources. Barely anyone lived there . . . not that a large local population would stop Jin's father. Emperor Aelius had decided to try taking it over while the Delians and Zaikudi fought over Posan, but that had been a fool's move. Both of the other countries had immediately switched their focus to Corsyca. They knew a threat when they saw one. Preventing Helosian land grabs was more important than controlling Posan.

Jin was just glad his friends and sister weren't involved. Eliana still had to finish her university coursework, so she had a few months until she joined the council with Kaius. More and more mages were being conscripted by the day, but Jin figured Cressida was safe. Her family owned Lodestar Industries, an engineering firm back in Kalama. They were too important and did too much for the army for her to die on the front lines. And Astrea? Well, Jin was very glad she wasn't a mage. Being the Imperial Stargazer's niece wouldn't save her from the front lines if she had any magical talent.

"It's ridiculous." Jin tossed his file onto the table. "My father's greed is going to destroy us all."

"Jin." Rasa's tone was sharp. "I don't disagree, but that's not why I called you all in here."

"Then what is it?" he asked.

"Your father isn't happy with how many recruits are flunking out of *our* training program."

"I don't know what to tell you," Jin said. "We're doing our best. It's a slow process to figure out who can handle what we do."

Jin didn't want anyone else to be dragged into this mess, but what he wanted didn't matter. This was going to happen whether he was involved or not. At least if he tried, he might be able to teach them some of what he'd learned. He might be able to save some of them.

"We've got thirty-two moving on to the next round of tests," Adi offered. "That's enough for eight teams."

"If they all pass," Dorin muttered.

"Probably six teams," Jin said. "I think another eight will drop out."

"Six teams." Rasa ran a hand through her hair, which she'd recently cropped short. It stood on end. "Your father wanted fifteen new teams by the end of the year."

"Let me talk to him." Though Jin doubted his father would listen to him, it was better than letting Rasa deal with the fallout alone. "Or have Zephyrine come do an evaluation and bring it back to the council. They'll believe her."

Rasa's lips pressed together. "You think Zephyrine would? I assumed she was too busy."

"I know she would."

"I'll reach out to her today."

"Are we going out any time soon?" Dorin asked. "Or are we stuck here?"

"For now, you're here," Rasa said. "I'm still trying to get the other trainers caught up on our drills and tests."

"Couldn't we be doing more out in the field?" Dorin asked.

"Orders are orders, Dorin. You're better off here, anyway."

"Are we done?" Jin asked. He didn't mean for it to sound so short, but he didn't want to listen to Dorin and Rasa bicker, nor did there seem to be much left to discuss. The situation was what it was.

"We're done," Rasa said. "I need to call Zephyrine anyway. Hopefully she can come out next week."

Dorin split off from Jin and Adi as soon as they left the meeting room. Typical. He didn't stick around much anymore if he didn't have to. How was his disinterest—his attitude—going to affect them when they went back into the field? Because despite what Rasa said, it was just a matter of time until they were given some new mission outside of Ironwing's walls.

"Dinner?" Adi asked as they left the officers' building and headed into the twilight.

Fort Ironwing hadn't changed much in the seven years Jin had been gone, but it was more crowded than he remembered. Maybe that was because now they were at war. Dozens and dozens of soldiers, young and middle-aged, milled around them, either heading off for training or whatever duties they were assigned while at the fort. A few new buildings had been erected, too.

"I was actually going to check in at the training center," Jin said.

"Got your eye on anyone in particular?" Adi asked. Jin nodded. "The twins?"

"Yes."

It was a conversation they'd had privately, just the two of them. Just like Jin knew it was only a matter of time before he was sent back into battle, he also knew it was only a matter of time before Rasa and Dorin both officially retired from the team. Rasa already had enough work to do in her new position, and she'd told Jin in private that she thought Dorin would be better suited to the job of instructor anyway. Jin agreed. He'd done well for years, but Dorin had never been the same after Lando died. It would also give him more time to be with his family.

And when Rasa and Dorin retired, Jin and Adi were going to need to replace them. That was part of the point of the training program. Jin just hoped he could build a team he trusted the way he'd trusted Rasa and Dorin over the years.

"Back to the silent brooding thing?" Adi quipped as they finally reached the training center's doors.

"Sorry," Jin said. "Just thinking."

A crowd milled around the edges of the largest gym in the building. This section alone was large enough to house a hundred trainees and a dozen more trainers. The crowd was large, but the gym floor was mostly empty.

"What do you think he's going to do to her?" one soldier whispered. He couldn't have been older than twenty, and his accent screamed Kalamian.

"I don't know," someone else said. "But you know how angry he gets."

"What's going on?" Jin asked as he placed a hand on the Kalamian soldier's shoulder.

"Just—" The kid paused. "Oh, Your Imperial Highness."

"Captain Auris," Jin corrected. He'd received the promotion when Rasa officially took over Zephyrine's old job, and he thought that title suited him much better. "What's going on?"

"That private," the kid said. "The one in the ring. She didn't dodge in time. It was her fourth try at the drill."

Jin ground his teeth together. He thought he'd already put a stop to this. When they'd been transferred to Fort Ironwing, he'd specifically met with Rasa and the fort's commander to go over acceptable training standards. The standards Zephyrine held everyone accountable to at Fort Avalon: challenging but supportive. Things had seemed to be changing.

"Adi, go get Rasa," Jin said. "Hurry."

As Adi hurried off, Jin shouldered his way to the front of the crowd and stepped onto the gym's dirt floor. Sure enough, Sergeant Koyalis had his back to the crowd and gym entrance. Jin knew that pose. The wide stance. The tight shoulders.

Jin hadn't seen the man much since arriving at Ironwing. They'd both been in a few meetings about training and drills, but otherwise, their paths hadn't crossed. In fact, other than those meetings, Jin hadn't seen Koyalis since the day he joined Zephyrine's team all those years ago.

"Do I really need to teach you this lesson again, Private Rusas?" Koyalis shouted. Jin flinched. "You are an embarrassment to this camp!"

Jin couldn't forget being on the receiving end of that exact same threat. Koyalis had treated him like absolute shit in his few months at Fort Ironwing. Koyalis had nearly broken him.

And of course, opposite Koyalis was one of the very privates Jin had been looking for. Lennor Rusas. Her twin brother, Civan, was the other he was interested in. Jin had overheard them talking about applying for Rasa's program, and he'd seen them in the gym. They were great. They were a year younger than Adi and had just been conscripted, and Jin finally understood why Zephyrine had approached him all those years ago. The twins had so much talent—they'd been professional mage athletes before the war—but they needed something different than what the regular trainers could offer.

Lennor's gaze darted to Jin, her expression tight. And that was when Jin noticed she was being held in place by the earthy floor of the gym. Koyalis wasn't even giving her a chance to dodge now.

"What are you looking at, Rusas?" Koyalis called. "This is your problem." He stalked forward, two jagged rocks floating near his shoulders. "You don't pay *attention*."

"Sergeant!" Jin called.

"Your Imperial Highness," Koyalis hissed as he turned. "What are you doing here?"

"Let her go, Koyalis." Jin owed this man nothing, not even the courtesy of a 'sir' anymore. Though his father had given Koyalis permission to beat the shit out of him years ago, Jin could finally pull rank. Not just with his imperial title, but his military one, too. "Take a fucking walk and cool down."

Koyalis chuckled, a low, nasty sound. "Found your backbone after all this time? And here I thought Zephyrine was soft on you."

"You mean she didn't abuse us?"

"We have to break you pathetic recruits somehow. That's how we build you back up."

"Take a *fucking* walk, Koyalis," Jin snapped. "I won't tell you again." He'd have to take this to Rasa, up the chain of command, but at least Jin had the power to do that now. He'd get Koyalis kicked out of the army if he could.

Koyalis watched him, his brown eyes questioning. Questioning what, Jin didn't know. His options, maybe. Koyalis's fingers twitched. There was no way he'd really try to fight Jin, right?

Wrong. Koyalis moved, his stance low as he punched those jagged rocks toward Jin. A series of earthen bullets followed. Jin kicked out, a wave of fire sweeping through Koyalis's rocks and burning them up like they were little more than dry grass. Rocky armor shot up from the ground and molded to Koyalis's body, protecting him from Jin's fire as it pushed past him and finally dissipated in the air.

"One more chance, Koyalis!" Jin called. "Take that walk and maybe you can save your career."

"Maybe your father would like to know his son is still a mouthy little brat," Koyalis spat.

Jin said nothing. Did nothing. He simply waited. People like Koyalis would always burn themselves out. Jin's father had wanted him to learn control, but he'd wanted Jin to learn it from the wrong person.

The gym's floor shook as Koyalis slammed his palms against it. An earthen wall sprang up from the floor. Jin jumped back. Stone after stone flew toward him, creating a maze of holes in the wall. Jin either dodged them or destroyed them with his fire, but Koyalis was pushing him further down the gym's long stretch, further away from Private Rusas.

"No fight in you, *Captain*?" Koyalis sneered as he forced the stone wall back into the ground. "You can't be on the defensive forever."

"You don't want to fight me."

"Oh, I really think I do."

Earth covered Koyalis's hands like rocky gloves. He punched out, sending the earth barreling down the length of the gym. Fire roared to life over Jin's palms. Two fireballs exploded out, eating the rocks in the air halfway between the two of them.

"You won't fight me?" Koyalis called. "Fine. I'll teach you a lesson another way."

Koyalis started back toward the middle of the gym. Lennor strained against the earth holding her body in place.

As Koyalis shot a rock toward Lennor, Jin's fire flared. A wall of flame shot down the gym, swallowing Koyalis's attack before it got near Lennor.

"Koyalis!"

Finally. Rasa and Adi had returned, a dozen guards at their heels. The crowd was clearing out.

"Colonel Foscari," Koyalis sneered. "Goodie, another of Zephyrine's lapdogs."

"Stand down," Rasa ordered.

"Why should I listen to you? People like you are this army's problem."

Jin almost laughed. It was ridiculous. Koyalis abused his trainees and accused them of not following orders, but he himself wouldn't listen to the chain of command. Did he not see his own hypocrisy?

"You can't fight all of us," Rasa said. The guards at her back were all tense. Ready. Waiting. Adi had slipped past them and was helping Lennor off the floor. "You're officially relieved of duty."

"What gives you the *right*?" Koyalis snapped. "You're not the commander of this base."

Rasa didn't respond. She tilted her head toward the sergeant, and one of the guards flicked his wrists. Metal soared through the air, binding around Koyalis's hands. As the guards hauled him away, he spat a series of curses and shouts over his shoulder. Jin didn't even so much as look at Koyalis. A man like that just wanted attention.

"You good?" Rasa asked Jin.

"Great."

"Get me a report in the morning." Then she was off, following the guards as they escorted a belligerent Koyalis out of the building.

"You didn't have to do that, Your Imperial Highness," Lennor muttered as Adi ushered her toward Jin.

"Captain Auris," he corrected, looking Lennor over. She seemed to be fine. Her straight brown hair was a bit dusty from Koyalis's earthmoving, and she had a few scrapes on her tan arms, but there was nothing serious. His shoulders relaxed. "And yes, I did. Koyalis has been up to that shit for years. Someone should've stopped him a long time ago."

She watched him, her small blue eyes curious but wary. "I thought you'd only been stationed at Ironwing for a couple of months."

"I was in your spot many years ago," Jin said. "He's a real dick."

Lennor's lips twitched, then she laughed. "Are you allowed to call him that, Captain Auris?"

"You think he doesn't deserve it?"

She shrugged one slender shoulder.

"You should apply to our program," he said. "You and your brother both should."

"How did you know that we were thinking about it?"

"We've been watching you," Adi said. When Lennor's eyes widened, he added, "Not in a creepy way! We've been trying to figure out who would do well on a team like ours."

"Applications close soon," Jin said. "I think you'd do well. It's not an easy program, though."

Lennor watched them both, then nodded. "I'll talk to my brother, Captain."

"I hope you do. Now go on, get cleaned up and get some dinner."

Lennor saluted quickly, then rushed out of the now-empty gym. Jin sighed and ran a hand over the back of his neck.

"You good?" Adi asked.

"I'm fine." Jin glanced at his friend, who was eyeing him warily. "I'm fine, Adi. Let's go get some dinner."

"Whatever you say, *Captain*."

Chapter 20
Autumn, Year 1019

Jin strolled the perimeter of the outdoor training rings on the western side of Fort Ironwing. Adi circled on the opposite side, both of them watching as young soldiers dressed in dark gray fought with each other. Four fighters were in each sparring circle, paired off in teams of two marked by either a red or yellow bandanna tied to their arms.

Part of Adi and Jin's jobs the last few months had included passing and failing recruits for the new special forces teams. This was their last bunch of trainees, twenty in all. Dorin had officially been transferred off the team at the end of the summer, and he'd made the move back to a base near Kalama so he could be closer to his family. He'd be spearheading a similar program down there while Rasa stayed on at Ironwing.

Since then, Jin and Adi had been on several missions as a pair, just the two of them. It hadn't been ideal, but Rasa hadn't had anyone to spare. But working with strangers wouldn't have been ideal, either. Teams had to trust each other on the battlefield, and that trust took time to build.

If the recruits passed today, they'd have a few more full teams to send out into the field. And by the looks of it, most of them would pass. Unless Adi saw something Jin didn't. Adi was good at that; he made an excellent teacher. He was patient and had an eye for detail.

"Alright, red fighters!" Adi shouted above the noise of fire, earth, water, and air. "This is it! Take down your yellow opponents in the next sixty seconds. We're done after that whether you win or not!"

Jin stopped as a pair of familiar brown-haired fighters caught his eye. Lennor and Civan Rusas. After that day in the gym, the twins had enrolled in Rasa's program. All of the new recruits were being fast-tracked through training. It wasn't like when Jin had to spend a year passing tests before Zephyrine even gave him a uniform, then another year before he got sent into the field. They were at war, as Rasa said, and needed people now.

As he watched the twins move in smooth, fluid motions around their yellow-flagged opponents, Jin couldn't help but be impressed. They were team of their own, much like he and Adi had become over the years. They didn't need to talk to communicate; the twins just seemed to anticipate each other's moves. Jin had been that way with Eliana once upon a time during their mage training growing up.

Just as Adi called time, Lennor knocked her blonde opponent on her back with a particularly strong gust of wind. Civan's water froze the other fighter, a skinny brunette boy no older than twenty, in place. Jin didn't know if he was more impressed by Civan's control over water or the fact that the kid managed to last the whole minute.

"Go ahead and take a break," Jin said as several recruits passed him. "Go get some dinner. Colonel Foscari will post announcements outside her office later tonight."

Soldiers thanked Jin as they passed, some of them still using his royal title despite the many times he'd asked them not to. The recruits continued on past Jin in a steady stream, and he told them all the same thing.

"Private Rusas," Jin said as Civan tried to slide past him. "Civan, Lennor."

The twins stopped in their tracks, only offering tight-lipped smiles. Both of them were tense. Did they not think they'd done well? Jin hadn't been the twins' only trainer since they'd enrolled in the program, but every time he'd seen them, they'd been improving. Civan was always quiet, but Lennor usually had more energy.

"Nice work out there today," he said to them both as other recruits ambled by. "Really. You two are a natural team."

"Thank you, Captain Auris," Lennor said as she ducked her head. A few strands of hair sprang out of her pigtail braids, and both her and her brother's delicate faces were slick with sweat. "That means a lot."

"We should get going," Civan murmured. Both twins saluted Jin before he could get in another word, then hurried after their peers.

Jin crossed his arms over his chest and watched them go. They ducked past Rasa, who was headed straight for Jin.

"What was that about?" Adi asked from Jin's right.

"Who, Lennor and Civan?" When Adi nodded, Jin said, "I don't know. I told them they did well. I think they're nervous."

"I would be, too," Adi said. "It reminds me of when I was still in school and teachers would post our grades after exams. I hated having to go find my name on their list."

"I never actually experienced that." Jin had always just had private tutors, ones who went to the palace just for the imperial siblings. "My tutors simply scolded me for not scoring higher marks."

"Didn't like school?" Adi asked.

"Not really."

"I did." Adi sighed wistfully but straightened as Rasa stopped in front of them. "Hi, Rasa."

"I got stuck in a meeting and didn't get to watch as much of their last session as I wanted to," Rasa said. "You two want to come back to my office and fill me in?"

Beyond Fort Ironwing's walls, Jin could just make out the tops of the trees that led into the Macadian Mountains to the northeast. The colors had started to change from vibrant green to rust red and yellow. Even the air had a sharp edge. It could've been peaceful had it not been for the trucks rolling by, soldiers shouting, and roar of airship engines as yet another ship headed for the front.

They made it to the nondescript building where Rasa's office was located with little incident. Ironwing, though functional, sprawling, and full of the latest tech, was also bland and utilitarian. It now served as the launching point for many of the troops going into Corsyca. Hundreds and hundreds of soldiers lived and trained here now, evidenced by the crowded hallways even in this building.

"Here we are," Rasa said with a sigh as she closed her office door behind them. "How about we just get into it?"

"Where do you want to start?" Jin asked.

Rasa circled around her desk, and Jin dropped into one of the hard chairs in front of it. Adi sat down next to him. Rasa pulled a thick stack of papers from a drawer, then set them on her desk and said, "How about we just go down the list alphabetically?"

So they did. With each name Rasa called off, Jin and Adi made their recommendations. Most were ready to move on, or as ready as they could be in the newer, shortened program. A handful needed a couple more weeks of training, but they weren't being flunked out at this stage. They'd made it past too many tests to simply get kicked out of the program. They just needed a little more time.

"And . . . Rusas," Rasa said. "Civan Rusas."

Adi shifted in his seat and nodded at Jin. "Well, Rasa," Jin said, "Adi and I actually wanted to talk to you about Civan and his sister, Lennor."

Rasa flipped to the next page in her stack, examining it quickly before she looked up at Jin. "What about them?"

"We want them for our team," Jin said.

"Oh?" Rasa's right eyebrow quirked up. "And what makes you think you get to make that decision?"

"It's your call," he conceded, "but you trust us. And Adi and I have talked."

"We have," Adi said. "Lennor and Civan already function well as a pair. We think it'll be easy to translate that into working as a squad."

"I do trust you." Rasa sighed. "I just don't want word to get out that I'm giving you special treatment, Jin."

"Is it special treatment, or is it trusting one of your captains' judgments?" Jin asked.

"You and I both know that's not how some people will see it."

"Maybe not, but does anyone have to know we requested them?"

"I suppose not." Tapping her fingers on the stack of papers, Rasa nodded. "Alright. Sure. You can have the Rusas twins."

"Thank you!" Adi exclaimed, then lowered his voice and repeated, "Thank you. Really."

"I need one more favor," Jin said, earning him an eye roll from Rasa. "When you talk to them tonight, can you send them over to the mess hall around the ninth bell? So that Adi and I can talk to them."

"You're lucky I like you, kid," Rasa teased. "Yes, I'll send them over. Now, let's get back to work, shall we?" She waved the stack of papers in the air. "We still have some names to get through, and I've got to get my paperwork sorted within the hour."

"I love that we're doing this," Adi said as he put the finishing touch of frosting on the small cake sitting on the counter.

Fort Ironwing's kitchen closed down after the eighth evening bell, though soldiers would sometimes use it to cook personal meals or help the fort's chef prepare ingredients for the next day. Now, it was empty except for Adi and Jin.

Jin glanced at the clock hanging over the wide sink on the far wall. It was nearly the ninth evening bell. If Rasa kept her promise—and Jin was sure she would—Lennor and Civan should be on their way to meet him and Adi.

It felt a little silly, to be making a cake to welcome two young soldiers to their team in the middle of a war. To welcome them when they'd likely be deploying within a few weeks once there was a new high priority target to take out. But when Jin had been in their position, new to the team and unsure of what to expect, Zephyrine had made him feel more at ease. She'd arranged that first phone call home to Eliana. And Eliana, even, had made Jin's transition a little easier by sending him those small care packages.

Jin didn't even know if Lennor or Civan liked chocolate, but he and Adi had agreed it was a good choice. Jin had actually done most of the baking, a recipe he'd learned from the chef back at Fort Avalon. Adi had taken charge of icing it; he had a much finer touch than Jin did thanks to years of practice.

Now, as Adi finished cleaning up the wooden countertops, Jin went to one of the refrigerators tucked in the corner. When he opened it, he reached for the beers he'd put in there a couple hours earlier. He also had no idea if Lennor or Civan liked beer, but Rasa had offered it to Jin the week before. Why not have one drink together before deploying?

In fact, beyond what he'd seen Lennor and Civan do in training the last few months, Jin knew very little about the twins. He knew they'd been professional mage athletes before the war. Their personnel files hadn't revealed much else, just that they grew up in the northwestern part of the empire, near the mountains that bordered Zaikud. They could both speak Zaikud thanks to their father's heritage, though they had no knowledge of the other continental languages. Knowing more of them used to be a requirement for the team, but Emperor Aelius had done away with that with the war raging on.

"Let's go out there," Jin said. "Don't want them to think we've forgotten about the meeting."

Bottles in hand, Jin followed Adi out to the mess hall. Most of the lights were off, though a few at each end of the long room were still buzzing with light. Adi picked a table in the corner closest to the kitchen and set the cake and a stack of small plates down. The cake was just large enough to serve the four of them. Jin set the beers down, then dropped onto one end of the bench.

"Do you think they'll care if I have my beer now?" Adi asked, already reaching for one of the dark bottles.

"Doubt it," Jin said, focusing on the metal doors at the opposite end of the room. "Might as well drink it while it's cold."

Just as Adi cracked the top off his beer, the doors creaked open. Lennor poked her head inside, her hair looking more red than brown under the mess hall's low lights. Her eyebrows rose a fraction, but she slipped inside the room and motioned for Civan to follow her. They both wore the black fatigues reserved for teams like Jin's. Like the ones he and Adi were both wearing.

"Captain Auris, Lieutenant Kuwat," Lennor said as the two of them approached the table. Her gaze flicked to the food and drinks, then back to Jin. "Colonel Foscari said you wanted to see us?"

"Please, have a seat," Jin said. "And please, call me Jin."

"Just Adi for me," Adi said. "We don't really do titles. Unless you want to annoy Jin."

"Oh, I wouldn't want to—" Lennor started, but Adi's chuckle cut her off.

"That's actually part of why we wanted to talk to you," Jin said as Lennor and Civan finally sat down. "I assume Rasa explained that you'll be joining our team specifically."

"She did," Lennor said. Civan nodded.

"Are you alright with the assignment?" Jin asked.

Lennor's eyebrows furrowed. "Of course we are. We were just surprised we'd get assigned to your team. We're so new . . ."

"We actually requested you," Adi said. "We've been impressed by the two of you. You've got good energy."

The corners of Lennor's lips quirked up. Even Civan, usually so stoic and quiet, ducked his head and smiled, revealing a small gap between his two front teeth. Jin swore a blush crept over bridge of the Tidebacker's slightly crooked nose.

"We know this transition isn't going to be easy," Jin said. "Both Adi and I have been where you two are now. And we both had people who helped ease that transition, so we wanted to try to do that for you, too." He nudged beers forward first. "If you don't want to drink, we won't ask you to. But if you'd like one, please take one."

Lennor's eyes darted to the beer Adi held in one hand, then Jin. "Really?"

"We won't be called up tonight." Jin had doubted it, too, long ago when Lando first offered him alcohol. "One beer is fine."

Civan reached for one and twisted off the lid. Jin smiled. So, Civan liked beer. This was good. Lennor reached for hers, still hesitant even as her brother took a sip.

"And a cake might seem morbid, but this place hardly ever has anything good," Adi said. "We thought we'd take matters into our own hands for tonight. Hopefully you like chocolate."

"I love chocolate," Civan said. Every time he spoke, his voice was a little quieter and rougher than Jin expected, like he needed a drink of water.

"Could never keep it in the house while we were growing up because Civan would eat it all," Lennor said. "I can't remember the last time we had chocolate, actually."

"Have as much as you want." Adi picked up the knife he'd brought out with the cake, then began slicing it. "Really. It's good. Jin's a pro with this recipe."

"You made this?" Lennor asked.

"With Adi's help, but yes." Jin smiled. "There's a lot you two will learn about us. First thing you need to know is that unless we're on a mission, we don't care much about protocol. As far as we're concerned, our ranks don't mean anything. We're a team, the four of us, and we need to know and trust each other if we're going to make it through this war."

"You say that like you've been through it." Lennor took the cake Adi passed to her and gently set the plate down on the table. "I thought the war just started."

"Adi and I have been out there a few times," Jin said. "And I served in the Delian-Helosian War."

"But you're so young."

Jin shrugged. "I was even younger back then. But my team helped me make it through, and I promise, I'm going to help you two get through this war. Both Adi and I are."

There wasn't much Jin could do for the other recruits who were now moving on to teams of their own. He'd taught them everything he could in the program, as had other trainers. It would be up to their team leaders to keep them safe now. But Lennor and Civan were his responsibility, and he'd be damned if he didn't do everything in his power to get them through to the other side.

Civan dug into his piece of cake, his shoulders sagging as he swallowed the first bite. Adi nudged Jin in the ribs, and Jin couldn't help but smile as Civan took another bite, then another. At least he had one way to win over the silent Tidebacker.

"Well . . ." Lennor's voice trailed off.

"You don't want us to help you through? Seems rather dark," Adi quipped.

"No! No, it's not that." She fiddled with the fork she held in her left hand. "I just . . . I don't know where to start. What do you need to know? What do *we*"—she gestured toward Civan—"need to know?"

There was so much Lennor and Civan needed to know. They needed to see how Jin and Adi worked together, and they needed to figure out how the four of them worked together and communicated. They needed to run drills. Jin needed to test them on their first aid skills. He needed to explain the team rules to them. And someday, Jin would need to tell them about just how strong his fireweaving really was. Someday.

"For tonight, let's just get to know each other," Jin said. "The real work will start first thing in the morning."

CHAPTER 21
WINTER, YEAR 1019

Lennor and Civan had been the right bet. The twins still had a lot to learn, but in the two months since they'd joined the team, they'd grown quickly.

Jin was lucky to have gotten his pick of people to fill the empty spots on his team. The twins' natural partnership made his job that much easier. It would make keeping them alive through the end of the war that much easier.

And now, they had their first mission as a team of four. Rasa had sent a runner to find Jin just an hour before to let him know they had to ship out. He'd gotten the team together in one of the meeting rooms in the officers building to brief them on the little he did know.

"So, you two ready?" Adi asked as Lennor finished tying off her two braids.

"As ready as we'll ever be," Civan murmured.

Lennor and Adi got on well. They both liked to chat and spent time between drills joking and socializing. But Civan often remained quiet. Observant. Jin wouldn't make the kid talk, though. He'd opened up to his old team in time, and Jin was sure Civan would if and when he wanted to. Besides, Civan communicated when it really mattered during drills and training.

"Ready," Lennor echoed as she shouldered her pack.

Jin grabbed his, slinging the knapsack over one shoulder, then nodded at his team. "Airship's waiting."

The late afternoon sun beat down on them, warm despite the early winter air. They headed south, straight through the middle of the fort to the sprawling airfield.

As they walked, the crowds of soldiers and officers cleared a path. This happened whenever one of Rasa's teams headed out; there were seven in total now. Zephyrine's old team, the one who had been on that skies forsaken mission to take out Vaiss with Jin and his team, had all been returned to trainer duty except for Bel, and they were leading one of the new groups. All of Rasa's teams had started to earn a reputation around Ironwing; what they did wasn't much of a secret anymore. And they were hard to miss, walking around in their all-black gear and body armor.

When they passed one group of soldiers, a young woman with dark blonde hair giggled and waved at Adi. Jin rolled his eyes, then rolled them again when Adi waved back at her.

"Don't let it go to your head, Adi."

"I was just being nice."

"I think she was being more than nice."

"Really?" Adi looked back over his shoulder. "All she did was wave."

Jin suppressed a smile. In all the time he'd known Adi, he'd only shown interest in one person, a soldier back at Fort Avalon who went by the nickname Bru. And Adi had claimed it was just a crush, that it didn't mean anything. The only thing Jin had known about Bru was that he, like Adi, often spent time in the garages at Avalon.

Nowadays, Adi seemed oblivious to whatever attention he did get. Jin got plenty of attention too. Nobody at Fort Avalon had looked at him differently, but here at Fort Ironwing, he—and the rest of Rasa's teams—were almost celebrities, especially as word spread about their missions. Jin simply ignored the attention as much as he could.

"Let's just focus on what we need to do, alright?"

"Always, Captain. Always."

Jin led the team up into the ship. It was a newer model, even smaller and faster than what Zephyrine used to send them out in during the Delian-Helosian War. It was a single story, just large enough to fit maybe eight adults. If they needed to sleep, they were going to have to do so on one of the wide benches lining two of the walls.

Rasa waited in the middle of the cabin, examining the small war table in front of her. Several figurines marked different locations and targets on the map laid out in the middle of the table. Jin dropped his pack onto one of the benches and joined her.

"Target?" he asked. Rasa hadn't given him any details earlier in the day. She'd just told him to meet at the airship at the fifth afternoon bell.

As Adi, Lennor, and Civan joined them, Rasa nodded. "Your target," she said, "is Delian Sergeant Berelle and her team. We've been tracking them in the Corsycan foothills for several days. Seems they're headed our way."

"Coming to Helosia?" Adi asked.

"Yes. You will intercept and eliminate them."

Across from Jin, Lennor shifted. This was their first mission as a team of four. This was the twins' first time going out into the field. At least it was a smaller target; no camps this time.

"How many are there?" Jin asked as the airship engines roared to life.

"Eight total," Rasa said. "Berelle's a Fireweaver. Two Tempests, Two Tephran, one Metalli, one Lightbringer, and one Tidebacker."

"The Delians are sending Lightbringers into the field?" Adi asked.

Healers, especially Lightbringers, were hard to come by with the war in full swing. They rarely went *onto* the battlefield, though some were trained to. Most healers were kept at camps and on airships, treating patients away from direct fighting until a ceasefire was announced. Even the continental powers, war-hungry as they were, sometimes stopped fighting for humanitarian reasons. When there were too many casualties, all sides stopped fighting to recover their dead and wounded. It was gruesome work, and Jin admired the healers for continuing on at all. How they dealt with so much death and pain, he wasn't sure.

Rasa shrugged. "Seems so. I'll leave the map and reports with you. I need to go. Bel's team is heading out in a couple of hours, and they still need to be briefed." She smiled at Lennor and Civan first, then Adi, then finally, Jin. "Good luck. See you tomorrow."

Rasa left through the narrow airship doorway, then the copilot climbed out of her chair and went to seal the door. Once that was done and she returned to the cockpit, the ship lurched into the air.

Jin grabbed the stack of reports off the table near the map and handed half of them to Adi. "Help me review these?"

"You got it." Adi took them and headed for one of the benches under a narrow window.

"What about us, Captain?" Civan asked.

It was the one habit Jin hadn't quite been able to break the twins of yet. Adi only ever called Jin by his title either as a joke or when in a room with people who valued hierarchy. The twins, however, always called Jin by his title when they were working. Lennor had finally started using his name when the team ate dinner together. That was progress.

"You two should get some rest," Jin said. "We should be at the drop point in a few hours. I need you in good shape for tonight."

Civan nodded and followed Adi. Lennor, however, hesitated.

"You good?" Jin asked her as he scanned the reports in his hand.

"Eight of them and four of us, Captain?" she asked. "You really think we can do this?"

"Len." He forced himself to look up from the reports. Jin put a hand on her shoulder. "Adi and I know you're ready. Trust us, and trust yourself."

Finally, Lennor flashed a half-smile. "Alright. Thanks, Captain." And then she, too, joined Civan and Adi.

Jin glanced over at his team once before focusing on the reports again. He just hoped he was right.

Navigating the Corsycan foothills in the snow at night was proving tougher than Jin had hoped it would be. Jin didn't dare summon any fire to melt the snow around them; it reached up to their ankles, not impossible to navigate but certainly slowing them down. Civan moved what snow he could with his tidebacking, but Jin didn't want him to tire himself out. They still had a hike to the spot where Sergeant Berelle's team was last known to have camped out.

Whether the sergeant and her team would be there was another matter entirely. The intel wasn't old, but it wasn't necessarily the most up-to-date either. *We will deal with that if it's an issue,* Jin reminded himself. That was what they always did. Besides, Berelle's team was also on foot; they probably wouldn't have made it too far with the snow and cold temperatures.

They had exactly six hours to hike the four miles to the location, find Berelle's team, take them out, and hike back to the pickup site. The snow would make that harder than it needed to be.

But they were almost at Berelle's last known location. It should be just over the next ridge; it wouldn't take them more than a couple of minutes to walk there. From here, though, that meant they were walking in with no visual confirmation of Berelle's presence. Not good.

Jin held his fist up, the sign for his team to stop. Behind him, all the soft crunches of snow ceased.

"What is it?" Adi asked.

"We're coming up on it," Jin said. "Need to find a way to take a look."

This wasn't like when they'd been doing reconnaissance on that ill-fated mission in Posan. The land there had been filled with tall evergreens and plenty of ways to get both cover and visuals. This part of Corsyca, though it had plenty of smaller trees and shrubs for cover, lacked anything substantial for them to climb. Most of the taller trees were narrow; they certainly wouldn't hold Jin or Adi's weight.

"There." Lennor pointed to one of the tall, narrow trees. "I can climb it."

From here, Jin couldn't tell exactly how thick the branches were, but it seemed safe to say they weren't going to be supportive. Both Lennor and her brother were slim and lithe, but she was also the shortest. If anyone was going to be able to do this, it was her. And Jin didn't see any other options anyway. They needed to know what was over there.

"Try it," Jin said. "But if it's unstable, come down."

"What am I looking for?" she asked.

"Any sign of life over that ridge."

"Do not fall," Civan warned as Lennor rolled her eyes.

She took off through the darkness, covering the couple hundred feet in no time at all. Only a sliver of the moon was out tonight, mostly covered by clouds promising fresh snow. Jin could barely make out Lennor's form as she climbed. Something invisible—her Tempest magic—gave her a boost to each branch as she ascended. Eventually, she stopped climbing.

"What's taking her so long?" Civan asked.

"It's only been a couple of minutes," Adi said.

Jin held his breath. But there. She descended, returning to the ground far more quickly than she'd been able to climb. Lennor started her jog back to them, skidding to a stop as fire cut a line through the snow.

Shit.

Five bodies were moving down the hill toward them. Were these their targets?

A spark of starlight, brilliant in the winter darkness, gave Jin his answer. Yes, this had to be Berelle's team. They'd never, in all his years doing this, encountered a Lightbringer like this. If this wasn't Berelle's team, that would be quite the coincidence.

"Go," Jin said to Civan. The Tidebacker crossed the last of the distance to meet his sister. Taking out the Lightbringer had to be their priority. There was no way that Lightbringer wouldn't be trying to save whoever Jin's team took down first. "Adi—"

"Got it."

They'd talked about this on the airship. Take down one, maybe two, to draw the Lightbringer in. And as Adi and Jin moved, taking down both a Tephran and Tempest, that spark of starlight moved closer. Perfect.

Until Berelle moved in with them, flames blasting through the air. Straight for Adi. Jin grabbed hold of her fire, welcoming the heat as its energy flowed through his body. Then he hurled that fire back at Berelle.

Light sparked to Jin's left. Adi grunted. Something crashed into the snow. Jin tensed. Despite his training screaming at him, he turned.

Adi stooped over who Jin assumed was the Lightbringer, pulling his dagger out of the man's gut with a sickening squelch. Red leaked into the otherwise clean snow.

Focus.

Jin's fiery shield burst to life in front of him. Berelle directed a fireball his way, stronger and harder than before. Jin's shield barely absorbed it.

He dropped it, moving half a step back. Berelle's next punch fell short. Jin kicked out, but she maneuvered away.

Water, wind, earth—it all crashed around Jin, and it took all of his energy to not check on his team. He needed to focus.

Berelle lunged, her flames melting the snow around them as fire spread through the air in a wide arc. Jin dropped to the ground. The smell of burning fabric made his eyes water. Rolling to his feet, Jin circled Berelle. She snarled at him, more flames flickering to life over her gloved hands and casting long shadows on the remaining snow.

He and Berelle continued their fiery dance. Every time one of them moved, the other anticipated. He needed to finish this.

Berelle's attention slipped, glancing away for just a second as someone shouted something in Delian. An opening.

Jin pulled his dagger from its sheath. He closed the distance between them in one stride and grabbed Berelle's jacket, pulling her closer as he drove the dagger home. Berelle shoved against Jin's arms, but he was stronger. He forced the blade through the woman's leather armor and into her gut. As Jin yanked his dagger back out, Berelle slumped to the ground, unmoving. Blood seeped into the snow.

"Good?" Adi asked, out of breath as he joined Jin.

"Yeah, you?" He had a few burns and scratches; it wasn't anything his med pack couldn't treat.

The twins had finally stopped, too. On the ground, Jin counted seven bodies among the mess of melted snow and rock. Seven. There were supposed to be eight.

"Who's left?" Jin asked. "There should be one—"

The sharp *bang bang bang bang* of an automatic rifle echoed in the otherwise silent night. Pain lanced Jin's left shoulder, burning as it spread through his back and arm. He stumbled. Pain flared on the left side of his torso, down near his hip.

"Sharpshooter!" Adi called as he wrapped one arm around Jin's mid-section. Jin groaned as Adi helped him slide to the ground.

Sharpshooter. There wasn't supposed to be a sharpshooter in the group. That had to be the Metalli, but Rasa would've warned them. Not all Metalli were sharpshooters; it was a very specific skill, combining shooting with magic. Rasa's intel had been wrong. It wasn't the first time.

"Down," Jin hissed. More shots rang through the night.

Jin's vision grew bleary, his mind trying to focus only on the pain. *Please, not the team.* His head pounded in time with his heart. *Please.* He didn't think he could even move. But he had to. He had to look.

Lennor stood frozen as a disk of water floated in front of her, something trapped inside. *A bullet.* No, not just one. Several. Civan had the bullets frozen in the air. That kind of speed was . . . something else.

Civan shoved his sister down with one hand as he turned toward the ridge. More shots rang out, and again, his water came up to block them.

"You see it?" Civan asked none of them in particular.

"Yeah." Jin saw it. The burst of light from the last shot had come from just over the ridge.

Cold, frozen earth shot up in front of Jin, a long wall that stretched toward where the twins were creeping closer. Adi helped Jin move back against the wall, and only when Jin braced himself against it did Adi finally let him go.

Darkness clouded the edge of Jin's vision. And as he closed his eyes, that Ilesourian fort came into view. The stone walls. The explosion in the hallway. Lando's panicked expression as Jin went down that day. *But you're not down.* Jin sucked in the cold Corsycan air and forced his eyes open. *Finish this.*

"Civan, draw them out," Jin rasped. "Adi, take them out. Len, cover them."

"You got it, Captain," Adi said, the twins trailing after him as they all moved into position.

Jin braced his back against Adi's earthen wall, slowly sliding toward the ground as pain pulsed through him with every beat of his heart. *Shit.* He'd never been shot before. Stabbed, cut, burned, pummeled with rocks and water and wind and fire. Never shot. Twice.

Another series of shots echoed through the Corsycan landscape. Jin's team didn't make a sound. Another shot, then the clatter of something against rock.

"Got 'em!" Adi called.

Jin loosed a breath. "You alright?" he asked as he stared out at the dark horizon. Warm blood leaked down his back, chest, and side.

"That first shot grazed Civan," Lennor said, her voice tight. "But we're fine."

Snow crunched. Jin looked toward his team. Civan was examining the large tear in his jacket sleeve as Adi held Lennor back.

"Adi," Jin croaked, "you and Len make sure they're all dead. Stay together. Civan, with me."

"Shouldn't I go with them?" Civan asked, hesitant.

"You know the rules," Jin said. Leave no one behind, leave no witnesses, and stick together. They were rules Rasa was now passing on to the new teams, the young mages who hadn't done this before. Jin just hoped they continued to make it through just as Lennor and Civan had tonight. "Besides, we need to take a look at that." Jin tilted his chin toward Civan's arm.

"Don't you mean we need to look at you?" Civan asked as he kneeled beside Jin.

"You first," Jin grunted.

"Captain—" Civan started, but Adi cut him off.

"Jin, come on."

"Just go check that we're clear," Jin said. "Let me worry about myself."

With a huff, Adi led Lennor away from their cover. Civan slipped his pack off his shoulders and started unbuckling it. "Captain—" he started again.

"Take your jacket off. Let me see." When Civan rolled his eyes, Jin added, "That's an order."

Civan unbuttoned his jacket, shucking it off with more than one wince. When Jin asked him to move closer, he did. Jin pulled at the ripped fabric of Civan's shirt with his good hand. An angry red wound tore across Civan's tan skin. Blood trickled down his arm. It would hurt, but he would live. Jin instructed Civan on how to patch himself up, and when he began to protest, Jin threw in another, "That's an order."

As Civan tended his own wound, Jin dug deep within himself, pulling on every ounce of energy he had to move his body and ignore the panic setting in. Despite how much it hurt, it didn't hurt as much as that day on Ilesouria. He had to focus on that. Jin gritted his teeth as he tried to get his knapsack off. By the time it fell from his shoulders, Jin was sweating. His breath came in short bursts.

"You can order me otherwise, but I'm not going to listen," Civan said as he crouched near Jin. "Let me help."

There was no way he'd be able to get his jacket or armor off. As Civan helped, Jin asked, "You wouldn't happen to secretly be a Purifier, would you?"

Civan laughed, low and deep. "No, Captain, I'm not."

"Damn." He let his head fall back against the wall and heaved a sigh. "Let's just get this done."

"I'm sorry I didn't stop these," Civan said as he opened Jin's pack. "I should've."

"I've been doing this long enough to know that kind of thinking doesn't get you anywhere." Jin sucked in a sharp breath. Pain ripped through his shoulder again. He might actually be sick. Or pass out. "You stopped what you could. What you did stop was incredible, honestly."

Civan pulled out Jin's med pack, a tiny black bag filled to the brim with whatever supplies would fit. "Does that happen often? Not knowing exactly who we'll be up against."

"Sometimes intel is bad. It happens. Not every mission, but some."

Civan simply nodded, then got to work in silence. By the time Adi and Lennor returned, Civan had finished inspecting, cleaning, and wrapping Jin's wounds. The bullet to his shoulder had gone clean through, and though he'd need a healer as soon as he could get to one, Jin doubted the wound would kill him. The one that hit his side only grazed him; his armor had stopped the worst of it. Civan had even dug up a couple of painkillers from his pack for Jin to take. Jin had insisted Civan take one of them.

"You two good?" Adi asked as he slid Jin's jacket back onto his shoulders.

"Let's just get out of here," Jin said.

Adi raised an eyebrow. "You sure you can move?"

"No, but we don't really have a choice." They couldn't just sit there all night. Jin would find a way to keep going.

Adi took the lead, Jin sandwiched between the twins. He peeked up at the sky, where the clouds were beginning to part and reveal a few twinkling stars. Lennor and Civan's first mission, done. Their first close calls, too. Jin was going to need to keep an eye on them and make sure they knew how to cope with what was coming. Because as Jin followed his team through the snowy Corsycan countryside, he had the feeling this was only the beginning for his new team.

CHAPTER 22
SUMMER, YEAR 1020

Twenty missions in six months. Jin and his team had barely been at Fort Ironwing since the winter solstice. None of them had even gotten to go visit their families for the celebration.

Coming back to Fort Ironwing after a mission was always a mix of relief and dread. Dread because it meant Jin had to see the ugly truth of the army's state. Rasa's other teams weren't doing as well as his. Not that they couldn't perform—they could. But the whole army was suffering casualties all the time, it seemed. Not just injuries that needed the attention of healers but devastating losses that were far outside the scope of what Jin remembered from the Delian-Helosian War—hundreds and hundreds lost in single weeks, sometimes single attacks. And while that was the reality of war, that didn't make it any easier.

He shouldered his knapsack as the airship's copilot unsealed the door. His team was a mess. They'd been in the Corsycan summer heat for three days with no showers. There hadn't even been a river to wash up in before the pickup. And Lennor and Adi had both suffered some injuries, albeit minor. They'd taken out a Zaikudi general and created an opening for a Helosian battalion to come in and rescue prisoners of war. That was a hard blow for the Zaikudi army, one Jin hoped would buy the Helosians some time before the next major offensive.

Now, all Jin wanted was to get his team to the healers and himself to his shower. And skies, he wanted a fucking coffee.

"Adi, Len," Jin said as they disembarked their airship, "go to the healers. Civan, do whatever you want. Rasa knows we need at least a few hours before we go back out."

"Back out?" Lennor groaned as she reached for her dirty, dusty braids. "I was hoping to keep blood and dirt out of my hair for a few days."

"Well, hopefully it'll be a few days," Jin said. But lately, the missions seemed endless. Time between them kept getting shorter. "Go. Get that"—he nodded at the thick white bandage covering her bicep—"looked at. You know where to find me if you need me."

He'd just branched off from the rest of his team and was cutting through Fort Ironwing's main plaza when a young woman with bronze skin and dark brown eyes approached him. The dagger insignia embroidered on her uniform denoted her non-mage rank.

"Your Imperial Highness," she said, "Colonel Foscari needs to speak with you. It's urgent."

Urgent? Jin didn't like the sound of urgent. "Does my team need to come with me?"

"She didn't say. She just said to come immediately."

Jin nodded. If Rasa didn't say, then he could go alone. Besides, Adi and Lennor really needed to go to the healers. Anything else would have to wait until they were patched up.

He headed straight for Rasa's office. He wove his way through the building, avoiding other officers and enlisted alike until he got to Rasa's door. The guard stationed outside opened it and motioned for Jin to go in.

Rasa was hunched over her desk, eyebrows pinched together as she stared at the phone. It was off the receiver.

"Rasa?" he half-whispered.

She stood and met him near the door. "Your father's on the phone."

"Is everything alright?" Jin's heart jumped to his throat. Had something happened to Eliana? Or one of his nieces?

"I'm not sure," Rasa said. "He'll only speak to you." She tilted her chin toward the desk. "Go. Take it. I'll make sure no one comes in."

A million possibilities ran through Jin's mind as he crossed the space to Rasa's desk and she exited the room. Eliana was hurt. Velia or Nina had fallen gravely ill. Apelo and Thana had gotten into an airship accident on one of their trips back to their estate in eastern Helosia. His father had found out about how strong Jin's magic really was. He was being transferred away from his team as some kind of punishment.

Jin sucked in a deep breath, then reached for the phone. "Hello?"

"Varojin." Aelius's voice was smooth and calm, all business. "Good. You're back."

"Airship just landed a few minutes ago."

Silence. Jin's heart thundered as he waited. And waited. And waited. He needed his father to just spit out the news, whatever it was.

"I assume Colonel Foscari told you this was urgent," Aelius said.

"She did. Is everything alright?"

"Yes. I need you to come home."

"Why?"

"Grand Duchess Ysabel has agreed to a summit for the autumn equinox, right here in Kalama. I'd like to put together an exhibition and hold a gala. Something to celebrate our shared histories."

That . . . that was the urgent reason for his father's call? Some party for a foreign head of state? Jin's pulse slowed.

"What does that have to do with me coming home?" Jin asked. "You want me to attend?"

"Attend, yes, but you will be organizing the entire event."

Jin couldn't stop the laugh that bubbled out of him. He ran a hand over his sweat-covered forehead. "I'm sorry, I don't think I heard you right."

"There's nothing funny about this, Varojin," his father snapped.

Rubbing his eyes, Jin sighed. This was not at all what he'd thought. Organizing a party? It didn't make sense.

"Why would you want to pull me out of the field now?" Jin asked. "Surely you know I'm practically out on a mission a week right now."

Jin hated that he and his team were out so often. Of course he hated it; he always had. But he needed to know why Aelius would pull him out now. The only time Jin had ever seen his father truly proud of him was that conversation years ago in Fort Avalon. *I have three heirs and one weapon.* The words still haunted him.

"Even soldiers cannot be in the field forever, Varojin. You need to learn how to be useful at home, too, and Colonel Foscari's other teams will be able to fill in the gap." He paused, then added, "Besides, I think you've earned a break."

Earned a break? Jin had never, not once in eight years, earned a break from his father. Not once in his twenty-six years of life had he ever been given a break. And even if his father had suddenly had a change of heart—which Jin doubted—it wasn't like anyone else was getting a break from the war.

"What about my team?" Jin asked. "What will they be doing?"

"That is for Colonel Foscari to figure out."

Jin didn't like the sound of that, but maybe he could convince Rasa to not send them out while he was gone.

"And another thing," Aelius continued. "I need you to come home immediately."

"Immediately?" Jin asked. It was almost the weekend, and the only ships running from Fort Ironwing to Kalama on weekends were supply ships. "I don't think I can get back until next week."

"Find a way," Aelius ordered. "You remember the Stargazer's girl?"

Jin's heart stopped. "Astrea Sovna?"

"Yes, that's her."

"What about her?"

"She's going to help you with this project," his father said. "I imagine the two of you will need plenty of time to work on this in case you screw it up."

Jin didn't know what to say. Nevermind his father's lack of confidence . . . Astrea? That was who Aelius had picked? Was this some kind of sick joke? Jin's stomach churned. His pulse pounded in his ears. This could not be happening.

"Is that really necessary?" he asked. "I'm sure I can manage it on my own."

"That's the thing, Varojin. I don't think you can. And Miss Sovna's background will be perfect for this. Is there a reason you don't want her help?"

Was that a challenge? Did his father somehow know Jin had fucked up the relationship that once mattered most to him? No, Aelius couldn't know that. Right?

"No, no," Jin said when the silence stretched on for a beat too long. "I simply assumed you'd want someone more experienced helping me since you have so little faith in my abilities." He didn't want to throw Astrea under the streetcar here, but anything to keep her out of this. Anything to keep her away from his father. To keep her away from Jin himself.

"It's a good opportunity for her career, Varojin. Helping one of the emperor's children on a diplomatic project . . . that's quite the accomplishment, don't you think?"

Jin ran his tongue over his teeth. He should've known better. There would be no getting her out of this, not when his father had so obviously made up his mind. And there would definitely be no getting himself out of it.

Fuck.

"Yes, of course," Jin said. "Of course it would be. You're right."

"Good. I'm glad you agree. So, return to Kalama immediately. I expect you to begin working with her on Monday."

His father didn't even give Jin time to respond. The line went dead. Slowly, Jin hung up the phone.

He was going home, and this time, he'd have to stick around.

He'd have to face every skies damned thing he hated about that place and the one skies damned mistake he couldn't forgive himself for.

"Fuck."

Jin's plans were in motion. As soon as he'd hung up with his father and regained some semblance of calm, Jin had found Rasa and his team. He'd explained the situation to them—everything except the part about Astrea—and that he had no way out of it. Rasa had agreed to put Lennor and Civan on training duty; they'd be helping train and test the next round of applicants to Rasa's program. Adi would be going to Kalama with Jin.

What Adi would do while Jin was in Kalama, he wasn't sure. Adi's younger sister, Noemi, had already returned home for summer break from university. Would Aelius care that Adi was coming to Kalama instead of staying close to the front? Aelius had said it was up to Rasa to decide what happened to Jin's team. Jin was just glad that Adi and

Rasa had agreed to this. Lennor, Civan, and Adi, for their parts, were just grateful to have some time away from the battlefield.

Now, Jin and Adi were on a small airship Rasa had agreed could take them to Kalama that night. They'd had just a few hours to get cleaned up and pack. The flight back to the capital would take most of the night.

"You finally gonna tell me why you're so nervous?" Adi asked as he settled onto one of the wide benches.

They'd been in the air for a few minutes, and the two pilots were the only other people on the ship. Thanks to their thick headphones and the roar of the engines, they wouldn't be able to hear Jin and Adi's conversation. Outside the windows, a smattering of stars were visible through the hazy clouds.

Jin ran a hand over his face and sighed. Finally, someone he could tell. Well, he supposed he could've told Rasa, but they had never really talked about this except for that first winter training expedition years ago.

"Do you remember Astrea?" Jin asked. "I believe I've mentioned her a few times."

"A few times?" Adi's eyebrows quirked up as he chuckled. The wound he'd sustained on his face during the Posan incident had scarred over, leaving a cut through his right eyebrow. "You've mentioned her far more than a few times."

Jin pinned Adi with a look, but the Earthmover simply grinned. And Jin couldn't even be mad; Adi was right. Jin talked about Astrea a lot when it was just the two of them, probably more than Adi wanted to hear.

But Adi made it so easy to just talk about everything. Their families, old friends, teen years, the missions. Everything. They talked about it all. And over the last few years, Jin had started really talking about Astrea again. One night after they'd both had a bit too much whiskey, Jin had told Adi everything he hadn't been able to when Rasa and Dorin interrupted their first talk about Astrea—their years of friendship, how he'd left without saying a word, ignored her letters, and felt he was justified in it all when he nearly died. How he'd changed his mind about that almost immediately after recovering.

Even after all this time—eight fucking years—Jin missed her. Aside from Adi, Astrea was the only person who Jin had ever really considered a true friend. Zephyrine was too, he supposed, but even their relationship was different. Same with Cressida.

For eight long years, Jin had lived with the regret and pain deep in his bones. He'd stared up at the constellations he'd once begged Astrea to teach him. On particularly difficult nights, he'd searched for the North Star and wondered if Astrea was looking for it. If she remembered everything he did. If maybe some small part of her missed him, too.

He supposed they'd both have changed some over the years; it would do no good to put sixteen-year-old Astrea on a pedestal in his memory. Though he was terrified to see her again, part of him was excited. Not just to see her but to learn everything about this new version of her.

"Well," Jin finally said, "last I heard from my sister, Astrea's a librarian now. And my father has assigned her to work on this project with me."

Adi slumped back against the wall and let out a low whistle. "Damn."

"I know."

"And you never wrote back to her?"

"No."

"Not once after all this time?"

Oh, Jin had written to her. He had a few dozen letters tucked neatly in his pack, the ones he'd written to her after missions and particularly hard days. Leaving them at the fort hadn't been an option, so he'd have to find a new spot to hide them in his room at the palace.

"No."

"This is gonna be rough."

"I know."

"For both of you."

"I know, Adi." Jin leaned forward on his knees and ran his hands through his curls. "I know. It's going to be impossible."

"And you have to stay through the autumn equinox?"

"I assume as much," Jin said. "That's when the gala is supposed to be. I doubt he'll let me leave before then."

"So, three months with Astrea." Adi nodded. "Damn. That's gonna be rough."

Jin groaned. He didn't know what would be worse: working with her or leaving her again when those three months were up.

PART 4: HOME

CHAPTER 23
SUMMER, YEAR 1020

The palace never seemed to change. Jin hadn't been home since before the Corsycan War had started, and yet, everything was exactly how it had always been. Even the guards' structured red uniforms hadn't changed at all.

Jin knocked on his father's office door. He'd only arrived in Kalama a few hours before—before dawn—and in that time, he'd gotten Adi settled in the barracks. Now, though, he had to talk to his father. It was still early enough in the morning that even the courtiers and politicians hadn't made their way to the palace yet. Eliana and Kaius were nowhere in sight.

As Emperor Aelius called out for him to enter, Jin sucked in a deep breath. This was it. He grabbed the cold metal doorknob, twisted it, and pushed into the room.

Even his father's office hadn't changed. Even his father hadn't changed. Aelius barely looked a day over forty, though he was already well into his fifties. Same dark brown hair, bright gold eyes, straight nose, tan skin. Even if Jin was a nearly perfect copy of his father and siblings, at least he'd started growing in his beard. His father was always clean-shaven.

"Varojin, good." Aelius didn't stand up from his desk. Didn't even offer a true greeting. "You're here."

"I am." Jin forced himself to cross the spacious office and take a seat in front of his father's desk. "I got back as quickly as I could."

"I'm glad to hear you can follow simple instructions," Aelius said. Jin bristled. "Now, on to business. Your project."

As Aelius rattled off the exact same information he'd given Jin on the phone the day before, he shuffled a few files around on his desk. Jin tried to pay attention, but none of the details were new, and he was so tired. He'd barely slept on the whole flight down from Fort Ironwing, and he'd barely slept for days before that while on that mission in Corsyca.

"You and Miss Sovna are to begin your work first thing on Monday morning," Aelius said. "A few days should be enough for you to settle in, yes?"

Settle in? His father was actually offering Jin time to settle in?

"Yes, that's plenty of time."

"Good. I'd hate to see you waste your time or mine, Varojin. I hope you understand how important this project is."

Jin, in fact, did not see why it was all that important. The Grand Duchy of Novaria was keen on neutrality and had been for as long as he could remember. He doubted Grand Duchess Ysabel would suddenly be keen on entering an alliance with Helosia, especially with the war. But there were more to summits and meetings than just formal alliances. There were trade agreements, goodwill gestures, and other smaller things that could add up. Maybe that was the grand duchess's play.

Besides, it was important to Jin because Astrea was being dragged into the whole mess.

"Of course, Father."

"I would hate for you and Miss Sovna to not take this seriously, Varojin."

"We will," he promised.

"It's important for our family and our country."

"I understand."

"Do you?"

"Yes."

Aelius smiled. "Good."

"Is there anything else I need to know?" Jin asked.

"No."

How was that supposed to help Jin? How was he supposed to take this seriously or not waste his father's time without further direction? Was this some kind of test?

"As I said, you'll be starting on Monday," Aelius continued. "You're dismissed."

Sitting in Zephyrine Kanakos's sprawling townhome and drinking coffee was not where Jin expected to be with the war raging on in Corsyca. The house, though large, had an understated feeling with its simple furniture and refined, muted color palette.

"You got married and didn't tell us?" Jin asked, his head tilting against the soft back of the armchair he sat in.

Small diamonds glittered on the gold band on her left ring finger as Zephyrine lifted her coffee cup. The band on her right ring finger was plain gold. "I did."

"And you didn't think we might like to know?"

"I didn't think you'd care. It's not exactly a love match."

If Zephyrine didn't love her partner, then what was the point of getting married? Some couples in Kalama, especially those in the aristocracy, married for other reasons, but Zephyrine never struck him as that type.

"Who is it?" Jin asked.

"Lord Anjou Lazarro."

"The shipping guy?"

Zephyrine's melodic laugh echoed through the parlor. "Yes. Though he'd hate to know that's how you've referred to him."

Lord Anjou Lazarro was from one of the smallest noble houses, but he'd made a fortune as a shipping magnate. He controlled at least half of the shipments coming in and out of Kalama daily.

"So, why did you marry him if it's not a love match?"

Zephyrine raised an eyebrow. "There are other reasons to tie myself to a person."

"Like?" Jin couldn't imagine what they might be.

"It looks good for the council." She took another sip of coffee. "And we tend to have the same worldviews."

"You mean . . . ?"

"I do."

Lord Anjou Lazarro was a rebel. Or, at least, that was what the newspapers were still calling anyone who disagreed with imperial policy. Jin had always thought it was a silly nickname; the so-called rebels didn't *do* anything except talk. They wanted Eliana to be named heir, and they wanted to end the war, but talk was just talk. Still, Jin kept himself out of politics as much as he could.

"And you thought that was a reason to get married?"

Zephyrine placed her coffee cup on the low table separating them. "I think you're just avoiding why you're really here by asking me about my personal life."

"I hardly think I'm avoiding—"

"Not that I'm not glad to see you, Jin, but this is unexpected. I've been getting reports from Rasa, and she didn't mention you coming home."

Jin sighed. "I'm home until the autumn equinox. My father only called me back yesterday."

Zephyrine's narrow eyebrows shot up. "Three months in Kalama?"

"Has he told the council about his meeting with Grand Duchess Ysabel?"

"Yes, we knew he was trying to set something up. That's what this is about?"

"He wants me to plan some exhibition and gala."

A loud laugh echoed through Zephyrine's parlor. "I'm sorry, he wants *you* to *what*?"

"I know. That was my reaction, too, until I realized he was being serious."

"That's not exactly what we've been teaching you to do out there all these years."

"I know." Jin set his cup down and scrubbed at his face with both hands. His beard prickled his palms; he needed to trim it when he got back to the palace. "Rasa's put Lennor and Civan on training duty until I return. I convinced her to let Adi come with me."

Zephyrine hadn't been out to Ironwing much in the last few months, nor had Jin's team really been there. But she'd met the twins on several visits she'd made to see how the training program was going and another time shortly after the twins' first mission. Officially, Zephyrine had been there to check in for the council and the emperor, but unofficially, she'd been there to check up on Jin, Adi, and Rasa.

"Why?" she asked.

"I thought he'd like to visit Noemi, but I knew Rasa wouldn't let me take the whole team." Selfishly, Jin wanted his closest friend nearby. But Rasa also had a job to do, whether or not any of them agreed with the war. And besides that, Aelius would start asking questions if Jin's whole team was suddenly off duty.

From across the sitting area, Zephyrine studied him. Her eyes narrowed, and her lips pursed. "Why are you actually nervous?" she asked.

"I'm—"

"I've been putting up with your bullshit for years, Jin. Out with it."

"I just don't want to be here. You know I don't like being home."

"True, but you've always hated what we do out in the field. I know that can't be everything."

Why did Zephyrine always have to be right? Jin sucked in a deep breath, then crossed his arms over his chest. "He's assigned Astrea to help me with the project."

"Ah."

That one syllable said it all. Zephyrine knew exactly what Jin was afraid of. She knew how Jin's actions had hurt not just Astrea but himself.

"I don't know what I'm going to do," he continued when Zephyrine remained quiet. "Three fucking months to stare my mistakes and imperial family future in the face."

It wasn't just that Jin was nervous about seeing Astrea again. Of course he was. He was nervous about his father calling him home. Because as much as Jin hated the wars and the fighting and the missions, he liked his team. He liked training other mages. And at least out there, Jin could try to help some of the soldiers forced into service. He could teach them how to protect themselves, give them a shot at making it home to their families. But here in Kalama? He couldn't do anything.

"Do you remember when I first found you at Fort Ironwing?" Zephyrine asked.

"Of course I remember." He'd been in the infirmary, just having taken another beating from Sergeant Koyalis. Zephyrine had found him there and not only delivered his mail but an opportunity.

"Eight years ago, I gave you a choice with very few details about what might be on the other side," she said. "Stay with Koyalis or join my team. And you joined my team."

"So?"

"Now you have another choice," Zephyrine said. "Do you want to stay detached from your life here, from your family and old friends? Or do you want to start repairing what you left behind and what you broke?"

"I—"

"I'm not done."

Jin kept his mouth shut.

"Because no matter what, someday, you won't be out in the field anymore. Look at me. Look at Rasa and Dorin. Your father giving you this new mission, here at home, is already proof enough that you won't be able to avoid Kalama forever."

Avoiding Kalama forever. When Jin was eighteen, even though he hadn't wanted to leave his sister or friends, it had seemed like leaving Kalama might be the one good thing to come out of his father forcing him into the military. But did he want to avoid it forever? This place had once been home. He'd once enjoyed his life here—parts of it, anyway.

Eliana was still here and would be for a long time. Apelo and Thana didn't live in Kalama anymore, but they brought Velia and Nina around the palace often enough. But Kaius was here too, as was Jin's father. So were the mistakes he'd made eight years ago.

"You really think this is my new path?" Jin asked.

"I know it is, kid."

Jin rolled his eyes. "You haven't called me that in years."

"And you're very much thinking like that kid you used to be, Jin. Take a step back. See this for what it is. It's the opportunity you've been waiting for."

"How do you know this is what I've been waiting for?"

She pinned him with a look. "It's not?"

Jin didn't know. He didn't know what he'd been waiting for or what he wanted. He didn't want to be within a thousand miles of his father, but Zephyrine had a point. He couldn't be a soldier forever. And he had to face his past eventually. Was this the opportunity he needed to do that?

"I don't know what to say to her," Jin finally said. "How do I explain why I made the choice I made?"

"Be honest."

"Wow, *never* thought of that."

"I'm being perfectly serious," Zephyrine said. "The sooner you can sit down and have a simple, reasonable conversation about what happened, the sooner both of you can move past it."

Jin swallowed hard. "And if she doesn't want to move past it?"

"That's her choice to make. It would be well within her right to tell you to fuck off." Zephyrine lifted her narrow shoulder. "But maybe she feels the same way you do. Stranger things have happened."

Jin pressed his lips together. He wasn't so sure. Zephyrine didn't know Astrea the way he did. What he'd done had definitely broken her heart. He'd broken his own with that choice. How was he supposed to fix that?

All he could do was try.

Chapter 24
Summer, Year 1020

Coming back to Kalama hadn't been Jin's idea, nor was going to the Whiskey Dream club. That had been Zephyrine and Adi's idea, though Adi had bailed last minute. Jin sighed as he walked into the packed building. Nobody took notice of him as he entered, and for that he was thankful. *At least one thing's working in my favor tonight.*

Blue lotus smoke choked the air, the crowds of gamblers and revelers loud despite the relatively early hour. It was barely even the seventh evening hour, and yet everyone was here. Kalamians liked to party, and Kalamians with money *really* liked to party. They also liked to show off what they could afford, evidenced by the jewels and rich fabrics draping off almost everyone he could see.

"Time for a drink?" Zephyrine's voice was light as she guided Jin into the club.

Jin didn't say anything as they shouldered their way toward the bar in the center of the room. A young man with blond hair was serving drinks at the far end, but Zephyrine waved him off when he made eye contact. She tilted her head in one direction, toward the black-haired man behind the bar. The blond tapped the man's shoulder.

"Ah!" Osin called as he turned and lumbered toward them. He was built like an ox, thick and muscular but not too tall. He tossed a striped towel over his shoulder before leaning on the bar. "There's a face I haven't seen in a while. How are you, Your Imperial Highness?"

"Good to see you too, Osin." Despite his sour mood, Jin smiled. On the few occasions Jin had ventured into this club over the years with Zephyrine, Osin had always been kind.

"Let me guess," the bartender said as he slapped two black paper napkins on the counter, "whiskey for the two of you."

"Make it a double," Jin said.

"Sure thing."

Osin grabbed a bottle from behind the counter, pouring the amber liquid into both of their glasses. Jin took a sip, welcoming the smooth burn of the alcohol.

"Anything in particular you two are looking to do tonight?" Osin asked. He gestured toward the bar with his thick, pale hand. "Just about everyone who's anyone is here."

"You and I have business, actually," Zephyrine said. "Maybe we can talk privately."

"Drag me out to the club and then dump me at the bar?" Jin asked. He'd meant it to be playful, but even to him, it sounded bitter. He just hated places like this; he'd expected to come in for one drink with Zephyrine to appease her, then leave.

"You'll find ways to keep yourself occupied," she said as she lifted her glass from the bartop. "Shall we?" she asked Osin.

The barkeep smiled. "I'll meet you in my office." As Zephyrine disappeared into the crowd once more, Osin looked at Jin. "Just tell Sergi if you need something."

"That's the blond?" Jin asked before tipping back another mouthful of whiskey.

"Indeed it is. He's one of the good ones."

As Osin rounded the bar and headed toward his office—one of the doors on the far wall—Jin watched the blond, Sergi. *One of the good ones.*

What, did he have a heavy hand when pouring drinks? Jin shook his head, picked up his whiskey, and moved down the length of the bar.

It had been such a long day. His and Adi's airship had only landed in Kalama that morning. Just a day ago, he'd come back from yet another mission in Corsyca. Hopefully Lennor and Civan were doing alright.

Drink in hand, Jin moved toward the right side of the club. A Delian woman was performing on the small stage, and a horde of people crowded the gambling tables. He scanned the faces there. Lord Hasko Magjan, of course, was seated at one table, his greedy hands pinching the waitress's behind as she turned to leave. The woman grimaced but said nothing as she hurried away. Jin forced his temper down . . . deep, deep down. Making a scene would do no good. Not tonight.

Lord Matliev was there, too, though his wife was nowhere to be found. Someone at the next table shouted with glee. The dealer slid a stack of coins to them as someone else cursed. Hopefully they weren't drinking too much, or Jin would end up breaking up a fight tonight, too.

There was Duke Pompilio, a blue lotus cigarette caught between his lips as he slapped a handful of cards down on the table closest to the stage. A woman leaned down next to him, her painted lips spreading into a wide smile as the duke's hand brushed her waist. Jin shook his head; the woman had to be at least fifteen years the duke's junior, closer to Jin's age than the duke's.

Nobody Jin would actually want to talk to was here. That list was small—Zephyrine, Rasa, Adi, Lennor, Civan, and even Dorin. He could talk to some of the nobles he'd passed, but they usually just reminded him why he hated being in Kalama. Gambling, alcohol, drugs—that was all fine. Even the duke's flirtations didn't actually bother Jin that much. That was the duke's private business and his business alone.

What bothered him was that the very people who were supposed to be in charge of the empire, running it for the benefit of the citizens, were partying in the capital and making business deals that would only benefit them. They had no regard for the soldiers on the Corsycan front, no regard for anyone but themselves. Jin doubted they even cared much for their own regions. When was the last time Duke Pompilio had even gone back to his dukedom to the west?

Jin shoved his temper down again. *Just find someplace to wait until Zephyrine's done*, he told himself. That would be the smart thing.

He wandered past the stage. The band's tempo picked up, and the crowd cheered. A few even began singing along off-key.

Maybe going back to the bar to wait was the best option.

Jin pivoted, intent on doing that, when he saw a familiar freckled face leading three people toward that very same bar. What the fuck was Nicos doing here?

If Nicos Masalis was here, that meant Jin's younger sister was, too. He was her personal guard, after all. And Eliana loved going to Kalama's clubs. Jin hadn't had much of a chance to call his sister since the war began, but on the few occasions they'd been able to talk, she'd told him about some of her nights out.

And if Eliana was here, that meant Cressida and Astrea were here with her. His sister wouldn't go out with anyone else. She'd told him that, too.

That had to be who was following Nicos to the bar. It had to be.

Tonight really couldn't be going less according to plan. He wasn't supposed to have to see her until Monday. He was supposed to have the weekend to figure out what he was going to do.

They obviously hadn't seen him. If Eliana had, she would have been running over to Jin in a heartbeat. *I probably should go say hello to her before she sees me first*, he reasoned. Eliana had no idea he was home yet; he'd thought to surprise her first thing in the morning at their family breakfast. But Jin couldn't make his feet move in that direction. What he really needed to do was stay out of it. That was what he'd been doing for years.

He turned back toward the stage, weaving through the crowd until he made it back to the table where Lord Matliev was passing a pair of dice back to the dealer.

"Oh!" A pair of surprised blue eyes met Jin's. "Prince Varojin, so lovely to see you! What a surprise."

"Lady Hiflow," Jin replied. She was seated next to Matliev, her blonde hair pulled up high to expose the low neckline of her gown. He hadn't seen her sitting there a few moments before, and now Jin really regretted his decision. He should've just gone to the bar and dealt with Eliana.

Ilara Hiflow's mother was a powerful merchant, and she'd arranged a loveless but aristocratic marriage for Ilara when she was just eighteen. It had been the talk of the court when Jin was seventeen. Her husband was some lesser nobleman, but a title was a title. Ilara spent most of her time trying to find other outlets for her energy. They'd played this game for years, even before Ilara's marriage. She'd always been trying to catch Jin's attention. After all, even a bastard prince was a bigger catch than a mere lord. Jin had no interest in Ilara, nor did he want to get stuck in the middle of such a distasteful situation.

"I didn't realize you were coming home, Your Imperial Highness," Ilara continued, touching her playing cards to her collarbones. "Maybe you can help me win a round. I don't understand this game."

"Don't let her fool you, Prince Varojin," Matliev said, the only acknowledgment of Jin's presence. He didn't look up from the dice being thrown onto the table. "Lady Hiflow knows exactly what she's doing. Just likes to pretend she doesn't so she can win big in the end."

"I do not!" she protested.

"I'm no good at cards anyway," Jin said, tone light. It was so easy to slip on his mask, to play the role these people expected of him. He hadn't been around the court much in the last eight years, but he'd been around it his whole life before that. "Wouldn't be much help."

"I bet that's not true, Prince Varojin," Ilara purred, one hand reaching out to touch Jin's.

He pulled it away, switching his whiskey glass into it and bringing the cup to his lips. From the corner of his eye, he saw Ilara frown.

"Trust me," Jin said with a practiced laugh, "you'll just lose more money if I offer any advice." He was actually quite good at any number of the card games popular in Kalama; they were popular among the soldiers at his base too. When Rasa's teams weren't on missions, they passed nights that way.

"Then maybe if you sit with me, you'll just be my good luck charm," Ilara tried.

Matliev laughed, deep and rumbly. "Prince Varojin, a good luck charm?" The man finally glanced up at Jin, then cleared his throat. "No offense, Your Imperial Highness."

Jin smiled his easy smile and tipped his glass in Matliev's direction even though he'd rather tell the man off. Just one more reason he hated coming home to Kalama. There was always someone to remind him that he wasn't the favorite Auris sibling at court. He didn't care about being popular, but the hostility was too much. That was the price he had to pay for his parents' mistake of having a child outside of the emperor's marriage.

As Ilara pulled another card from a stack on the table, Jin peeked at the bar over his shoulder. His sister was speaking with someone, though Jin didn't immediately recognize who in the haze of blue lotus smoke drifting in the club.

Eliana and Nicos headed off with two men. Jin glanced back to the card table. Ilara was in a position to win, if her cards were any indication;

Jin could see both her and Matliev's hands from his position between them.

Jin looked over his shoulder again. Cressida was talking to Astrea, pink cocktails in crystal glasses in both their hands. Astrea looked upset about something. Even after all these years, her eyebrows still pulled together the same way they used to when she was unhappy. She tucked a strand of dark, wavy hair behind her ear as she stared down at her glass.

That familiar ache settled in Jin's chest as he watched the two women. How was it that on the few occasions he'd ever come home, he seemed to always see Astrea from afar? He supposed that was bound to happen, considering her closeness with Eliana and the fact that she lived on palace grounds, but it hurt. He wanted to go talk with her, apologize for the way he'd fucked up years ago, but this was neither the time nor place. He needed to figure out what he was going to say to her. He needed a plan.

Ilara's screech made Jin whip around to the table. His muscles tensed, then relaxed. The dealer pushed a stack of coins and paper lire toward her. She grinned.

"You *are* my good luck charm, Your Imperial Highness!" she exclaimed.

"Imagine that," he murmured, already looking toward the bar again. Cressida was dashing off into the crowd, and Astrea was alone at the bar. Her shoulders sagged as she picked up the cocktails and headed in another direction.

As Ilara began counting her winnings, Jin slipped back into the crowd. He tracked Astrea's lavender dress among the clubgoers dressed in a variety of jewel tones. Even his own all-black ensemble blended in better than hers.

Astrea headed toward one of the seating areas on the far side of the bar. He stopped in his tracks. What was he thinking? He couldn't go talk to her. She'd probably throw a drink in his face. Not that he didn't deserve it. Maybe he should let her.

"You left!" Ilara's voice was behind him again, and Jin had to stop himself from cringing.

"Cards aren't how I want to spend my evening, Lady Hiflow," he said. "You'll have to excuse me. I thought you were going to play another round."

"We don't have to play cards." She leaned toward him, lowering her voice as she said, "We can do whatever you want. My husband isn't here tonight."

"I'm actually supposed to be meeting a friend," Jin lied. "I'm sure she's expecting me."

Ilara's thin lips pulled into a frown. "Your friend?"

"Apologies, Lady Hiflow."

Jin circled the bar, searching the crowd for Astrea again. She'd always been average height, and that combined with her dark hair and the blue lotus smoke made her impossible to find among the sea of people.

But there. A flash of lavender near one side of the club drew his attention.

A man was talking to Astrea. He looked angry, and his hand snapped out as he grabbed her arm.

More importantly, Astrea looked scared.

Jin swore under his breath. Making a scene hadn't been the plan. None of this had. And whether Jin had spoken one word to Astrea in the last eight years or not, he wasn't going to let some asshole upset her.

As Jin weaved through the crowd, he saw Astrea try to pull away from the man. Fuck, why did he have to touch her? He shoved his temper down again; upsetting her by bringing more attention to the situation was the last thing he wanted to do.

Just as Jin stepped up behind Astrea, she pulled back again, but the man's hold on her was firm. Jin crossed his arms over his chest. Up close, there was no hiding who this man was. Lord Victor Nazarov, another low-born noble surviving on whatever leftover money he'd inherited. Jin didn't have much of a history with Nazarov, but he knew how the younger sons of nobles acted. Entitled. Overcompensating.

"Is there a problem here?" Jin asked, his heart hammering despite his steady voice. He wasn't nervous about confronting Nazarov. No, Jin knew he could have Nazarov begging on the floor in just a few seconds.

Astrea went stone still, her body even more rigid now. Jin's stomach twisted.

"Your Imperial Highness." Victor Nazarov dropped Astrea's arm. "I didn't know you were back in the city."

"Get lost, Victor." Jin took half a step forward. "Now."

Victor Nazarov inclined his head, then turned and retreated into the darkness of the crowd. Jin was grateful. He wasn't sure he could control his temper any longer.

Astrea didn't move. Jin wasn't sure she would. But slowly, she turned toward him. Jin schooled his features, embracing that mask Lady Hiflow and Lord Matliev bought into.

Skies, Astrea really had grown up in the years he'd been gone. She looked good. So good. She was all soft curves, from her wide hips to her small bust to her rosy cheeks. He forced himself not to look too much. He forced himself not to breathe in the way she smelled like peony despite the blue lotus smoke in the room. Instead, he focused on those skies damned brilliant silver eyes of hers.

She said nothing, but she didn't have to. The tight shoulders. Those furrowed eyebrows. The slight pout of her lips. She was nervous. That's how she always looked when she was nervous.

Fuck.

Jin held onto his mask as he smiled. "Hello, Astrea."

ALSO BY H.E. BAUMAN

Under Darkened Skies: Darkened Skies Book One
Into Whispering Shadows: Darkened Skies Book Two

ACKNOWLEDGMENTS

Every book takes a village, and I can't thank mine enough.

To my editor and my beta readers, thank you for your thoughtful feedback and your enthusiasm. It's hard to keep perspective on your own work, so having your input is invaluable.

To my family and friends, thank you for supporting my books and your encouragement and enthusiasm.

And to my readers, thank you for loving my characters and the world I'm creating. None of it would be possible without you.

About the Author

H.E. Bauman is a fantasy author fascinated with all things magical. After spending her childhood obsessed with writing stories, she went on to receive her bachelor's in English and has continued writing ever since. When she's not reading or writing, she enjoys playing tennis, immersing herself in video games, and spending time with her family.

If you want to get in touch, visit H.E.'s website or follow her on social media.

Made in United States
Orlando, FL
10 July 2023